THE
MURDER
BOOK

THE MURDER BOOK

A Cold Case Investigation

LISSA MARIE REDMOND

MIDNIGHT INK
WOODBURY, MINNESOTA

FIRST EDITION
First Printing, 2019

Book design by Bob Gaul
Book format by Samantha Penn
Cover design by Kevin R. Brown
Cover illustration by Dominick Finelle / The July Group
Editing by Nicole Nugent

Midnight Ink, an imprint of Llewellyn Worldwide Ltd.

Library of Congress Cataloging-in-Publication Data
Names: Redmond, Lissa Marie, author.
Title: The murder book / Lissa Marie Redmond.
Description: First edition. | Woodbury, Minnesota : Midnight Ink, [2019] |
   Series: A cold case investigation ; 2.
Identifiers: LCCN 2018041422 (print) | LCCN 2018042601 (ebook) | ISBN
   9780738755663 (ebook) | ISBN 9780738754277 (alk. paper)
Subjects: | GSAFD: Mystery fiction.
Classification: LCC PS3618.E4352 (ebook) | LCC PS3618.E4352 M87 2019 (print)
   | DDC 813/.6—dc23
LC record available at https://lccn.loc.gov/2018041422

Midnight Ink
Llewellyn Worldwide Ltd.
2143 Wooddale Drive
Woodbury, MN 55125-2989
www.midnightinkbooks.com

Printed in the United States of America

For my mom

Author's Note

I was born and raised in Buffalo, New York. I have never lived anywhere else and hope my great love for the city shines through. This book takes place in Buffalo, but it is a work of fiction. In the spirit of full disclosure, I took many liberties with locations in this novel. The gated community Lauren lives in does not exist. Garden Valley resembles a neighboring town south of the city, but you won't find it on a map. Real roles—such as mayor, Erie County district attorney, and the police commissioner—are populated with fictional people who in no way resemble any living person. I took great pains to create fictional characters to populate the very real Buffalo that I love. Hopefully my fellow Buffalonians will forgive the literary license I took.

"Homicide is killing me," Shane Reese complained, slinging his duffel bag over his shoulder. "We've been here for almost twelve hours. You almost done?" He was standing in the main office of the Buffalo Police Cold Case Homicide unit, his tie hanging loose, his hand on the door knob. It was Friday night, and he was ready to get out of there.

"Not yet." Lauren Riley smoothed some papers flat across her desk. They had been in the office for almost twelve hours for two days in a row, so she understood his eagerness to go. And was slightly jealous because her touch of OCD wouldn't allow her to leave until she was finished. "You can kill that light, though. I'm only going to be a few more minutes."

The second floor of police headquarters was already empty. The rest of the detectives from the other squads had gone out to start their weekends. The "regular" Homicide guys had caught a particularly nasty murder first thing that day and were out canvassing in the Black

Rock neighborhood. They had needed Reese and Riley to help out in the morning but had everything under control by the late afternoon. Then she and Reese split off to do follow-up on their own cold cases.

Lauren could hear their radio squawking next to her computer. One crew was still going house to house to talk to the neighbors, while the other crew was hunting down any cameras local businesses might have pointed toward the scene. They wouldn't be going home anytime soon. In the meantime, the Homicide wing was left deserted and probably would be for the night

"Not for nothing, but it's already past seven," Reese pointed out, still trying to convince her to go home. Five foot eleven, athletically built, and almost seven years younger than her, Lauren liked to consider biracial Reese the annoying little brother she'd never had. He ran a hand over his close-cropped hair, so short that Lauren called it the five o'clock shadow on his head. "We should've been out of here an hour ago."

She tugged on the rubber band holding her own thick blond hair back. It was too tight and had been giving her a headache. "I just want to type these notes up or I'll forget something from the interview."

"I know it went better than expected, but we have time," Reese told her. "You don't have to do all of this right now." Riley and Reese had gone to the holding center to talk to a prostitute about the murder of a young gangbanger. Francine hadn't known anything about that boy, but she had known an awful lot about another murder they'd been working on. In fact, she'd seen her boyfriend kill a fellow heroin fiend over a money dispute and steal the junkie's benefit card. She'd known where he'd stashed it in his mother's house. Eddie, the boyfriend, was in jail upstate for a separate possession charge, so there was no worry about him ditching the card before they got a search warrant on Monday.

"If only Eddie hadn't been sleeping with the woman in the cell next to hers," Lauren said. The two women had a lot to talk about and all the time in the world to do it. Lauren smiled to herself. "Hell hath no fury like a junkie scorned."

Reese narrowed his green eyes at her, but she acted like she didn't notice. She wasn't in the mood to spar with him, although it was one of her favorite pastimes. She knew she'd get more done without the witty banter. Some days it seemed like everything just fell into place and she was going to take advantage of it. "Put an overtime slip in," he reminded her, giving up. "Don't forget to lock the office."

She waved her hand at him and turned toward her laptop. She had a brand-new city-issued iPad in her bag but liked to work with a real keyboard instead of the touch screen. Reese told her she could buy keyboards for the iPad, but that seemed to defeat the purpose of having one. "Okay, Dad. See you Monday."

Lauren heard the door open and Reese laugh. "You're unbelievable."

It shut behind him, leaving her in the dark gloom of the office, except for the glow of her computer screen. She was almost forty now and typed better in the near dark. She had a pair of readers tucked in her desk drawer, but she only put them on when no one was around. They were just another little reminder that she was older than she sometimes felt. She pulled them out and perched them on her nose, feeling her age.

All around her were cardboard boxes, stacked in preparation for the impending move to a new building. The city had finally sprung for some new digs for the police department and now the detectives had to pack and work their cases at the same time. The clutter scattered about the office made her claustrophobic, so she combatted that feeling by diving deep into her paperwork.

Engrossed in typing her notes for the search warrant, Lauren didn't look up when she heard the office door open. "What'd you forget, Reese? Your condoms?" she called out absently, fingers still pounding the keys.

The first blow hit her in the right side, knocking the wind out of her and sending her glasses flying as she crashed to the floor. The second was a vicious stomp, directly on her head, causing her to black out for a moment. When she opened her eyes to the dim light, Lauren could see the legs of her ancient metal office chair, and the worn pile of the filthy gray industrial-grade carpet. Her left hand looked out of place on the ground next to her head. Lauren's first thought was how odd it was that she was on the floor. Her second was an awareness of a sticky wetness spreading around the left side of her.

Then she tried to breathe.

Like a goldfish out of its bowl, her eyes darted around, her chest heaved, but she could not seem to take in air. A fierce panic set in as her body desperately struggled to manage a breath. A sickly, thick, sucking sound accompanied every attempt.

Someone was walking around her office. She tried to call for help, to get their attention, because there must have been some kind of accident. Her heart thundered in her chest as her mind raced: something horrific had happened to her, she couldn't take a breath, she was dying.

I'm dying. That fact was the only clear and concrete thing she knew in that moment.

She was dying.

As her vision began to fade, she saw two things pass by her limp, useless hand: a pair of city-issue boots and the unmistakable olive-green cover of the Murder Book.

2

All around her, there were strange sounds, like the buzzing of flies very close to her ear. Her throat hurt, burned, as if someone had poured turpentine down her mouth and threw a match.

Pulling in a breath, she tasted something pepperminty, only not. This was not where she was supposed to be. She was supposed to be somewhere else. Thoughts were coming to her in disjointed clusters of sensation and awakening.

If I could just open my eyes, Lauren thought. *I could figure this out.*

The brightness hit her like a boxing glove to the temple. She immediately squeezed her eyes shut again. Someone in the room must have noticed because the buzz became a loud frenzy around her head. There was something on her face, a mask, pinching the bridge of her nose. Unfamiliar voices were swirling around her, interspersed with electronic beeps and the shuffling of shoes. Lauren's hands batted out weakly, trying to get that thing off her face, until someone took hold of both her wrists and held them to her sides. She let out a croak of protest.

"Riley, it's okay." Reese's voice popped into her head above sounds of the rest of the commotion going on around her. "You're in the hospital. You're okay, girl. You're okay."

She forced herself to open her eyes again. Blinking, blinking, blinking, the frame of the curtain that snaked around the top of her bed came into focus. The room was too white, too bright. She was lying in a bed surrounded by monitors. Everything was foreign; nothing was right. A man started passing a penlight in front of her eyes, causing her to snap them shut again. "Don't do that," she rasped. It was barely a whisper. "Reese?"

A hand came down on her shoulder. "I'm right here."

She yanked her right hand free from her side. It seemed like it had been encased in cement somehow and reached up to touch his wrist. She willed her eyes open again. Shane Reese was standing above her, baseball cap on, dark circles under his green eyes. "You look like hell," she said.

He laughed. Not a happy, *you told a good one* kind of laugh, but a half-hysterical, half-relieved version. He clutched at her gown for a second, then released his grip a little. "Thanks. You look great, by the way."

Someone slipped a blood pressure cuff around her left arm and it began to inflate. Her right hand had an IV line taped to it, the tubing snaking up to a bag hanging from a metal pole next to the bed. The saline, if that's what it was, hung an inch from Reese's head. It didn't make any sense. "What am I doing here? What happened to me?"

He swallowed before he answered and Lauren thought she had never seen him look so old and tired. "Do you remember anything after I left you on Friday night in the office? Anything at all?"

She shook her head. "I don't know. What do you mean, Friday? What day is this?"

"This is Sunday."

"Sunday?" Now she began to panic, she could hear the pulse monitor hanging next her start to beep faster. "My daughters. What about Lindsey and Erin? Are they okay? Please—"

"No, no, no." He tried to calm her. "They're fine. I sent them home to get some sleep. Lindsey got in on Saturday night and Erin made it here today. They are fine. You're in the ICU now. They're moving you to a regular room soon."

The confusion was too much; tears began to run down her cheeks. "Why am I here, Reese? What happened?" She felt an itch in her right side. When her hand went to scratch it, she felt gauze and plastic. Lead lines stuck out from her chest connecting her to various equipment. A furious beeping pulsed from a machine above her head. "Is that a tube? Oh, God. Reese, do I have a tube in my chest?"

A doctor swooped in and grabbed Reese by his free arm. "You're going to have to leave now. She's too upset. We have to bring her pressure down."

"No!" Lauren didn't recognize her own voice. It was shallow and raspy and forced. She began to shake uncontrollably. "He needs to stay. I want him to stay."

The thin, balding doctor turned to her. "He needs to leave. Just for a while. He can come back soon. Just until we can evaluate you. You had surgery and we need to make sure that you're recovering properly." His face was ruddy and flushed, like he'd been standing out in the wind all day.

"No. Don't leave, Reese." His hand was still on her shoulder. She managed to grab onto his wrist now. Lauren could feel the tension in his fingers through her hospital gown.

7

"We need to work on her." The doctor's patience was wearing thin, but Reese's was no better.

"Yeah? Call the police," he challenged. They locked eyes for a second and the doctor turned away. Reese wasn't going to budge. Lauren heard the doctor ask the nurse to get Security. Her eyes started to lose focus.

"What happened to me, Reese?" Lauren asked in a fading voice.

"I forgot my baseball hat. I came back and found you."

She was breathing hard. Why was it so hard to breathe? Why did she have a tube in her chest? And why was this answer so difficult? "But what *happened* to me?" she insisted in a forced whisper.

"Someone stabbed you." His voice was soft and far away. She tried to hang onto the sound of it, to keep her head above the water closing in. "Someone came into the Cold Case office while you were alone and stabbed you."

The dark crept back over her and she was gone again.

3

When Lauren woke, it was morning—or so she assumed from the angle of the sunlight coming through the gray blinds of her window—but she still wasn't sure what day it was. She coughed, coughed again, and tried to remember why she was in a hospital bed with an oxygen mask on her face.

She recognized the telltale signs of a standard hospital room: cold, sterile, and white. White walls, white sheets, a white board on the wall with red and blue marker scribbles on it. She vaguely remembered seeing Reese, but it was her daughters who filled her mind now. *They should be away at college,* she thought absently, *it's not Thanksgiving yet.*

Lindsey and Erin were both asleep on those plastic hospital recliners they wheel in for family members. Lindsey, with her blond hair that was just like her mom's, was sitting straight up, like she had fallen asleep mid-sentence. Erin, on the other hand, was sprawled over the chair like she had melted into it, short dark hair spiked up in every direction. Lauren moved her hand to touch the tube in her side and everything from before came flooding back—what there was anyway. Reese said she had been stabbed.

"Hey," a familiar voice said from over her shoulder, "it looks like someone's awake."

She twisted her head to see her mom rising from her own recliner positioned at the back-right corner, behind her original line of sight. Lauren hadn't seen her mom in over a year, since she last came up from Florida with her dad for a visit. Then, her parents had looked tan and radiant, true snowbirds who flourished in the vitamin D after years of hard Buffalo winters. Only these snowbirds had never come back, choosing to sell their South Buffalo home and get a condo in Tampa. Now her mother looked gaunt and drawn. Naturally thin and tall like Lauren, she looked emaciated from stress. Charlotte Healy's gray-blond bob hung limply around her face. Her purple sweatshirt and gray pants draped off her size-zero frame, the lines in her forehead etched in worry as she stepped to the side of Lauren's bed.

"Where's Dad?" Lauren's voice sounded muffled and rough, like she was breathing through wet sand. She reached up and touched the oxygen mask over her mouth and nose. Coughing, a stab of pain radiated up her right side, making her bend forward a little.

Her mom eased her back down against the bed with one hand, mindful not to interfere with any of the sensors they had stuck all over her. "He finally went back to your house to take a shower. We had to practically pry your partner from your side. He went home last night, but he'll be back. He hasn't left you since it happened. Jill is back at the house too. I hope you don't mind."

I guess it pays to have a five-bedroom, four-bath house that your ex-husband gave you in the divorce settlement when you get stabbed, Lauren thought, still trying to wrap her head around the situation. *Even my sister is here.*

Mrs. Healy gently took Lauren's hand in hers, careful of the IV. "The doctors say if your partner hadn't come when he did and given you first aid until the ambulance showed up, you'd be dead." Tears welled up in her eyes, threatening to spill over onto her cheeks.

"How are the girls?" Lauren motioned to her sleeping daughters. Erin gave a half snort and rolled face first into the arm of the chair. *She's nineteen now, but still looks like she's twelve.* Lauren drank in the sight of her baby for a second. It still caused a lump to rise in her throat when she watched her daughters sleep. Raising them as a working single mom had taught her to sneak moments with them whenever she could, especially late at night after a long shift, just watching them dream.

"Relieved that you're going to be okay." Her mom clutched at Lauren's hand with both of hers and the tears fell freely. "We all are. You're going to be okay."

She bent forward and touched her forehead to Lauren's shoulder and sobbed. After half a minute, she sucked in her breath and tried to get herself under control. She straightened up and smoothed the hair back from Lauren's forehead. "You're going to be okay," she repeated, as though it were a mantra she'd been chanting to herself all night.

A nurse popped her head in the door. "Glad to see you awake, my lady. Do you mind if I get some vitals from you?"

Her red Crocs squeaked as she crossed the room, clipboard in hand. Suddenly Lauren was unmercifully thirsty. "Could I have some water?" she choked out as the young woman slipped a blood pressure cuff around her left bicep.

"Let me check with your doctor and if he says yes, I'll bring you some." She squeezed, squeezed, squeezed the bulb, tightening the cuff.

Lauren watched with detached fascination as the nurse, her ID clipped to her scrubs proclaiming her as Anna Dunkin, fastened a monitor on her index finger, swiped her forehead with a thermometer, and gently clamped down on her wrist to take her pulse. The nurse was one of those women who were as tall as they were round, including her chubby, cheerful face. *This can't be happening to me,* Lauren thought as Anna checked the bandages on her tube. *Who would do this to me?* But she knew neither the nurse nor her mother was the right person to answer that question.

"Am I at the Erie County Medical Center?" she asked Anna as she finished writing up her stats.

"Yes, you are," she replied in that placating, fake cheerful voice nurses adopt to soothe patients. "And half your co-workers are crammed in the waiting room down the hall. I hope no one has a cat up a tree in the city of Buffalo today."

"That's firefighters," Lauren replied.

"See? She still has a sense of humor. Right, Mom?" The nurse gave Lauren's mother's arm a little squeeze. "I'll find the doctor, tell him you're awake and thirsty, okay?"

Lauren nodded and watched Anna squeak out of the room. "Is it true? Are there cops here?"

Her mom sniffed, wiped her nose with the back of her arm, like she'd always told Lauren not to do, and said, "It seems like every cop in the city was here when we came in this morning. You were still in the ICU. The mayor was here. Mr. Church, the district attorney too." She stopped herself for a moment to catch her breath before she went on. "Your commissioner met with your father and I as soon as we came in. What a fantastic lady. She told us, whatever we needed, she'd get. She ordered a policeman to guard your door."

Lauren looked toward the door. There was no window in it, only a fire exit diagram taped at eye level. There was sandpaper in her throat when she spoke. "There's a cop out there now?"

"It's a different one every couple of hours." Her mom leaned over and pulled Lauren's pillow higher so she could sit up better. Lauren winced at the pain in her side as she tried to adjust herself. "I guess everyone wants to volunteer for the duty, to help. It's very sweet. Every time I go downstairs for coffee, there's a new face. It was very comforting while you were still unconscious."

The beeping monitor above Lauren's head picked up steam. "You have to call Reese. Get him back here, now."

"Why? What's wrong? What's the matter, honey?" Her mother's face turned pale at Lauren's reaction. She reached over Lauren's head and began hitting the nurse call button.

"Because it was a cop who did this to me."

4

Lauren was convinced she'd die of thirst before either the doctor or Reese showed up. Erin had woken up and put Chapstick on her cracked lips for her. They were so parched they were beginning to bleed. Even with the Chapstick, she kept licking at them, her tongue rough and dry, until Anna brought in a tan plastic pitcher of water. She would have foregone the whole cup and straw and chugged, but the nurse insisted she sip it slowly as she held the cup for Lauren like she was a baby. By that point she would have lapped at a mud puddle like a dog, the thirst was so powerful.

Lindsey repositioned her pillow for her while Erin stood by with the lip balm. Their silence underscored the deep anxiety they wore on their faces. It was as if at any moment one of them would say something and both would slip into tears.

"The doctor is on his way," Anna told Lauren, refilling the cup. Lauren held the mask away from her face, waiting for more water.

"How long do I have to keep this tube in?" The sight of the plastic sticking from her side made her want to gag a little. She tried not to think about it, but every time she moved she got a painful reminder. As a cop, she'd seen tubes sticking out of every orifice imaginable, but it was different seeing something like this come out of your own body as opposed to someone else's.

"He'll go over all of that with you." Anna lifted the cup back to Lauren's mouth just as Reese burst through the door.

"Look at you, partner! Sitting up, having a drink." He gave Lindsey and Erin both quick hugs before making his way to the side of Lauren's bed. Mrs. Healy put a hand on Reese's shoulder and mouthed the words *thank you* to him, making Lauren wonder what everyone had been saying about her the last few days.

"Reese, we need to talk— " she said and then coughed, which felt like someone was jamming ice picks in her chest, bringing tears to her eyes.

"Slow down," Anna admonished gently, pulling the cup away. Lauren wanted to reach out and snatch it back from her hand.

There was a single knock on the door and the man Lauren took to be her doctor strolled in. He was in his mid-fifties, Asian, with jet black hair graying at the temples, combed straight back off his forehead. He had his hands stuffed in the pockets of his white coat and a stethoscope draped around his neck. "Awake and alert," he smiled, drifting across the room toward Lauren. He glanced at all of her company. "And the gang's all here."

"Girls, let's go get some coffee so the doctor has some space," Mrs. Healy suggested. Erin and Lindsey both brushed past Reese and gave their mom a half hug and kiss before following their grandmother out of the room.

"How's the pain?" the doctor asked. He was tall and carried a confident air about him, like having a knifed cop with a chest tube sticking out of her was the least of his worries. His name tag read *Dr. Samuel Patel* and the only initials she could swear to were "MD." The rest she would have needed her readers for.

"It only hurts when I talk or breathe or try to move," she said to him quietly, trying to lessen the pain.

He took her chart from Anna with a knowing grin. "You still have your sense of humor. That's a very good sign." *Apparently losing your sense of humor was a one-way ticket to the morgue,* Lauren thought as he flipped through the pages and made a couple of notes.

Motioning toward Reese, she told the doctor, "This is my partner, Shane Reese."

Dr. Patel clasped the chart behind his back. "Shane and I have gotten to know each other very well over the last couple days. He even promised to take me shooting down at your police range."

Pulling the mask way from her face so Reese could get the full effect, she said, "Suck up," setting off a new round of coughing.

"Easy, easy," the doctor said, stepping up with the stethoscope, pressing the cold metal disc to her chest. "Breathe for me." He moved the disc around. "Again."

Lauren dutifully sucked in and out as he pressed his scope all over her chest and back. Finally satisfied that she was indeed breathing, he pulled the ends of the scope from his ears and slung it around his neck. "Everything is sounding better."

"This"—she took a stuttering breath—"sounds better?"

"So much better than when you were brought in," the nurse agreed.

"Can you excuse us?" Reese asked Anna, giving her his famous thousand-watt smile, but there was tension in his voice.

She seemed to realize her overstep and became flustered. "Oh, sure. Of course. Lauren, I'll be back to check on you in a little while." A flush of red colored her chubby cheeks.

"Thank you, Anna," Dr. Patel told her as she rushed out the door.

Poor kid, Lauren thought, *she just wants to help. But this ain't her party.*

"How am I doing now?" Lauren asked.

Dr. Patel's eyebrows knit together. "You were stabbed between your fourth and fifth rib, puncturing your right lung. You were also hit in the head with a blunt object—"

"Probably a flashlight," Reese chimed in.

"Possibly a flashlight." The doctor gave Reese a look to shut him up. "This caused a slight concussion. We inserted the chest tube to assist you with your breathing. It's not permanent. You're very lucky, Lauren. If Shane here hadn't found you when he did, you probably wouldn't be here to enjoy my company right now."

"I forgot my baseball hat," Reese explained, his face getting red. "I saw you on the floor, you were turning blue and you weren't moving. I thought you were dead already."

Ignoring the emotion in Reese's voice, Lauren peeked under the thin green gown down at the chest tube sticking out between her right breast and armpit. "What's this doing?"

"Draining fluid. We don't want liquid to accumulate in the thoracic cavity and cause pressure. Like I said, it's temporary. Right now we're mostly concerned with the internal scarring, but we're watching that closely."

"No more bikinis for me." Lauren turned her face away from the tubing, back to Reese and the doctor.

"The scar won't look that bad when you're all healed up," Dr. Patel assured her.

"It looked pretty bad to me when I saw her lying on the floor," Reese said.

Dr. Patel reached over and gently felt the lump on the top of her head. "It wasn't good," he agreed as he probed. "But I still have to worry about the effects of the concussion as well. Do you know what month it is?"

Lauren winced and the doctor pulled his hand back. "November."

"That's good. How about the day?"

Lauren shook her head. "It was November ninth on Friday. I don't know what day it is now."

The doctor nodded and made a note on her chart. "Excellent. It's Monday the twelfth."

"That's Veteran's Day," she said softly, trying to picture the calendar in her head.

"Yeah, thanks for ruining all my plans," Reese joked. An Army veteran, he'd seen action in the Gulf. *Veteran's Day is special to him, and here I am,* she thought, *taking that away from him.*

Seeing the strained look wash over her face, Reese backtracked. "I'm only kidding. I didn't have any plans, really."

Not believing him, Lauren tried to concentrate on the doctor. She'd make it up to Reese somehow. As if her getting attacked was an inconsiderate thing to do to him.

"Do you remember Friday? What did you have for breakfast?" Sticking a finger up, he started moving it back and forth before she could answer. "Follow my finger with just your eyes."

Eyes sliding along with his finger, Lauren replied, "Nothing. I drank coffee until lunch. Then I drank more coffee with a sandwich."

The smile crept back over his face. "Good and how about the incident itself? Do you remember anything of that?"

She shook her head. "I was typing. I heard the door, thought it was Reese. Didn't bother turning around. Next thing I know, something hit me in the side and then someone was stomping on my head. Sorry, Columbo. No flashlight. The blunt object was a city-issue boot."

"A boot? Are you sure?" Reese asked.

"I saw a black city-issue boot and the hem of our polyester uniform pants. I'm sure."

Reese took a deep breath. "This is what we know: someone stole Craig Garcia's swipe card off his desk sometime Friday during the day when they were handling that homicide. He logged it as missing to our report technician, but she assumed he'd just left it at home again. She told him to look for it when he was done for the day and she'd put a message out in the morning if he couldn't find it."

"There had to be twenty cops milling around Friday afternoon," Lauren said.

"At least. There were three scenes, two suspects, seven witnesses. It was a clusterfuck. They propped the door open and people were popping in and out half the day." That was common practice since only a Homicide detective's swipe card worked on the main door into the wing. They'd prop it open with a chair so the street cops could bring witnesses in and out. Then the cops would have to wait around to bring the witnesses home after they'd been interviewed. You'd have officers in the hallway, in the break room, sitting at detectives' desks playing with their pens; it was chaos.

"Did you get any kind of look at the suspect?"

Lauren closed her eyes, tried to concentrate. "He hit me from behind. I went down, and he stomped on me. I think I blacked out for a second or so." The rug, the legs of the chair, and the thick black laces slowly formed a picture in her mind. She opened her eyes to the blinding light of the window. "It was definitely a man. And he had the Murder Book in his hand. But I couldn't lift my head to see his face."

"As far as I can tell, that's the only thing missing. Whoever it was attempted to get into the file room. The camera on the door shows a shadow turning the knob, but the window is frosted. He must have gone into the Cold Case office to try to get the key and found you there."

"Who the hell would want to steal one of our files? It's all fair game; even the public can file a Freedom of Information Act form and get a copy."

"You know that's only partly true." Reese gripped the rails of her hospital bed with both hands. "They're still active investigations, so they wouldn't get suspect information, crime scene photos, witness information."

She let out a dry breath. "Do you have any leads?"

"We're trying to narrow down exactly who was actually in the office, but it's hard. The swipe card system only keeps records of people who enter, not who leave. And with the doors propped, we can't even count on that. The department has cameras on the front door of headquarters and on the Cathedral side door, but not the Church Street side. We assume that's how whoever did this got out."

"Through the Church Street door?"

"Actually, there is a camera in that little hallway because that's the door the prisoners still use to pick up their property, but it doesn't show the street. It looks like whoever did this went through the underground parking lot, where the top brass keep their cars, onto Church Street. There aren't any cameras in there, either."

Figures, Lauren thought bitterly, *the brass doesn't want anyone to know when they're coming or going. There are a gazillion cameras all over the city, but none pointed at them. And whoever attacked me knew it.*

"Could it have been someone impersonating a police officer?" It was Dr. Patel's turn to play detective. "Anybody can buy those pants and some black boots at any uniform shop in the city. It's not illegal."

Reese shot that idea down immediately. "Not a chance. You'd have to get into the building, get up into Homicide, steal Garcia's swipe, and then hang around somewhere in the building, all while avoiding the cameras."

"It could be any cop in the department," Lauren said. "You can't rule anyone out. Not even the guys sitting outside my door right now."

"We have extra security in place," Dr. Patel assured her. "One of our peace officers is at the nurses' station, logging in and out everyone who comes to see you, including the officers guarding your door."

With a grim smile, Reese moved his Buffalo Bills sweatshirt to the side, showing Lauren his .40-caliber off-duty gun. He let the material fall back into place. "Nothing is going to happen to you while you're in here."

"Who caught the case? Not you." She knew Reese would be unofficially in control of the investigation because no one would be able to stop him, but the captain would have to assign a detective not as close to Lauren. Someone else had to be in charge on paper.

"Joy Walsh is the lead detective on your attack. She'll be here to interview you later today or tomorrow."

Lauren nodded. "She's a good detective. Did she look into Craig Garcia?" It was a joke, of sorts. Everyone knew she and Craig didn't like each other.

Laughing, Reese said, "He was the first person to get interviewed and cleared. He was on Hudson Street doing a canvass for the homicide when you got stabbed."

Gingerly touching her side, she asked, "How long is this tube going to be in me? Will I be able to go back to work?" Lauren's blue eyes met the liquid brown of the Indian doctor's.

"It should be out in a day or two. I want you out of work for at least three to six weeks, and then I'd want you back on light duty only."

Lauren shook her head. "That's not going to happen. I need to be back to work as soon as possible."

"You can't be out there chasing criminals. You've suffered a serious injury, Lauren."

"With all due respect, doctor, I haven't done many foot pursuits since I got to Cold Case. Most of my suspects are a little long in the tooth at this point. The only way I'm running now is if a zombie is chasing me."

Dr. Patel crossed his arms. "We're not even at a place in your recovery where we should be discussing it. I'm more worried about your safety when you leave here. I was told you live alone."

She glanced at Reese, who had mirrored the doctor's crossed-arm pose.

"Not anymore," Reese informed them both. "I just moved in."

5

The living arrangements had been decided upon while she was still unconscious. "I have my parents, my kids, my sister, all staying at my house," Lauren protested after Dr. Patel had the good sense to leave and avoid the brewing argument. "Where the hell are you going to stay? The old doghouse in the backyard?"

"Don't get your blood pressure up," Reese said. "When your family clears out, I'm going to take the downstairs guest room. You won't even know I'm there."

Lauren's house had an old servant's quarters on the first floor that had been converted to a bedroom with its own bath and separate entrance. Her daughters used to love it when they had sleepovers, stuffing the room with five or six friends, sometimes trying to sneak out. But Lauren knew the game and caught them. Most of the time.

With the doctor gone, her family drifted back into her room one by one. Lindsey, Erin, then her mom and dad, followed by her sister, Jill, who must have shown up while the doctor was in. Reese faded into the background, keeping a watchful eye. *My own personal bulldog,* Lauren thought as he leaned up against the far wall.

"It's the Healy family reunion," Lauren said as her sister came to her bedside, hugging her gently. Jill was dark, like her father, like Erin. And tall, like her and their mom and Lindsey.

"It shouldn't have taken this," her dad said, standing on the other side of Jill, holding Lauren's hand, being careful of the IV.

"Your place looks like a funeral home," Jill said, forcing a smile. "There must be a hundred flower arrangements there. We keep taking them from the nurses' station every time one of us goes back to your house."

Born four years apart, Lauren hadn't had much of a relationship with Jill growing up. Lauren had always been a handful; Jill has always been the good girl. Jill, the little sister who went to college, got married, had three boys. She had done all the right things, in the right order, unlike her messed up older sister, who got knocked up a month before she graduated high school by the neighborhood loser.

While Jill was making honor roll in high school, Lauren was changing diapers and working overnights as a waitress. Maybe that had been Jill's inspiration, her motivation to excel in school, graduate magna cum laude, marry a steady, stable man who made a decent living. Jill was Martha Stewart to Lauren's Angelina Jolie. The only thing they had in common was the unwavering love for their children.

"Thanks for coming, Jill," Lauren told her, and she meant it. It was hard for Jill to get away. She lived in Portland, Oregon, and two of her sons were still in middle school. The youngest, Evan, had just started kindergarten in September.

Now it was Jill's turn for the tears to well up. "We thought we'd lost you," she whispered, leaning down, draping an arm around Lauren's neck. "I spent twelve hours in planes and airports not knowing if I was coming home to a funeral. I've never been so scared in my life."

Lauren's dad put a hand on his younger daughter's shoulder. Lauren watched his Adam's apple bob up and down in his throat.

"I'm okay now," Lauren whispered in her sister's ear. "I'm okay."

"Don't you ever do this to us again," her father warned, wiping a tear from his eye.

"I promise," she said. "I will not let someone stab me in my office ever again." In the background, she heard Erin suck back a sob and her heart clenched up. All these years she spent protecting her children and here she was, flat on her back, helpless.

Anna the nurse brought her more meds and more chairs to accommodate her family. Lauren tried to keep up with the conversations swirling around her, the words and voices and faces. In the end, the stress and strain proved too much, and she found herself drifting off while talking to Lindsey.

At least she didn't dream.

6

Arguing with Reese and her family about Reese coming to live with her was futile, and Lauren knew it. Better to just go along and pretend he was going to move in. It took two more days before Dr. Patel removed the chest tube. Now she had matching scars on her right side, front and back. Once the tube was out, the face mask was reduced to two irritating tubes stuck into her nostrils. Her stitches itched like crazy, it still hurt to breathe, but even she could tell she was getting better.

Better enough to get interviewed by Joy Walsh on Thursday night. Joy, with her crazy short, dark choppy hair and gum-chewing habit, came in like a hurricane with Ben Lema following after her.

Lauren's parents exited, taking Lindsey and Erin down to the coffee shop on the first floor. "You two don't need to hear this again," Dad told them, herding them out the door. Lauren suspected her daughters would be caffeine addicts like their mom by the time she left the hospital. Reese had gone out to get a pizza for the nurses. It was always good to butter up the people changing your bedpans.

"How are you feeling?" Joy asked, snapping her gum. "You look good. Your color, I mean. I saw you in the ICU and you looked like shit."

Lauren had to laugh at Joy's approach. There wasn't a ladylike bone in her body, and Lauren appreciated it. "It's better to look good than to feel good, right?"

"Are they letting you have caffeine yet?" Joy asked.

Lauren glanced up at the apparatus hanging above her head. "If you could just dump a cup into my IV bag, I wouldn't tell the nurses who did it and I'd be in your debt forever."

"Sorry, friend," Joy said. "Fresh out of java."

Giving an encouraging smile, Ben added, "We're all just glad you're on the mend."

"Have you got anything?" Lauren asked the mismatched detectives. Both in their early forties, they were a study in contrasts. Where Joy was a swirling mass of energy, Ben was the neat, quiet thinker type, with his sand-colored hair neatly combed to the side and eyebrows so light they looked almost invisible. He was fantastic in the interrogation room, and his patience was legendary. An hour, three hours, or ten hours; he could literally wait out a confession without ever raising his voice or showing signs of getting tired. He stood slightly behind Joy in his charcoal gray suit, letting her take the lead.

"We've been working with Reese as much as we can. He's been up here ninety percent of the time, but I swear every time he goes downstairs for coffee, he checks in." Joy ran a hand through her crazy mop of hair. "I have a copy of the new file you were working on when you were attacked, and Reese gave us the rundown on the two cases you were working hardest."

"The Thu Chang murder and the Jolene Jefferson case."

"Your suspect in Jolene's case is in Folsom Prison in Louisiana for another murder," Joy told her, but Lauren was already well aware. The next stop in that case was a trip down South and if Reese had his way, preferably during the famous Folsom Prison Rodeo. "We didn't find any family ties to the police department. None in the Thu Chang murder, either. We're not ruling anything out, but your work on those two cases doesn't seem to be related to your stabbing."

"The murder that happened earlier that day? You think that's connected to me?"

"We know someone stole Garcia's swipe and keys off his desk sometime between when the homicide occurred, roughly nine a.m., and six o'clock, when Garcia told Marilyn it was missing. That was right before she closed up the main office for the night and Garcia and the rest of his crew went out to finish their canvass."

"It was a messy situation," Lauren remembered. "Three scenes. Multiple witnesses. Me and Reese both pitched in and took statements. Every interview room was full. All the chairs in the hallway occupied."

"We have every cop we know that was in the Homicide office that day making a list of every single person they remember seeing," Joy said. "Between detectives, uniforms, report technicians, and cleaners, we're up to forty-six people. And we haven't got some of the reports yet. You know how coppers are."

Did she ever. Joy and Ben would be chasing those pieces of paper for the next week.

"I want you to look at the list of names we have so far." Joy produced a piece of paper from her folio and put it face down on the tray table next to Lauren's bed. Lauren picked it up and scanned it, silently wishing for her readers. "I want you to go over them and tell us if you've ever had any problems with anyone on it. I mean any problems at all."

"You know that me and Garcia have had problems, right?"

She and Craig Garcia had had a confrontation when she first got to the Homicide squad. Over the years they'd had continual squabbles: a snide word here, a smirk there, a snarky note about one of her cases posted where everyone could see. It was a constant battle of micro-aggressions. But sometimes those could bloom into outright aggression.

Both detectives nodded in unison. "Already checked and cleared," Joy said. "He wasn't too happy we came to him first."

Ben added, "And it's not a secret there's no love lost between you and Vatasha Anthony, either."

Vatasha. There was no reason for the animosity between the two women, they just didn't like each other. Still, Lauren was certain that she saw a man's boot.

"I think this kid, Connor Adams, cut me off in front of headquarters at the end of October." She was reaching now, she knew. Then a name jumped out at her. "Patrick Harrington got a reprimand for not doing a report for a domestic violence victim back when I was in the Special Offense squad. The victim called the office when he pulled away without doing a thing. I got him on the radio and asked him to go back and take a report. He refused, so I drove out to her house and did it myself. His lieutenant got wind of it and let him have it. That was years ago, though."

"A reprimand in your file follows you around your career like herpes," Joy said, making a note. "That can kill a promotion."

"You think that Harrington blamed you?" Ben asked.

"I know he did, but I wasn't the one who told his lieutenant what happened. As far as I was concerned, everything was handled." Lauren remembered walking by him at a party a few weeks later and hearing him call her a bitch, then pretended not to notice her when she turned around. After that incident, he'd never said another word to her. She'd seen him a hundred times since, all without so much as a dirty look.

"Did you run into him in the office the morning of the homicide?" Joy asked.

She shook her head. "No. But I wasn't looking for him, either." Lauren had more questions about that day. She tried to steer the conversation away from Harrington for the moment. "And the swipe cards? What do they say about who was there?"

"We got the records, but that propped door throws everything off. People were just coming and going at will. We should have a scene integrity sheet for the Homicide office, too, not just the crime scenes," Ben threw in. "We do have all the camera footage from within a two-block radius of headquarters."

"And?" Lauren prompted.

"It shows a lot of cops coming and going from headquarters until a little after six, but only Reese leaving at 7:05, and then him coming back into the building at 7:18. The next thing you see is a swarm of ambulances, patrol cars, and fire trucks."

"To help me." Somehow, she felt shame in that. That she hadn't been able to protect herself in her own office. That Reese had to be the cavalry that came in and saved the day for her. She changed the subject: "Reese said the person who attacked me tried to get into the file room."

Joy nodded. "The video from inside the room shows a shadow. Damn frosted glass. But it does appear that someone was trying keys and turning the knob."

"Whoever did this was smart," Ben continued. "We don't think you were the intended target, but he did plan the break in. He stole the swipe card and the keys during the day, hid out somewhere, and came back to the office after he thought it was all closed up. It looks like he couldn't get into the file room for some reason, even with the stolen keys, and went into your office for the Murder Book. He just didn't plan on you staying late on a Friday night."

"The captain changed the locks last year on the file room. It used to be everyone in Homicide had a key. Now only Cold Case, the captain, and the day RT have one."

"Why'd he do that?" Ben asked. "I didn't even know my key didn't work anymore."

"Twenty-two people in Homicide, four in Cold Case, two report technicians, and one captain equals a lot of people with access to files that are considered evidence in and of themselves. The DA's office wanted us to limit the access if we could. Like you said, you didn't even know the lock was changed. You probably just asked Marilyn, the RT, when you needed to see an old file and gave it back to her when you were done anyway."

Ben smiled. "Guilty."

Joy opened the folder she'd brought with her, poised her pen over it and asked, "What do you remember?"

Lauren dutifully went over her attack for the hundredth time, trying not to leave out any details, although there wasn't much to say, it happened so fast.

"You're sure whoever it was took your Murder Book?" Ben asked. Joy and Ben both knew Lauren used that book on an almost daily basis. Since none of the Homicide files were digitized before the year 2000, it had been her best way to look up cases quickly. Lauren was often seen wandering between her office and the file room with that distinctive green binder under her arm, looking for an old file.

She nodded. "Right in his black-gloved hand."

"You saw them? City-issue gloves?" Joy tried to clarify.

31

"I'm not sure about the gloves, but the boots were definitely issued by the city. That's all I really saw. I passed out pretty quick."

"You tell us, Lauren," Ben said, "if someone was trying to get into the file room and couldn't, why would they steal the Murder Book instead?"

That was the million-dollar question, wasn't it? Lauren had been thinking about that a lot over the last few days and had come to only one conclusion. "If there was a file a cop didn't want anyone to look at from twenty years ago, it's only on paper in that room. If you took the file and burned it, there'd be no way to piece together that investigation again. All the original notes, reports, everything, are in those files. Sure, you could get the crime report off microfiche and the crime scene photos from photography, but the entire investigation would be lost."

"And the book?" Ben asked.

"It's my indexing system. Say all you had was a year and a street, I could flip to that year and look the homicide up by street." Lauren's eyes searched around, looking for something. "Give me a pen and paper."

Joy flipped the legal pad inside her leather folio to a new page and handed over the pen she'd been using. Lauren quickly sketched out what a page in the Murder Book looked like:

DATE/TIME-VICTIM NAME-RACE/GENDER-ADDRESS-METHOD-ADRESSS OF OCCURENCE-ARREST

"See?" She held the drawing up for them. "I could look up all the white females strangled in 1998. Or all the males shot on Cherry Street, if you didn't have a year. It was the original database. Some brilliant copper thought it up in the eighties. The oldest entries are handwritten. Those are the cases that aren't in the computer yet. I make sure the RTs add all the previous years' homicides every January, and it works like a charm."

"And now someone took the book," Ben said as he and Joy bent over the sketch. "What would be the point? Why would someone want to steal it?"

"To hide something."

"Hide what?" Joy asked, taking the paper from Lauren's hand.

"A murder." Closing her eyes, Lauren eased herself back against her pillows. She suddenly felt exhausted. "Finding an old cold case from limited information just got a hell of a lot harder."

7

The removal of the chest tube seemed to signal that the worst was over. Lauren told her daughters they should go back to school; that she was out of the woods, and she should be home for Thanksgiving break the following week. They protested, of course, but knew she was right. Sitting there staring at their mom and her IV drip wasn't helping anything, and their school work was piling up.

Before they would leave, the girls made her do something Lauren swore she'd never do. Something that she had fought against for years. "I don't want to tweet or be on Instagram or Snapchat," she protested as Lindsey positioned Lauren's personal laptop on a pillow in front of her.

"I'm just signing you up for Facebook," Lindsey told her mom. "All the old people are on Facebook."

Rolling her eyes, Lauren entered her email address. "I don't want any perverts contacting me on this thing."

"We'll set the privacy to the highest level," Erin assured her. "Only friends of friends will even be able to find you, and you can block anyone you want. I do it all the time."

"Who are my friends?" Lauren stared at the blank profile page as Lindsey started dragging and dropping pictures from her hard drive into the empty spaces.

"Me and Erin," Lindsey told her, "once we friend request you. Accept us, Mom. Don't ignore the request. Maybe Reese could be your friend. Grandma too."

"Your grandmother is on Facebook?"

"Don't look so shocked," Erin admonished her, typing something in under the ABOUT section. "Grandma is on Twitter too. We tweet all the time."

"I barely know what that means."

"Facebook means we can message you and post pictures to your wall and check in at places, so you'll know where we are. And you can, too, so we'll know where you are," Lindsey explained.

"Can't we just text each other?"

"You don't look at your text messages until you go to bed sometimes," Lindsey said. It was true; Lauren hated her cell phone. She carried her work phone during the day and often left her personal one at home. She figured anyone who had to get ahold of her would know how to reach her.

Giving in on the social media stance made Lindsey and Erin feel better about having to go back to school. They said they'd feel more *attached* to her, which was a generational thing, Lauren knew. They felt most connected through technology, which Lauren thought was sad. That's why she'd held off for so long, depending on their Saturday three-way calls to stay connected. She prayed social media wouldn't end those conversations, but she knew she had to embrace social media somewhat to stay close to her girls. Consoling herself with the fact she'd be able to spy on her daughters—even if it wasn't really spying if you and your friends put your whole life on the Internet anyway—Lauren finished setting up her account and accepted her first two friend requests: Lindsey Riley and Erin Riley.

8

Erin left first, crying and still wanting to cling to her mom. Lauren's dad stood sentry in the background, hands stuffed deep in his pockets, ready to drive Erin to the airport. "I'll be home next week," she told Lauren. "As soon as my last class lets out on Wednesday, I'll be back."

"I know, honey. I'll be fine." Lauren kissed her daughter's forehead, trying not to show the full ache of separation that washed over her every time either of her daughters left her.

Lindsey took off first thing the next morning, on Friday, exactly one week after the attack. "Listen," Lindsey brushed back her blond hair, so similar to Lauren's, "I'm only leaving because Reese is coming to live with you. If you kick him out, I'll drop out of school to stay with you."

"You two are unbelievable." Lauren looked from Lindsey to her partner. Reese was conveniently lounging on one of the chairs. "Ganging up on me. Hitting me where you know it hurts."

Reese shrugged and pulled his baseball cap down over his eyes. "We can't help it if you're stubborn and we have to resort to drastic measures."

"He only stays until I go back on full duty, which I intend to do within a month."

Reese snorted from under his cap and feigned sleep. Kissing her mom on her forehead, Lindsey's eyebrows were knit together in frustration. "Don't be difficult, Mom. I'll be home for dinner next Thursday, checking up on you. I mean it, you better be good and do what Reese says."

"I'll try." Lindsey knew it was the best she was going to get out of Lauren.

Putting a smile on her face, Lindsey brightened, "See you soon. If anything happens, I'll be on the next plane home."

Watching her daughters leave was more painful than the chest tube. Her mom, dad, and sister all left that same day, right after Lindsey, echoing the Thanksgiving reunion speech and threats to come live with her if she didn't behave herself. As stressful as seeing her mom and sister usually was, this time it had been different. The realization of your own mortality tends to dull the edges on old grudges.

With no one left to sit and stare at her but Reese, Dr. Patel was encouraging Lauren to get up and walk the halls now that her tube was out and she was "healing nicely." Lauren waited until Reese went home to take a shower before she attempted to waddle the hallway dragging her IV bag along with her. She hated the hospital gown, hated the slippers, and hated the tubes up her nose most of all, so she pulled those out before she took her stroll.

A cop was still assigned to guard her door. That day it was a young guy she'd never seen before, sitting in a hard-backed plastic chair, playing Candy Crush on his iPhone. Looking up as Lauren managed to slide out the door with her apparatus in tow, he gave her a smile. "Hey, Detective. I'm Roger Weeks. I work out of the Delta District."

He stood up, stuffed his phone in his shirt pocket, and stuck out his hand. She noticed his uniform shirt was pressed and neat, the way a rookie's always was. The pleat lines in his pants were so sharp you could cut a finger on them. *I wonder if he still lives with his mother,* Lauren thought as she waved him off with her free hand.

"You're fine. I just need to take a walk. I'm only allowed to go as far as the nurses' station. You sit. Play your game."

"Whatever you want," he replied, sinking down in the chair, eyeing her like she was a zoo animal finally allowed to roam the grounds.

He looks like a baby, she thought, stepping carefully down the hall, using her IV pole for support when needed. *I'm literally old enough to be his mother. Maybe I should offer to iron his pants. Make myself useful.*

The hallway in front of her was clear except for an empty hospital bed propped against the wall. She stuck her hand under one of the sanitizing dispensers, covering it in foam, then rubbed them together. *Force of habit,* she thought, *these places are so nasty with germs.* Up ahead she could see some activity at the nurses' station. Her two favorite nurses, Anna and Juan, were bent over paperwork while Kent, ECMC Public Safety, was staring at the computer in front of him on the desk.

"Hey, chica," Juan called when he saw her making her way toward them. Today he was wearing scrubs with happy green aliens all over them. "Slow down, this ain't the Indy 500."

"Are those mine?" Lauren motioned towards a huge pink and purple bouquet of flowers twice as wide around as she was. A white ribbon was tied off in an elaborate bow around the glass vase stuffed with stems.

Anna pushed them forward so Lauren could see them better. "Your partner said he would grab them on his next run home. Not enough room in his car." She gave them an admiring glance. "I have to say, these are the best ones yet. And you've gotten a lot."

Juan plucked the card from the little plastic trident stuck between the blooms and held it out to her. "Go ahead. Who are they from? The president?"

Lauren shook her head with a smile. "Cut it out, Juan. You're going to make me blush."

"That's why we call him Don Juan," Anna joked as Lauren struggled to get the card out of the tiny envelope.

Printed in neat black block letters was: GET BETTER SOON. DAVID SPENCER XOXO

Lauren dropped the card on the floor and looked around. "When did these get here?" Lauren demanded. Shooting her good arm out, she slapped her palm to the wall to steady herself. Kent looked up from his emails, startled.

Both Anna and Juan came around the nurses' station at the sudden change in her demeanor. "What? What's wrong?" Anna asked as Juan grabbed her on her good side and held her up, easing her to the station desk.

"Did you see who left these?" Lauren had Anna by the front of her scrubs with one hand.

"It was a kid," Anna told her, gently trying to break her grip. "I thought he might be one of your daughters' boyfriends. Good-looking, nineteen or twenty. He was here a half hour ago. He wanted to see you, but he wasn't on the list."

"He said okay and asked if he could leave them for you." Kent stood up. "Is everything all right?"

Waving at Kent to sit back down, her voice dropped an octave. "Help me back to my room." She let Anna go and hooked her arm around Juan.

"What's the matter?" Juan pressed. "Was that kid the one who hurt you?"

"No," Lauren told him as he guided her gently down the hallway. "Not me."

A year ago, Lauren had made a mistake. A huge mistake. One that almost got her killed in her own backyard. She had agreed to help with the defense of a now twenty-year-old man who had been charged with murdering the beautiful wife of a wealthy local business owner. As the case dragged on she began to have doubts over David Spencer's innocence. David developed an unhealthy fixation on Lauren, at one point causing her to storm out of the holding center after he caressed her hair. His lawyer, Frank Violanti, insisted it was just the hormones of an incarcerated teenager, that David's boundaries had been eroded by the stress he was under.

Lauren should have known better, but truth be told, her need to stick it to her ex-fiancé, Joe Wheeler, who was the arresting officer, clouded her common sense. After her first divorce, she thought Wheeler had been the kind of strong-willed man that would be good for her and her young daughters. She couldn't have been more wrong. After she finally dumped him, he'd transferred from the Buffalo Police Department to suburban Garden Valley, where she'd had little to no contact with him over the years, right up until he'd arrested David Spencer for the murder of Kathrine Vine.

Lauren had taken so many physical beatings from that man when they were together, she wanted to prove to him she was stronger and better without him. Joe hadn't liked that. He'd punched her in the mouth, knocking her to the ground at David's arraignment. She hadn't told anyone in authority about that at first; she hadn't wanted anything to interfere with David's trial. Lauren had needed to see Joe beaten in a courtroom, to feel the humiliation of an acquittal in his first big arrest and be the cause behind it.

Her underestimation of Joe Wheeler's level of hatred toward her could have cost her her life. Their tumultuous relationship finally peaked when she caught him sneaking into her backyard, and Lauren had no doubt what he had been planning to do to her. But without an overt violent act, Joe had only gotten arrested for trespass and harassment, the legal equivalent of parking tickets.

She'd managed to get Joe Wheeler suspended for stalking her after the trial was over. He'd had no choice but to plead guilty to the harassment in Buffalo City Court, but his departmental charges were still pending. He was about to lose his job. Maybe.

Had Joy Walsh given Wheeler the once-over yet? Did Garden Valley cops wear the same type of boots as Buffalo cops? Lauren didn't think Wheeler would risk sneaking into headquarters, not to steal the Murder Book. She couldn't think of any reason for him to take that.

Lauren shouldn't have let her pride dictate her actions. She knew that. She shouldn't have let her hatred for Wheeler trump her common sense. She should have given David's lawyer her retainer back and walked away. But she didn't, and when the jury read the verdict of not guilty, she was positive that not only had David Spencer murdered Kathrine Vine, but that he had also killed his girlfriend, Amber Anderson, whose body was found decomposing in the woods south of the city on the last day of the trial.

Lauren had been monitoring David Spencer over the last twelve months. Keeping tabs. It hadn't reached the point of obsession, more like a constant vigilance on her part. Even Reese didn't know how closely she was tracking him because she kept it at a distance from their regular case load. She never confronted David, hadn't spoken a word to him since they walked out of the courtroom, had had no direct contact at all. As the months stretched into a year, she had begun to slack in her surveillance. He had kept out of trouble, out of the public eye and, perhaps most importantly, away from her.

And now this, a visit to her hospital room. She had no explanation for what his motive could possibly be. Lauren knew one thing for sure: David Spencer was dangerous. Even when he was playing nice. Hell, *especially* when he was playing nice.

Lauren had Juan and Anna get her settled back in bed, then swore them to secrecy about the flowers. "Give them to your mom, throw them out, just get rid of them now."

"You sure you don't want me to tell your cop friend outside?" Juan was trying to untangle her lines.

"And interrupt his video game? I trust you and Anna to protect me more than that kid." Lauren struggled to get the tubes back into her nose.

"I did take karate lessons in seventh grade."

"And for that, Juan, I am truly in your debt. Just make a note on the visitors list that if a David Spencer shows up again, don't accept anything, and call my room right away."

"Will do, but is this guy someone we should be worried about?" Anna asked.

"I don't think so. It's a bit complicated, is all." There was too much to explain and not enough wind left in her lungs. "Just don't tell Reese. I'll handle it."

"Get some rest, chica." Juan propped her pillow behind her back. "I'll come back and check on you in a little while."

"Just don't karate chop me."

Juan made a double-strike motion for her with a goofy look on his face. She managed to crack a phony smile for him as they walked out the door even though her stomach was twisted in knots.

43

Damn David Spencer.

He was the last thing she needed complicating her life. Grabbing her cell phone off the table next to her bed, she turned it over in her hand. Part of her wanted to call Frank Violanti and tell him to keep his creepy little client/godson on a leash. But the sane part of her knew that any contact with Violanti was poison and might, in some mysterious way, prolong her stay in the hospital.

Her smart phone showed she had 123 unopened texts and 452 emails. Some of them were from her ex-husband, Mark, and three were from a cousin who wanted her to follow up on his divorce case. Chucking the phone back on the table, she tried to take a deep breath and relax. Her private investigations would wait. And so could Mark. If she played nice and followed directions, Dr. Patel had told her she could be home early next week. No good adding drama to the mix at this point in the game. *I can be patient*, she thought as her phone dinged to report another incoming text from some well-wisher. *More patient than whoever attacked me, because when I get out of here, I'm going after him hard.*

9

By the time Reese got back from delivering the pizzas and flirting with the nurses, Lauren had managed to calm herself down. The last thing she needed was Reese going off to find David Spencer and losing his temper on him. It wasn't David Spencer who stabbed her; she knew this, and she wouldn't let him become a distraction from the person who did. She'd take care of David herself when she got out of the hospital.

"Can you have pizza?" Slinging a pizza box across the small table by the window, Reese flipped the top up to reveal half a pie: extra cheese, extra sausage.

"I don't think I'm allowed to have that."

Reese made a grunting noise as he stuffed a slice in his mouth, making sure to chew with it open for added effect.

Lauren's lip curled in disgust. "I can actually hear your arteries harden."

"This is so good."

"Don't they miss you at work?"

He tried to lasso a ropey piece of cheese hanging from his mouth using his tongue. "Nope," he told her when he successfully inhaled the cheese. "The commissioner has made you my assignment."

"It's not that I don't appreciate everything you've done. I do. I don't think I would have made it through all this without your help." The sincerity in her voice stopped Reese's pizza-fest cold. That was not how their relationship worked. Lauren insulted him, he insulted her, all was right in the world. "But you don't have to stay here. You've done enough for me."

"One: you can never do enough for a friend." He wiped his mouth with a napkin and picked up another slice. "Two: I just told you that the police department made you my job for now. And three: you are not the boss of me, so sit there and shut up. I'm trying to enjoy my food. You should actually eat something sometime. You probably love getting fed by a tube."

Watching him attack the second slice was like watching a wolf devour a deer. "You know what? Take the sausage off that small piece for me."

A huge smile spread across his face as he plucked the meat from her pizza.

"Did you wash your hands?" she asked as he handed over the goods.

"Probably not."

She bit into the warm, gooey cheese. "I figured."

10

The police department had made no progress on her assault when Reese wheeled her out of the Erie County Medical Center to a waiting patrol car on Sunday. With only four days until Thanksgiving, Lauren had begged to be released, promised she'd be faithful in her follow-ups, and sworn she'd take it easy while following her doctor's orders. Dr. Patel finally gave in, and Reese notified the chain of command so a proper police escort could be arranged from the hospital.

Lauren took in the sea of faces surrounding her as Reese slowly pushed her wheelchair to the waiting police vehicle. A line of cops had formed on either side to keep the swarm of media back. There was a leak somewhere in either the police department or the DA's office—had been for a while—and Lauren was positive that whoever it was had made sure to give the press the exact time of her release.

Reporters called out questions. Bystanders filmed her with their cell phones. *Look at me,* she thought bitterly as she tried to fake a smile, *I'm the dumbass who managed to get beaten and stabbed inside police headquarters!* Cameras and microphones filled her vision as she got into the backseat of the chief of E-District's Chevy Tahoe.

Reese climbed in next to her as Benny Hughes twisted around in his seat to greet her. "It's good to see you, Lauren. You really scared us there for a minute."

Chief Benny Hughes had worked as a lieutenant with her in the Special Offense squad, also known as the Sex Offense squad or SOS, before getting promoted. It was good to see his smiling face. "Thanks, Benny. I mean, Chief," she fumbled.

"I don't know what to call myself sometimes," he told her, putting the truck into gear and flipping on the overhead lights. "You call me Benny. Just don't call me Bunny Hedges."

"I forgot about that." She explained to Reese, "A lady left a message for him, only the cleaner had answered the phone and it got posted as Lieutenant Bunny Hedges. You know the guys in the squad had a field day."

Reese smirked. "I love hearing all your old-timey cop stories."

Hughes raised an eyebrow at him in the rearview mirror. "Don't get on my bad side now, kid. It's tragic enough I'm going to take all your money in the playoffs this year."

Listening to them go back and forth about their fantasy football teams, Lauren leaned her head against her window, feeling the cool of November through the glass against her skin. Outside, the trees had shed the majority of their leaves but were still painted up in reds and oranges and yellows. She loved fall, loved the crisp autumn air, the pumpkin pies, and crunchy scarlet apples. Buffalo was known for its snow and terrible winters, but it should have been known for its spectacular falls.

Benny killed the lights once they were clear of the paparazzi in the parking lot and was now taking his time to get her over to her house.

Awarded her mini mansion, clear and paid for, in her second divorce settlement, Lauren lived in a gated community off of Millionaire's Row on Delaware Avenue. At the turn of the twentieth century, there had been more millionaires in Buffalo than anywhere else in the country, and the legacy of that was the number of opulent mansions left behind by the grain and steel barons. Most had been converted into business use, but a few were still private residences. While Lauren's house was not on their grand scale, it was still an impressive dwelling for a city cop, detective or not.

Benny pulled into the driveway, which was blessedly free of the press. That was one good thing about having an actual guard stopping people trying to get in: the press was thwarted in their coverage of her homecoming. Wondering if her lawn service had watered them while she was gone, Lauren noticed that her yellow and orange chrysanthemums were still blooming beautifully in their pots along the front of her two-story Colonial. Thankfully, she had taken down all her Halloween decorations two days before she got attacked. It would have been more than a little freaky to come home to a lawn full of plastic tombstones.

The burly chief got out and grabbed her bag from the front seat. She didn't have much; Reese had taken almost everything back to her house the night before in preparation for this homecoming. Benny came around the front of the car to help her out and give her a deep hug. "I'm glad you're okay," he whispered in her ear. "Don't scare us like that again."

Reese took the bag, gave the chief half a man-hug, then held on to Lauren's arm as they went up the front walk. Out of nowhere her neighbor Dayla came tearing up Lauren's driveway wearing high heels, an orange maxi dress, and a thick brown sweater. Benny almost restrained her until Reese waved him off. "She's with us," he told the chief.

49

"I'm so happy you're home! They wouldn't even let me see you. Can you believe that?"

She had Lauren around the neck, hopping up and down as much as her stilettos would allow. Lauren never knew what look Dayla was going to be sporting on any given day. Dayla was married to a prominent local plastic surgeon and had had at least six procedures since Lauren moved in. She'd taken the weave out of her jet-black hair sometime since Lauren had been hospitalized, leaving the locks to flow in natural curls against her coffee-colored skin. Beautiful and careless, Lauren's best friend gave her the worst advice but was the greatest company.

"And you!" She stuck a manicured finger in Reese's face. "Shane Reese, you should have told them to let me in. Shame on you."

"Dayla, if I'd have known you were on the floor, don't you think I would have welcomed you in instead of incurring your wrath?" Reese tried to maneuver around Dayla's flailing arms.

"On that note," Benny said, backing up, still not quite sure what to make of the tornado that was Dayla, "I'll be going. Lauren, call or text me if you need anything. Reese, see you at the last football party. And um ..." He looked at Dayla, who still had Lauren in a chokehold. "It was nice meeting you. Goodbye, all."

"You scared away my friend," Lauren told Dayla, untangling herself from her grip.

Waving to him as he drove away, Dayla admonished her, "He has police stuff to go and do. I get to take care of you now. You need a good dose of black-girl magic."

Hearing Reese suppress a laugh from behind her, Lauren let Dayla guide her up the front walk to the door. The lawn had been freshly cut and the leaves raked, although some stragglers blew across the path in front of them. Reese fished Lauren's keys out of his back pocket and opened the front door.

"What the hell is that?" Lauren asked, looking down.

"It's a dog." Reese brushed past her, set her bag on the floor, and started to rub the little white dog under his chin. The dog jumped up, licking at his face in pure happiness.

"I know it's a dog, but why is it in my house?"

"This is Watson, my West Highland Terrier." Reese fell back and let the dog fully pounce on him, jumping on his chest, barking and licking.

"He's been here a couple days now. Shane had me taking Watson out for walks while he was at the hospital with you." Dayla eased Lauren farther into the hallway so she could shut the door behind them.

"How long have you had a dog? And how did I not know?"

He sat up, cradling Watson in his arms like a baby. "You don't know everything about me. Four months ago an old friend was moving to Missouri and couldn't take him. I always loved the little guy when I was over at his apartment, so Watson came to live with me."

"And his name just happens to be Watson?"

Reese shrugged and let the dog go. He promptly ran over to Lauren and jumped up on her shins. She bent down as far as she could and scratched his ears.

"It was actually Wilson, but that's my grandfather's name, so I altered it a little."

Maybe it was the shock of the dog, or maybe the relief of being in her own home, but suddenly Lauren was overpowered by the smell of hundreds of flowers. Looking around her living room, still scratching Watson, Lauren absorbed the sight of dozens of floral arrangements covering every conceivable surface. Some were even set off to the side of each step going up her staircase. "What am I going to do with all of these?"

"Every day I've been taking a few to a nursing home, but as soon as I clear a spot, another vase arrives." Dayla reached over to pluck a lily out of an arrangement and tuck it behind her ear. "That one there is from Mark." She pointed to an enormous, elaborate arrangement of roses and lilies. "He also sent a robe and slipper set, new three-hundred-dollar pajamas with the tags still attached, and left twelve messages for you on your twentieth-century land line answering machine."

Wrinkling her nose, she motioned to Mark's flowers. "Get rid of those next."

Dayla admired her new floral accessory in the hall mirror, muttering, "Harsh." Lauren ignored Dayla's attempt to bait her into a conversation about her ex-husband.

"I think you found a new friend," Reese observed with a grin. Looking down, Lauren realized she was standing with Watson in her arms. Despite the painful ache in her side that warned her to not strain herself, she didn't have the heart to put the soft white dog down. Perfectly content, Watson had closed his eyes, ears flat against his head, enjoying the attention.

"He's a little sweetie." Lauren had been going back and forth for over a year about getting a puppy. Growing up, her family had always had dogs. She'd almost caved in to her daughters a couple of times but then came to her senses that they weren't home enough to care for a puppy the way they needed to be. Now with this little ball of pure love in her arms, she remembered why a dog might be the best thing for her.

"Go upstairs and get settled in," Dayla said. "I'll take care of everything."

"You won't even know me and Watson are here," Reese assured her. "He has a crate in my room and hardly ever barks. He's so mellow."

"Thanks, guys." Feeling tired, Lauren started to climb the flower-strewn staircase.

"Can I have my dog back?" Reese called as she reached the landing, still holding the snoozing Westie.

Disappearing with Watson onto the second floor, Lauren called back, "We're good."

11

$\mathbf{B}$eing home did feel good, especially knowing Lindsey and Erin would be back in less than four days. She talked to them on the phone every night, and she was even getting the hang of the whole Facebook thing, including stalking people she hadn't seen in years and poring over their photos. It was crazy what normal people posted for the entire world to see. They'd been using Facebook to track suspects and witnesses for years, but it always seemed like such a foreign thing to her, like something aliens from another planet might do, not people she knew and loved.

With the companionship of her new best friend, Watson, who followed her around the house all day long, she had no urge to rush off to try to figure out who shanked her just yet. Because she was home from the hospital, that meant Reese was back at work and could bring back information to her about developments in the case first-hand. All she had to do was wait for him to walk in the door so she could grill him.

Living with Reese turned out to be surprisingly easy. But it had only been a day. He would retreat into his wing and watch sports, giving Lauren the space she needed. With Watson to keep her company while she was healing, she was in a good place, all things considered.

David Spencer's visit to the hospital still nagged at her, though. She had gotten him off on a murder he most certainly had committed, lied to her, used her. She couldn't imagine what else he could possibly want from her. Nothing good, anyway. Not a nice chat or to hold her hand, that was for sure. No, people like him had to have ulterior motives. Their entire lives were ulterior motives.

Now that she was home from the hospital, she decided to find out what was going on in David Spencer's sick little brain.

Unused since her attack, her home office in the basement definitely needed a good dusting. Setting Watson on the carpeted floor, she sat down at her desk and fired up her computer. She used her iPad to Facebook-surf in bed; this computer was strictly for business. Having a private investigator's license meant having access to several excellent, but expensive, databases. She couldn't legally use the law enforcement resources at work for her PI business, but that really wasn't a hindrance. People's whole lives were documented on the Internet. Having her own account on Facebook reinforced that truth. You just had to know how to do a proper search.

As Watson shuffled around the floor, sniffing feverishly at this newfound territory, Lauren typed David's name and date of birth into her favorite public records database.

Interesting. David had changed his address two months ago from his mom's place to a house in a section of Clarence, north of the city. A woman named Melissa St. John was listed as the property owner. Running a check on her name revealed Melissa's age to be twenty-nine. *What kind of game is he playing?* she thought as she printed out their address: 1462 East Goose Lake Road. That was an expensive section of Clarence, very high-end new builds.

Lauren had only just been released from the hospital. Her doctor, her partner, her parents, and her kids would have a fit if she went off to talk to David Spencer on her own. She wasn't even supposed to drive yet.

"Well, Watson," she announced to her tail-wagging sidekick, "looks like I'm going on a road trip tomorrow."

12

Watching Reese inhale the pancakes she made him for breakfast the next morning brought back memories of long-ago hectic Tuesday mornings with the girls rushing to get ready for school, hopefully not forgetting their lunch bags or gym clothes, and her reminding them not to drip syrup on their uniforms.

Now she was having coffee while Reese ate with his fingers, alternately shoving a piece in his mouth, then giving Watson some and letting him lick his fingers clean, then popping another piece in his own mouth.

"No wonder you're single," Lauren observed, sipping black coffee from an oversized mug.

"If I had a dollar for every time you said that…" Reese picked at another pancake while Watson's tail wagged furiously in anticipation.

"I don't think maple syrup is good for dogs."

"Don't tell me how to raise my kid," Reese said good-naturedly, wiping his mouth with a napkin. Standing up, he pulled his jacket off the back of the kitchen chair, slung it over his arm, and went over to the sink to wash. Watson jumped on his legs, wanting to be picked up. "Sorry, boy. My hands are all sticky. I wouldn't want you to have to get another bath because your stepmom kissed your white fur with her red lipstick on."

"That was Dayla," Lauren protested, clearing the dishes from the table. She waited for Reese to finish wiping his hands. He moved aside, stuffing his arms in his jacket as he went. Lauren stacked the plates on the granite countertop next to the sink. Running the water, she gave it a second to heat up before she began to clean the tableware.

Reese nuzzled his face close to Watson's nose. "It's a good thing you have all your shots then, isn't it, Watson?"

"Hey! Be nice."

"I'm sorry, Lauren. But every time she's here, I feel like she's undressing me with her eyes. I'm not some piece of meat."

Lauren cocked an eyebrow as she rinsed the plates. Seeing Lauren's skepticism, Reese continued: "I'm a proud biracial man and I admit I let myself get used by the opposite sex quite often, but Dayla's different." He shuddered as he scooped up his portable police radio. "It's like she wants to *consume* me."

"She is a happily married woman who loves to make you squirm." Lauren noticed one of her good bowls was missing from the cabinet and wondered if it was sitting on the floor of Reese's bedroom attracting bugs.

Reese was still busy pleading his case. "She'd make me squirm, all right. And buck. And kick. And bite."

"Go to work. Find out who attacked me." She began to line the dishes in the dishwasher, plates in a neat row, thinking the only thing that got consumed that day was seven pancakes, five slices of bacon, and half a jug of orange juice. "Have a good day."

Waving as he cracked open the back door, he called, "Bye, my best friend! Have a wonderful day! You too, Lauren."

She threw a dish cloth at him, but he'd already shut the door. Watson ran over, picked it up with his mouth and gave it a good shake. Kneeling down, she tugged on the cloth, and Watson playfully pulled back. "You won't rat on me, will you?" She gave him a scratch between the ears and let go of the cloth. "Not my good boy."

13

Driving turned out to be much more painful than she thought it would. Every turn, bump, or pothole was its own slice of shiny white agony. The stab wound in her back began itching again, making her twist in her seat to try to scratch it while the seat belt strangled her. *Maybe this wasn't such a good idea*, she thought as she pulled onto the thruway. Still, she had to know. She had to see David in person and get to the bottom of his visit. She knew he hadn't gone away to college after he was acquitted of murder, like he had planned. She also knew that his lawyer/godfather had given him a job in his office. She wondered how that had turned out. Frank Violanti was never the easiest person to get along with.

The traffic was light for ten in the morning on a Tuesday. The sun was bright, the sky was clear. It was another perfect late-fall day. But it was Buffalo, so the specter of a freak storm always hung over their heads.

Listening to music on her iPhone synced to the car's sound system as she drove, Lauren sang along. She loved to drive, loved taking road trips by herself, although she hadn't done it in a while. There was something peaceful to her about the long stretches of highway, and it helped take her mind off her lingering pain.

She hit a hard right onto the exit and thought how grateful she was that the guys down at the police garage had disabled her airbags after she got her new SUV earlier in the year. It wasn't strictly legal, it was an old cab driver trick, but she couldn't afford replacing the bags every time she smacked into something. That white powder was a bitch to clean out.

Passing Amherst's Big Blue Water Tower, the traffic epicenter of the Buffalo Niagara Region, Lauren turned off her music. She wasn't as familiar with the Northtowns as the Southtowns and had to rely on her Ford Escape's GPS. As a joke, Lindsey had changed the voice to sound like an Englishman the last time she'd been home. Lauren had never gotten around to changing it back. Now Jeeves was dutifully telling her to take the next left in one quarter of a mile.

She slowly drove down East Goose Lake Road, checking the house numbers from the mailboxes at the end of the long driveways. *This is what my ex-mother-in-law would have called "new money" in her passive-aggressive tone,* Lauren thought as she rounded another corner, *as opposed to what I was, which was "no money."* Being married to the ridiculously wealthy Mark Hathaway for a year had had its advantages, but so had their divorce, like getting away from Mama Hathaway.

Double-checking the address before she pulled in, Lauren couldn't help but be surprised at how over-the-top Melissa St. John's house was, even for this neighborhood. Twice the size of the houses that flanked it on either side, the modern three-story monstrosity boasted terraces, huge oval glass windows, and an elaborate layout that looked like it belonged on a spaceship rather than in Clarence, New York.

A silver Lexus sedan and a black Cadillac SUV sat parked in front of the garage door. She pulled her Ford in behind the Caddy and hit the ignition button. As long as she lived, she would never get used to the keyless entry feature in her car.

As Lauren made her way up the front walk, she saw one of the blinds move in a window to her right. She had her off-duty Barretta holstered in the small of her back, but she made no reach for it. This was strictly an informal visit, like the one David Spencer paid to her hospital room. Lauren rarely carried a weapon off duty. The gun was just a precaution due to recent events.

The front door looked more like a porthole to Narnia, with dark wood infused with stained glass and metal. Maybe more Steampunk than Narnia, she decided as her eyes roamed over the front of the house. Someone had definitcly mixed their genres in the design.

Lauren was just about to ring the bell when the enormous door swung inward. "Can I help you?"

Standing in front of her was a tall, thin redhead who appeared to twinkle. Everything on her sparkled. From the rhinestones bedazzled into her skinny jeans, to the sequins on her low-cut top, right down to a misty shimmer in her dyed red hair. Erin and Lindsey had gone through a sparkles stage when they were thirteen and fourteen, respectively, that had included copious amounts of the shimmering body lotion that this woman seemed to have bathed in. Lauren's daughters had outgrown the fad; this woman hadn't gotten the memo it was over yet.

"Hi," Lauren said as lightly as she could manage. "Is David Spencer here?"

The glittering young woman's green eyes narrowed. "I'm his girl-friend, Melissa."

Nothing like staking your claim right off the bat, Lauren thought as she gave Lady Dazzle her best heartwarming smile. "Hi, Melissa."

It didn't melt the ice. "Why do you want to see David?" she asked, looking Lauren up and down.

"I'm Lauren Riley. I worked on his legal case last year—"

"Now I know who you are." She cut Lauren off with a snap of her fingers. "You're the one who got stabbed."

"Is David here?" Lauren asked again, feeling her temper starting to spike. Getting stabbed and drop-kicked in the head had definitely reduced her tolerance for jealous banter from someone covered head to toe in fairy dust.

"I'm here." David materialized on the side of Miss Sparkles-a-Lot.

The first thing that struck Lauren about his appearance was his hair: he'd dyed it blond. He was taller than she remembered, well over six feet. Six-two, if she had to guess. And muscular. He hadn't lost that prison build he'd gained, only added to it. He looked older than twenty; the little boy sweetness that had pulled her into his case had disappeared.

Coming around his girlfriend, he eased himself into her place in the doorway, effectively pushing her off to the side. "Melissa, why don't you put some coffee on? We can sit down in the living room."

"I just need a minute of your time," Lauren said, not giving him an inch. "I don't need to come inside."

"Okay." Now he sounded a little uncertain. Turning to his much older girlfriend he asked, "Can you go make me a cup?" Leaning over, he gave Melissa a light kiss on her glossed lips. She softened, nodded, and headed down the hallway, high-heeled shoes clicking the whole way.

"I'm sorry about Melissa. She has this jealousy thing." David walked out of the house, closing the door behind him, forcing Lauren back down a step onto the walk. He was wearing a crisp white tee shirt and jeans ripped at the knees but was also barefoot. "She had gastric bypass last year and lost over a hundred pounds, so she's got some self-esteem issues."

"A big mansion like this? A good-looking young boyfriend like you? I'd say she's doing all right."

David crossed his arms and leaned against the doorway. *Still so handsome,* Lauren thought, *so convincing.*

"I met Melissa when I was working for Frank after you got me out of jail. She was one of Uncle Frank's personal injury clients. She got a huge settlement from an amusement park accident. Melissa designed this house herself."

That figures. Lauren glanced around the rest of the residence, with its oval windows, almost like portholes, set in castle-like walls and a construction she had no words for sticking up from the left side resembling a midevil tower. *Where else would a grown-ass fairy princess live?*

"You still working for Violanti?" she asked.

"I used to. Not anymore. I'm surprised you didn't know that."

Lauren ignored the dig. David waited a moment for a reaction that didn't come, then said, "Melissa's family is into flipping houses. It's good money. I manage a lot of their properties for them now."

"Why did you come to the hospital?" No use prolonging the conversation with small talk.

He feigned shock that she would even ask such a question. "I wanted to see you, make sure you were okay. You saved my life, you know? I'd be in prison right now if it wasn't for you."

"You'd be in prison right now because you murdered Katherine Vine."

64

"No." He shook his finger at her like she had when she warned Watson off from chewing on her couch leg that morning. "I'm innocent. A jury said so. Because you did such a great job on my behalf. I owe my freedom and my life to you."

"Cut the act with me. We both know you killed Katherine Vine and Amber Anderson. And I'm here to tell you that a bunch of roses won't change my opinion of that. Or you playing house with Glinda the Good Witch of the East."

His brown eyes looked amused. He was getting to her, and he was getting off on it. "One thing I know about you, Detective Riley," he countered, leaning forward as though they were conspiring together, "is that if you could prove anything you just said, I'd be in Attica Correctional Facility right now. But here I am, out and free as a bird. All because of you."

"You little prick," she hissed and took a step back.

"How does your side feel? Where the guy stabbed you? I bet it still hurts. I have to tell you, that's such a bullshit move, to stab someone in the back when they're not looking. That's a coward right there. He should have at least shown you his face."

"Because if we'd been face to face, it would have been a fair fight?" she asked incredulously.

"No, because if you're going to do something to someone, it doesn't mean anything if the person doesn't know who's responsible. You man up and show yourself."

"That's a really sick and twisted thought, even for you, David."

His smile was dazzling. "You have no clue."

Talking as she turned to leave, she told him, "Don't contact me again."

"Speaking of contact, Detective Riley, you didn't happen to get my new address by illegally abusing your position at the police department and running my name without probable cause?"

She turned on her heel, facing him again as Melissa put a cup of steaming coffee into his hand. "Heavens, no. You should know, better than anyone, that you can find out just about anything on anybody using the plain old Internet. Especially an address."

"That's good. I should write that down. I think I'll use that line sometime," he called as she walked to her car. "It was great to see you again, Lauren. I hope they catch the guy who hurt you. He deserves anything he gets."

Asshole, she thought, as she poked hard at the ignition button with her finger, causing a new round of pain to flare up her back and side.

14

Seething the whole ride home, Lauren tried the breathing methods her therapist had taught her. Physical and occupational therapy were supposed to take up her mornings twice a week. It would have been more, but she had flat-out refused. In more pain after she left than when she went in, Lauren figured she was better off doing things her way. Unfortunately, the department's doctor disagreed and refused to let her go back to work until both of the therapists cleared her.

She hadn't even made it through her front door before her cell began buzzing in her pocket. Glancing at the name, she wasn't surprised. Who else would David have called after a visit from her?

"What's up, Violanti?"

"You tell me. I see on the news you got shanked at work and now you're out in Clarence harassing my client."

Frank Violanti had been the defense attorney who convinced her to work on David Spencer's case. Short, abrasive, and extremely effective in the courtroom, Violanti had pulled off the upset of the decade getting David acquitted of murder last year. She had told Violanti after the trial she would never stop trying to put David back in jail. Probably a bad move on her part, but it seemed necessary at the time, to let him know she was determined to atone for her mistakes.

"It wasn't harassment." She bent to give an adoring, excited Watson a pet on the head so he wouldn't start barking. "It was a friendly drop by to say thank you for the lovely flowers he brought me in the hospital."

Pausing to digest that for a second, Frank Violanti continued with a more subdued tone. "He visited you in the hospital?"

"Yes, but don't fret. He didn't get in to see me and he is not a suspect in my attack. So you may rest easy that David's psychotic tendencies are focused elsewhere right now. Maybe on his shiny older girlfriend?"

"I know, I know." He sighed into the phone. "Melissa St. John is a couple sandwiches short of a picnic lunch and David somehow latched on to her. It may make him a manipulative leech but not a murderer."

"If you say so, Counselor. I have to let you go now. I have healing things to do." She set herself down on her living room sofa, the exhaustion of the excursion beginning to kick in. Watson crawled up and laid his head dutifully in her lap.

"Listen, just stay away from David, Lauren. He didn't go away to the SUNY college like he'd planned, but he is taking their online classes, for criminal justice. And he's acing them. At the rate he's going he'll have his degree in a year."

"What a sad commentary on higher education in New York State."

"I get it, Lauren. I do. We aren't on the same page, and I respect that, but David is smart. Like documenting with me that you came to his house today."

"You think he'd hurt me?" she asked bluntly.

"Physically? No. He *likes* you, which may be worse. Just stay clear of him and call me if anything like the hospital ever happens again."

"All right. If he shows up on my doorstep, you'll be my first call. Or second call."

He paused, picking his next words carefully. "How are you doing? Are there any leads on who attacked you?"

Looking over at the pile of stills from the file room's surveillance camera scattered across her dining room table, she frowned into the phone. "They're working on it."

"If there's anything I can do ..."

"Yeah. No. That won't be necessary. I'll be back to Cold Case soon, same as I ever was. Thanks for the call."

"Lauren, I just meant—"

"Thanks, Frank." She clicked and ended the call. The last thing she wanted was a sentimental talk with Frank Violanti. Working with him on David's case, they had developed a mutual respect for each other, dangerously bordering on friendship. All that was smashed when Lauren realized that David had conned them both and yet Violanti still defended him.

Resting her head against the back of the sofa, gently stroking the fur between Watson's ears, she allowed herself to pass out and didn't wake up until Reese came home from work, six hours later.

15

"**H**i, honey, I'm home. How was your day?" Reese called, waking her. Lounging on the sofa with her clothes sweaty and wrinkled, Lauren watched Watson launch himself at Reese the moment he walked through the door.

The little dog was so excited, he knocked Reese's baseball cap off. Knowing Watson wouldn't be content unless he received maximum attention, Reese scooped him up and carried him into the living room. "I see you had another productive day."

"Sorry there's no dinner on the table tonight. I got a little busy with this whole letting myself heal thing."

"No worries. I brought you a present, though. To get the little gray cells working again." He plopped a manila folder in danger of bursting onto her coffee table. "Here's all the copies of reports that matter in your case right now. I figure you don't need to see every random piece of paper in the file."

"But I will." She bent forward, fanning the paperwork in front of her.

"I know, but this is a start. Nobody knows what happened to you better than you." He put Watson down and sat next to Lauren, pointing out various documents. "They did a camera canvass. It didn't take a genius to figure out where all the city cameras are located because the administration sends an updated list to the districts and squads every month."

He pulled an aerial photo from the stack, probably taken from the sheriff department's helicopter, which showed headquarters bounded on the east by Franklin Street, on the north by Church Street, and on the west by a tiny building belonging to the Diocese of Buffalo. It also showed the commercial parking lot behind headquarters and the entrance to the Skyway bridge. Reese tapped a spot behind St. Joseph Cathedral, the seat of the Diocese in Buffalo and Police Headquarters' majestic neighbor immediately to the south on Franklin Street.

"We think whoever did this probably slipped out the Church Street side, cut through the empty parking lot, and had his car parked here under the entrance to the Skyway." The spot he showed her was considered a plum parking spot for headquarters. Seven or eight vehicles could squeeze under that no-man's land beneath the elevated portion of Route 5 that ran from the Pennsylvania state line right into downtown. Neither a personal vehicle nor a cop car would stand out; either could be found wedged under the concrete overpass at any given time. "From there he could have cut down any of these little side streets, hopped on South Park Avenue here, or jumped on the thruway here."

"No cameras in the parking lot?" she asked hopefully.

"Nope. I guess having a commercial lot directly next to police headquarters would cut down on people breaking into cars. Besides, it's entirely sold out to monthly parking permit holders and locked on Fridays by six. Which means you can't get in, but you can still get out if you parked earlier in the day. It's only open on the weekends if there's an event at the arena, like a Sabres game or a concert, which there wasn't. We checked all the permit holders, and none of them were cheap-ass cops."

"Which doesn't mean a cop's girlfriend or brother-in-law doesn't have a permit there."

"It's a possibility, for sure. We're not ruling it out. Whether he parked in the lot or under the Skyway, he made sure to avoid every camera."

She let that sink in for a moment. "Whoever it was did his homework."

"Looks like it. Maybe he even saw me turn the office light out."

"I hadn't thought of that." She hadn't been sitting in the dark very long before she heard the door open.

"He could have seen it from the street outside, or from the inside."

"Which would mean he would have been watching our window from the other side of the building across the courtyard," she pointed out. "That would explain how he showed up so quickly after you left."

The courtyard was actually the roof of the basement, surrounded on four sides by the walls that made up headquarters. If someone wanted to, they could crawl out a first-floor window and walk around the debris and weed-filled area; Lauren had seen maintenance do that on occasion. For a while, when she first got to Cold Case and found herself staring out into that depressing void, she had the urge to throw sunflower seeds out her window, to see if they'd grow. She never did it, but she kept tabs on a small tree in the west corner that was now a good three feet high.

"He could have been waiting on any of the floors if he was already in the building. In one of the empty offices." With the impending move, the powers that be had already packed away a lot of the administrative offices and left them vacant. Up to half the building was probably unused at this point.

"He sees the light go off, swipes in to try to get into the file room, can't, and heads into Cold Case," Reese summarized.

"Where he sees me typing in the dark and tries to kill me," Lauren finished up. "And you have no leads."

"Ah, ah, ah, my doubting friend." Reese waved a yellow piece of paper with his telltale scribble on it in front of her face. "I got a phone call an hour ago from Carl Church. If you're feeling up to it, he'd like to meet with you, me, Joy, and Ben tomorrow. He thinks he may have something."

"Carl Church, the Erie County District Attorney who hates my guts, may have a lead in my stabbing?"

"I haven't heard anyone say 'hates my guts' since third grade," Reese said. "And he only dislikes you because you beat him in the Katherine Vine murder trial and got an acquittal."

"Which I shouldn't have done."

"Take off your hair shirt for a second and focus."

"Tomorrow is the day before Thanksgiving. Erin and my parents are coming in. Lindsey will be here first thing Thursday morning—"

Annoyed, Reese cut her off. "He says he may have information regarding your case. Do you think you'll be able to put the bon bons down, turn off *The View*, and come and hear what the man has to say tomorrow at eleven?"

It would mean she'd have to miss physical therapy. "Yes, sir. I'd love to hear what Mr. Church has to say."

"Good. And seriously: what's for dinner?"

16

Lauren nervously got dressed the next morning, flinging outfits across her bed, trying on and taking off blouses, twisting as much as she could to look at herself in the full-length mirror in her bedroom. *Not good*, she told herself, looking up and down. The freckles that had made her look cute and youthful had faded to brown spots across her nose. She'd gone from thin to gaunt since the incident. People, especially other women, were always saying how lucky she was to be naturally thin. But she also heard the whispers from those same women about how she must have some sort of eating disorder too. Now she looked like she was giving them proof. *I look like a washed out, understuffed scarecrow,* she thought, touching her shoulder-length blond hair. *Complete with straw.*

Taking a step back from her usual uniform of black pants with a black jacket and solid-colored blouse, she chose instead a loose-fitting boat neck tunic her mother had gotten her for Christmas last year. She had never worn it, but it matched perfectly with her navy pants and favorite flats. She was technically off duty, no need to dress the part. Hell, she was the *victim* in all this. She wondered if she should bring a handkerchief to put in her handbag in case she got emotional.

Scolding herself all the way downstairs for being insensitive to her victims, she realized why she was so nervous. Because of all the shitty things that had happened to her, including getting her ass kicked on a daily basis by her ex-fiancé, she had never really considered herself a victim. Even when Wheeler came to her house last year intending to kill her. Yes, she had been furious. Yes, she felt like the cops couldn't help her, and yes, she had to wait until David Spencer's murder trial was over before she could pursue charges, but she never, ever would have called herself a victim. *Victimized*, yes. But a *victim*, no.

Now she knew there was no other definition for what she had been. Or what she was now.

Reese was holding the morning paper in his hand as he stood at the bottom of the stairs, dressed in his lone court suit, looking to her much like a character from a 1950s TV show.

"What's wrong?" she asked. "You have that look on your face."

"Did you see the morning paper?" He held it out to her.

"How could I see it if you have it in your hands?" She snagged it from him and he followed her into the kitchen.

"Someone leaked our entire timeline of your stabbing. Down to the freaking minute. Talk about giving the bad guy a head start."

She shook the paper out to read the headline. It quoted "law enforcement sources" and gave details right down to the time she had logged onto her computer. "This has got to be someone in our office," she fumed. "Who else would have this information?"

"It's either our Homicide squad, the brass, or someone in the DA's office." Reese took the paper back, folded it neatly, and placed it on the kitchen table. "Just leave that there for now. I don't want you to have a stroke before our meeting."

Getting up, she poured herself a cup of coffee, ignoring the comment. "Where's Watson?"

"In the backyard. He loves to run around back there. I used to feel guilty when I went to work, him sitting in his crate all day at my place."

"It really isn't fair," she agreed, still thinking about the article. "He should stay here with me when you go back home. It's much more pet-friendly. You don't have any yard." Reese had inherited his great-aunt's cottage over on Beyer Place in South Buffalo a couple of months back. It was tiny and minimal maintenance, perfect for a bachelor like him.

"Nice try, but the dog comes with me. Besides, I'm right across the street from Cazenovia Park."

She glanced out the window, watching Watson chase a little yellow butterfly around the backyard. "We'll see," she told him.

The drive to the district attorney's office was uneventful, except for the conversation Reese had with one of his current girlfriends. She was complaining that he hadn't come over the night before like he'd said he was going to. He countered with the old, "Things have been crazy at work." Using skills that he had been honing since his teens, he got her calmed down, they made some new plans, and they ended up with the woman looking forward to seeing him again on their next date. Lauren shook her head in mild disgust after they'd clicked off.

"What?" He was genuinely baffled at Lauren's reaction.

"You can't treat people like that."

"Like what? I didn't feel like hanging out with her last night. I was tired. I don't owe her any explanation. We're not a couple."

"You are the reason I don't date," she said. "I can't stand the lying and the games."

"I seem to remember some lying and games on your part not so long ago, Miss High and Mighty." He was referring to her affair with her very remarried ex-husband that had sparked and ended over the course of the David Spencer arrest, trial, and acquittal.

"And look what that got the two of us."

"Him, a divorce. And you dumping him after he did the very thing you asked him to do so you could be together."

She pulled the elastic band out of her ponytail, shook her hair out, then put it back up again. Reese would have said that action was her tell when he hit too close to a nerve. "He was a cheat. He cheated on me. He cheated on his second wife. Why would I put myself through that again?"

"Hey, I'm not saying you didn't make the right decision. I think you did. But don't go throwing stones at my house."

He had a point; she was being unfair. "Sorry."

"Apology accepted."

Reese parked on Franklin Street in front of headquarters and they walked over to the district attorney's office across Church Street. Lauren wished she had worn a heavier jacket as they made their way up the stone steps and into the building. The wind had kicked up from the lake, whipping her hair around her face, causing a strand to stick to the pale lip gloss she was wearing.

The deputies knew Lauren and Reese, so they didn't make them take everything out of their pockets, remove their belts, or go through the metal detector. An old-timer with two days' worth of beard and a nasty scar on his chin gave a very loud, "Good morning, Detectives," so that the seven people in line holding their pants up with their hands didn't riot.

Riley and Reese walked past the roped-off medallion set into the floor, which declared that on that very spot in the year 1901 the body of President William McKinley had lain in state after his assassination at the Pan-American Exposition. He'd been hit by two pistol shots from point-blank range, and Lauren had always been amazed at the stories of how the first bullet had reportedly "bounced" off the president's chest. On the other hand, the second one killed him. A lucky break followed by a tough one. *The story of my life,* she thought.

Carl Church's office was on the sixth floor of the new wing of the Erie County Courthouse. Taking the elevator up, Lauren realized she had not spoken to Carl Church in person since before the David Spencer trial last October. Whenever she and Reese had needed something, they would request it of the DA's office and either ADA Kevin King handled it, or it got handled by someone else; anyone but Church.

Prior to the trial, she and Church had worked quite closely together on cold cases. From an elected official's standpoint, cold cases were a win-win for the police department and the district attorney's office: cases long thought to have been forgotten were revived, pleasing the families, who were happy just to know their loved ones hadn't been forever overlooked. If a case was solved, it was like a baseball grand slam; killer off the street, justice to the victim, closure for the family. Good publicity all around.

Her being hired by David Spencer's defense had cost her that good relationship with Carl Church, who was running for re-election next year. She didn't blame him for wanting to cut ties with her. Almost as soon as the polls had closed earlier that month, the countdown to the next election had started, and it was projected to be a nasty fight. She knew his opponent, Sam Schultz. He was a former police officer and assistant district attorney himself, now in private practice. Sam was sure to make hay about the loss of Katherine Vine's murder trial during the campaign, if only because Church had decided to try the case himself.

Church had always enjoyed a healthy Democratic landslide in Buffalo. This had always been a blue-collar, working-class town. The rise of the Republicans in recent elections meant that next year Church would have a serious contender for the first time since he won his first primary all those years ago. So it was surprising to her that Church was meeting with her personally. She would have thought he'd just call in the lead detectives assigned to the case. Unless he was working on something.

With a long election season looming, he wouldn't be a survivor if he didn't have an angle.

Carl Church was waiting for Reese and Riley in his office. Homicide Detectives Joy Walsh and Ben Lema were already there, sitting in the brown leather seats in front of Church's impressive desk. Behind him, an American flag stood in the corner, a reminder of his days serving his country in the Marine Corps. Church rose when they walked in, flanked by the red-headed Kevin King, who was standing to the left of him. Kevin King, AKA The Kinger, as he referred to himself, was the Cold Case squad's unofficially assigned assistant district attorney. The Kinger strode forward, shaking Lauren and Reese's hands before stepping back in place. Church motioned for them to sit in the two unoccupied seats next to Joy and Ben.

"I came to see you in the hospital," Church began, addressing Lauren directly. "You were unconscious; they didn't know if you were going to pull through. I was with Commissioner Bennett, and we met with your family after. I have to tell you, in all my years as district attorney, I've never felt so helpless."

Lauren's eyes slid from Church's earnest face to Reese's and back. She didn't know how to handle such a heartfelt admission from Carl

Church. All could not be forgiven so easily, could it? Lauren couldn't help feeling skeptical. After all, she'd earned his disappointment in her when she'd gone over to the "other side."

"I'm glad you're back and doing so well," he continued. "That's why I thought it was important for you to hear this yourself. I'll let Kevin tell you what we've got."

Clearing his throat, Kevin King set a small black digital recorder down on the desk. "About fifteen years ago, the county decided to upgrade our phone system. During the upgrade some of our interdepartmental numbers were inadvertently switched around. One of them was the number for the old confidential tip line we used to use in the early nineties during the crack epidemic. The investigators back then used to call it the Snitch Board. People would call in, leave information, and get an ID number to write down. If the information led to an arrest and conviction, they'd be in line to collect any reward money. When they upgraded the system, that number was reassigned to one of the phone lines down in Archives."

That sounded logical to Lauren. When they created the Cold Case squad in 2005, they gave it the old auto impound number. Every once in a while, someone would call about a car that had been seized in some long-ago drug raid. "This is the Cold Case Homicide squad number. Unless someone murdered your car twenty years ago, I can't help you," had been Reese's standard response until Lauren put a stop to it.

"The phone messages that come into the district attorney's office directly are carefully recorded and logged. They have to be, for evidentiary purposes. The Archive numbers aren't made available to the public, so their phone calls and messages aren't monitored. Two days ago one of the secretaries found three messages on the phone with the old Snitch Board's number. Luckily, Sharon is sharp and recognized the date and the possible significance and notified her supervisor right away."

King pressed the play button on the recorder. A tinny mechanical voice announced the date and time: "Friday, November ninth, eight-oh-one a.m." Then it clicked over to an older women's voice. "Yes. Hello. I want to talk to someone about a murder. I—I'll call back."

There was a two-second pause and the next message played: "Friday, November ninth, ten-twenty-six a.m." Another audio hiccup, then the same woman's voice. "Hello, I need to talk to someone in your office about a murder that happened a long time ago, and I'd really appreciate it if someone picked up the phone." The caller paused. "Hello? I need someone to pick up the phone. I can't call the precinct. Please pick up." A few seconds passed, then, "Please, someone. Pick up the phone. I'm calling about a murder here." There were some muffled sounds in the background, then the sound of the caller disconnecting.

"Friday, November ninth, twelve-sixteen p.m." The caller was already speaking when the message started recording, "What kind of useless shit is this? I'm trying to report a Goddamn homicide and no one there can pick up the Goddamn phone? This here is *eyewitness* information and I need to talk to a real person. When I used to call this number, I'd say, 'It's Peaches,' and someone would snatch up the fucking phone." The frustration in the caller's voice was spiking. "You know what I'm gonna do? Call the Homicide office. Because this here is the real deal. The *real* deal. And someone is going to finally pay for this shit." The speaker cut off suddenly, leaving the listeners in Carl Church's office straining forward to hear the rest of a message that wasn't there. Silence followed as the four detectives processed what they had just heard.

"One of the cops answered the phone in Homicide when she called," Joy murmured, almost to herself.

"And maybe didn't like what she had to say," Reese added.

"There's our motive for the break-in," Ben said.

"You think it's possible?" Lauren asked, looking to the other detectives. "That this woman called the office and said something that caused someone to try to steal a file and the Murder Book?"

"You said back at the hospital," Ben reminded her, "that finding a cold case without the Murder Book would be next to impossible. Maybe whoever answered that phone in the Homicide office didn't want anyone to find the file she was talking about."

"We don't know what to conclude. Obviously, we tried to trace the call." Church sat back in his overstuffed leather chair. "It was a burner phone. Untraceable. The cell tower information puts the caller somewhere on the lower West Side, which tells us almost nothing."

"Is the phone number still in service?" Reese asked.

"It was shut off later that same day," King responded.

"Does anyone recognize that woman's voice?" Church asked the four detectives. They all shook their heads.

"Can we get a copy of this?" Ben tapped the face of the digital recorder.

King reached into a folder on the desk and slid over three discs encased in paper sleeves with the date of the robbery and assault written across them in black Sharpie. "Done. I'll email digital copies to all of you. You can take this recorder too." He handed it to Ben. "We'll leave it up to you to check with your report technicians, see if they recognize the voice. See if they know someone who calls herself Peaches. Maybe she's a frequent flyer. If she calls a lot, maybe you'll get lucky."

"If she called all the time, she wouldn't be leaving messages on a tip line that hasn't been used in fifteen years," Lauren pointed out.

Reese reached over and clamped his hand down on her forearm, the signal for her to shut up. He ought to know; she used it on him ten times a week. Lauren swallowed her next comment, and thought to herself, *No wonder we don't let the victims in on every step of the investigation—these people are my co-workers and I'm pissed off that no one answered that Goddamn phone.*

"We're trying to keep this as quiet as possible. As you know, there have been problems with leaks to the press lately concerning homicide investigations." Church steepled his fingers in front of his chin. "Whether that leak is coming from your office or ours, when I find out who it is I will make sure the closest that person ever gets to a homicide investigation is a *Law and Order* marathon on TV."

More of a problem for the regular Homicide squad, someone had been leaking key information on current investigations to the press for the last six months—a lot of it not always accurate—causing problems for both the detectives investigating and the assistant district attorneys prosecuting the cases. Lauren had her suspicions about who the sieve might be, but she'd never put a name out there in something like this without proof.

Whoever was doing it was jeopardizing the integrity not only of her case, but of all their murder investigations, and compromising the effectiveness of the DA's office to prosecute the killers.

"Except for our secretary, her supervisor, and the people in this room, no one knows about the existence of these messages," Church went on. "Let's make sure to keep it that way until we know for sure whether they are directly related to Lauren's assault."

"Here's the phone information, the cell tower tracking, and transcripts of the calls. I did those myself." King passed a folder to Joy and another to Ben.

"Thanks," she said, paging through the records he just gave her.

"Make sure, when you question your report technicians, they know they'll be facing charges if one word is leaked of any of this," Church asserted. "Not a single syllable of this goes to the street."

"Marilyn and Tess have both been with us a long time," Ben said, standing up. "If they weren't one hundred percent trustworthy, they would have been gone a long time ago."

The two RTs were the heartbeat of the Homicide squad. Marilyn worked the day shift, Tess afternoons. It was no exaggeration to say that the Homicide squad would come to a complete and total stop if it weren't for the two of them. The Homicide detectives were fiercely loyal to their RTs, who kept track of their overtime, vacation days, birthdays, anniversaries, sent flowers when someone was sick, reminded them to call their wives, juggled their messages, and basically managed their work lives. Lauren could see how pissed off Ben was that Carl Church insinuated one of them may be a leak. Following his lead, she stood up. The meeting had ended itself.

"We'll follow up and keep you in the loop," Joy said as she leaned over the desk to shake Church's then Kevin King's hand.

Reese and Ben followed suit until it was just Lauren standing there awkwardly facing them. "I'd shake your hands," she told them, "but I don't want to reach over and bust a stitch."

Church held his palms up. "Not a problem. Just get better, okay? I'm so pleased you were well enough to come here today. We need you over in Cold Case."

"Yeah," King agreed, "just get back to work soon."

Words she never thought she'd hear come from Carl Church's mouth, or Kevin King's while he was in Church's presence. *Be nice,* she reminded herself, *they're trying to be good.* Still, it was hard to think all was forgiven after everything that had happened. She couldn't believe Church would just let it go. Or maybe she was the one who needed to let go of the past. "Thanks, guys. I'll do my best."

The four detectives filed out into the reception area. "Marilyn's at the office now," Ben told Lauren and Reese. "I want her to listen to this right away."

"I'll go see Tony down in the Communications office and get him to pull up all the incoming calls to the Homicide or Cold Case offices that day. If we can find a burner call, we can get an idea of who was up in the Homicide squad during that time frame." Joy's mind was on overdrive as she stabbed the down button for the elevator six times.

"I want to come over," Lauren said as the door slid open. "See the scene of my crime."

"You up for it?" Ben asked, positioning himself against the back wall.

"As ready as I'll ever be," she replied, hitting the door close button.

17

There's no such thing as lunchtime at police headquarters. You got something to eat when you caught some downtime, whether you were a detective, a report technician, a cleaner, or the commissioner. At twelve thirty in the afternoon, the poor lobby RTs had a line of people at the front window stretching almost out the door. Linda, the RT on duty, looked up from the elderly woman she was helping when Lauren and her entourage came in.

"Lauren!" she called, making everyone in line turn and stare. "I'm so glad to see you! And you look so good!"

Lauren's hand snaked around to her right side and settled over her wound. It felt like she was wearing her scars on the outside for all the world to see. "Thanks, Linda. I'm just here for a visit, though."

Lauren heard a man say to his companion, "That must be the one who got stabbed."

"Feel better," Linda called after them as she pressed the buzzer for the inner hallway door. *Maybe I'll use the Church Street exit when I leave,*

Lauren thought as they waited for the world's slowest elevator to take them to the third floor, *bc stealthy like the guy who shoved a blade between my ribs and pounded my head.*

The elevator was so old it didn't even bong when the door rumbled open. The others would have taken the stairs to the third floor, but Lauren knew they were trying to be considerate of her injuries. After what felt like an hour of upward travel, she stepped out into the Homicide wing.

To her left was the chief of detectives' office, his own RT sitting sentry behind a glass wall so she could screen his visitors. Her back was to the group, and she didn't turn around from her computer. *Just as well*, thought Lauren. *I'm in no mood for small talk.*

Reaching over, Joy swiped the door open to the Homicide office with a quick snap of her wrist. Going in first, Reese held the door for the others as they filed through. The smell of old coffee, cheap disinfectant, and bad cologne hung in the air. *Mario must be working*, Lauren mused, *rocking that funky cologne he wears.* Everyone knew not to use the phone after Mario did, unless they wanted to smell like an elderly Italian gigolo with no sense of moderation.

Nothing had changed. It was still the beat-up, run-down, overworked office space it had been since Lauren had started working there. The only difference was the moving equipment parked in the hallway.

The crew that was on duty came out of the back office to say their hellos and how glad they were she was all right. She awkwardly accepted their hugs with her good arm, stitches blazing by the time they were through.

"Detective Lauren Riley!" Lauren turned to the familiar voice. "Nobody told me you were coming!"

Marilyn, the Queen Mother of the Homicide squad, charged down the hallway and threw her arms around Lauren's neck. A breast cancer survivor, Marilyn wore her brown and blond streaked hair short, framing her fiftyish face. The tears Lauren felt on her neck were real and came from a place of joy: Marilyn loved her detectives. Some needed her more than others, but she considered all of them family, and the feeling was reciprocated.

"It's good to see you," Lauren told her, still holding on, ignoring the pain in her side. "Hell, it's good to still be here."

Marilyn nodded into her shoulder, stepped back and wiped her eyes. "I know the feeling. You scared the hell out of me." Then the mother hen came out as she asked, "What are you doing here? Why aren't you home resting?"

"Actually, Marilyn," Ben interrupted, "we need your help. Can we borrow you for a second?"

She looked from Lauren to Reese, then back to Ben. "Of course, you can. What's going on?"

"Why don't we go into the Cold Case office?" Joy suggested. "It's a little more private."

Lenny the cleaner didn't look up from his emptying of a trash can into the huge rolling tote he pushed around for just such occasions. He was born deaf, and with his back to them, hadn't acknowledged their presence. But they knew he was aware the foursome had come in. He tended to mind his own business, like he'd always done over the forty years he'd been cleaning headquarters. Able to lip read from a distance, Lenny probably knew more secrets about the Homicide squad and its members than anyone else. He'd always chosen to keep them to himself.

The problem was the woman in the chair sitting next to his tote, clutching a cheap pleather purse with a gaudy fringe tassel close to her chest. "Mister," she was saying to Lenny, who continued his work by lining a trash can with a new plastic bag. "My boyfriend has been in there for an hour. I have to go. Mister? Mister?"

Lenny could speak a few words with difficulty, of course, but almost never did. He chose to move onto the next trash can, ignoring her.

"This is bullshit. I've been here for an hour," she cried aloud, for everyone to hear. "And this loser is ignoring me."

"Come on," Marilyn said, abruptly turning toward the woman. "Come sit out here in the hallway. That loser is deaf and can't hear you complain."

"Nobody told me he was deaf," the woman mumbled, getting up and sheepishly following Marilyn's directions.

Lauren saw Lenny smirk as he dumped another trash can into his tote. "Maybe," Marilyn went on as she sat the twenty-something woman down on the bench that lined one side of the long hallway outside the office, "if you and your boyfriend would just tell the truth instead of lying about witnessing the shooting, you'd both be home now."

The woman pulled her purse up against her chest like a shield. "It's none of my business. I don't have to say nothing."

"It's your business because the victim is your cousin. And you don't have to say *anything*," Marilyn corrected.

"That's what I said. I don't have to say nothing."

Marilyn shook her head and called into the side office, "Mario? Can you come out and keep an eye on Miss Leoni here? Reggie is taking a statement."

"I'm coming," Lauren heard Mario reply. The five of them ducked into the Cold Case office before they could be overwhelmed by his aroma.

"Just another day in the Homicide office." Marilyn shut the door behind them.

Lauren's desk was torn apart, her computer gone. Black smudges dotted her desk where they had tried to lift prints, leaving behind the black powder. Her chair was gone. For good, she hoped. She couldn't imagine sitting in that cheap, wobbly thing ever again. Or her desk. She'd have to move to the empty one by the interview room in the corner until they relocated headquarters to their new building.

Everyone pulled up a chair to the mess table where Reese and Lauren usually dissected their case files, pulling them apart and organizing them on the long, faux wood tabletop. It was free of clutter now; Reese and Riley hadn't opened a new case in two months. Joy sat herself at the head of the table, putting the folder Kevin King had given her down in front of her. Lauren's eyes immediately fell onto the bald spot on the floor, next to her desk. A large patch of the carpet had been cut out, revealing the stained floorboards underneath.

That's where my blood soaked through, Lauren thought as her eyes wandered over the black, discolored wood. *This is where I almost died.* The memory of blood in her mouth flooded her brain, causing her to grip the sides of her chair with both hands, steadying herself, stomach reeling.

"Marilyn," Ben said, snapping Lauren back to the matter at hand, "I want you to listen to this recording we received from the DA's office and tell us if you've ever heard this woman's voice before. If she's ever left a message, or if you've spoken to her on the phone. Maybe if she's ever been here in the office. Anything at all."

He hit the Play button. Marilyn sat with her hands clasped in front of her, listening carefully to the audio recording. When it was finished, she asked to hear it again. Shaking her head slowly from side to side, she said, "No. I've never spoken to that person, and I know for a fact that she didn't leave a message in this office on the ninth."

"Could someone else have answered the phone?" Joy asked.

"Don't you work here? You know the phone doesn't stop ringing. There were fifty frigging cops up here that day. Any one of them could have answered the phone."

"Maybe Tess will recognize the voice," Reese said hopefully, leaning back in his chair. "Does the name Peaches ring a bell?"

"Not a one. And how does the DA's office not know where this came from? Don't they have super-secret spy gear to trace this kind of stuff?" Marilyn asked.

"It didn't come in on the main line." Ben reached over and took the recorder back. "It came in through one of the phones down in Archives. An old number that used to be a confidential tip line."

"The old Snitch Board? I remember that," Marilyn said. "Prisoners used to leave all kinds of messages at all hours of the night. Charlie Daley was in charge of following up on them when he was head of the Narcotics Squad. He'd keep the crack-house tips and pass the homicide stuff along to us. Why is the DA's office using our old number?"

As Joy explained the inadvertent switching of the phone numbers, Lauren's mind thought back to Charlie Dailey.

Charlie Daley had retired as a lieutenant out of narcotics fifteen years before. In charge of the drug squad during the bloodiest years Buffalo had ever seen, he'd been a legend in the nineties for his leadership and attention to detail. While half the Narcotics Squad went to prison for being dirty, his crew proved to be squeaky clean, no matter how hard the Feds tried to prove otherwise.

"Is Charlie still alive?" Reese asked.

Marilyn gave him a look. "Sure, he's still alive. And just because he's old enough to have changed your diapers, I'd show him some respect if you go and see him, or he'll slap that smart mouth of yours."

Reese held up his hands in mock surrender. "Why does everyone think the worst of me? I'm pretty charming, Marilyn. Admit it."

She wasn't admitting anything. "I don't think you're his type, darling."

"Did you know Charlie?" Joy asked Ben. Joy had about ten years on the job; Ben, maybe sixteen or seventeen.

Ben nodded. "A little. But he was here in headquarters, and I was on patrol. He retired a year or two after I got on. I went to his retirement party at O'Flannan's pub, though. Great time. I think I'm still hungover."

"I know him," Lauren said, trying to stem the wave of nausea that was passing over her. In her head blood was filling her mouth, hot and thick and salty, threatening to make her vomit. She choked it back with a visible effort. Marilyn put her hand on Lauren's arm.

Swallowing hard, Lauren managed, "I used to hook for him. He'll talk to me."

18

Before Lauren got her detective's badge, she had been a prostitute.
With less than a year out of the academy, Lauren got to work with
Narcotics and Vice, posing as a prostitute. Working undercover, she
dressed in the oldest, beat-up jeans she could find, spilled coffee down
the front of ripped tee shirts, and rubbed dark-purple eye shadow into
the lower corners of her eyes to transform from a fresh-faced police
officer in her early twenties to a strung-out hype selling her body for
drug money. After seeing her roll around with a suspect while assist-
ing on one of his raids, Charlie Daley had handpicked her for the detail, thinking she had the stomach for the disgusting, perverted johns
she'd have to encounter. She did. And for three months she had been
pulled out of her precinct and plopped down into the shadows on the
corners.

They never had to wait more than five minutes for Lauren to get
propositioned.

The detail was Charlie's baby. He had the idea that drugs and prostitution were so closely linked that to tackle one would help combat the other. In the three months she was a decoy, she witnessed and made arrests for drug deals, assaults, robberies, and domestics. Prostitutes are invisible. To the denizens of the drug trade, the gangbangers, and the users, prostitutes were a fixture, like lamp posts or fire hydrants. Always in the background, forgotten and invisible until their services were needed. But also vulnerable to abuse from all sides: the johns, the pimps, the other hypes.

Lauren discovered a great sympathy for the women and men out there selling their bodies to survive. Because that's what it boiled down to, survival. To reach the point where you have to stand on the corner and sell yourself, you have to have endured enough physical, mental, and emotional anguish to wall yourself off from the rest of your life. When Lauren would talk to the street walkers, after they'd been arrested for threatening Lauren for standing on their corners, she'd find out they were mothers. And daughters. And sisters. Many had graduated high school. Or they had a family in the suburbs who were waiting for them to come home. They were more than just the bodies they were selling. Somewhere in their past they'd taken a wrong turn that had led to another, and now they lived on the corners, day to day, hour to hour, and didn't think much about the future. They didn't know if they had one.

One of the first things Lauren did when she got to Cold Case was to pull every unsolved murder of prostitutes she could find. She and Reese solved a couple, a few were still looking promising, but most had gone back to the shelves. Still, it was Charlie Daley who taught her that these people mattered.

She, too, had been at Charlie's retirement party. Lauren had still been engaged to Joe Wheeler at the time and had to beg him to let her go to the party. Joe had been so controlling that he took the night off to go with her, just in case some other cop got any ideas about who she was with.

Even with Joe hovering by her side all night, it had been a great time. Charlie had been well loved and respected. When he gave his speech, he pointed out Lauren specifically, telling everyone gathered at the Bison Rod and Gun Club, "That kid right there, she's going to run this department someday." Lauren had swelled with pride, even though Joe was squeezing her hand so hard she lost feeling in her fingers.

She hadn't seen Charlie since. She'd heard rumors he was living with a psychic south of the city in the Town of Lily Dale, famous for its lifestyle of spiritualism. Then she'd heard he was working as a railroad cop. The last word she had on him was that he was working in Lackawanna at a cemetery as a maintenance man.

"I forgot you were a hooker," Reese commented on their way home. "Is that why I'm always broke?"

"There ain't enough money in the world to pay me for servicing you," she said.

"Between you and Marilyn, my manhood has been completely diminished today."

"Not completely. You managed to get another date with the woman you blew off last night."

"Oh, yeah." Reese poked at the radio, trying to find a good station. "I forgot."

They had stopped by the union office on the first floor, at Marilyn's suggestion, to grab Charlie Daley's most recent address. They got it, but no phone number. When Joy had run his name through the computer, it showed Daley hadn't had a valid driver's license in over five years.

Reese and Riley had left Joy and Ben behind at headquarters. They had wanted to follow up on the angle of the burner call coming in. Reese was supposed to take Lauren home.

"I'd like to say I hated every minute of that Vice gig, but it was just the opposite," Lauren said. "I loved seeing the look on those guys faces when they realized their cars were getting impounded and they were going to jail for six hours."

"Six hours? That's all?"

"Long enough to get an appearance ticket and for their wives to find out."

Lauren heard Reese give a low whistle, then say, "I'd rather stay in jail."

She smiled. "Exactly." More than one had begged to stay behind bars rather than go home to confront their wives.

Her smile faded as the reality of the situation hit her. "You know the cop that stole the Murder Book is going to try again to get the file he was after."

Reese nodded in agreement. "He wanted it bad enough to kill for it."

"Joy and Ben are running down phone numbers. They should be scooping Daley up right now. Once that file leaves the room, the homicide might as well never have happened." The sick feeling in her gut had returned. It was only a matter of time before the motivated cop took another shot at getting into that file room.

Reese drummed his fingers on top of the steering wheel, one of his nervous habits when he had pent-up energy to spend. "You want to go knock on Charlie Daley's door? Like right now?"

"We're going the wrong way," Lauren pointed out.

He made a U-turn in the middle of Delaware Avenue, causing cars in both directions to screech to a stop, colorful language coming at them from the other drivers. "Now we're not." He grinned and headed for the Skyway.

19

The cemetery was just past Our Lady of Victory Basilica on Ridge Road in the city of Lackawanna. Buffalo's southernmost neighbor in Erie county, Lackawanna was famous for two things: the Bethlehem Steel plant and Father Nelson Henry Baker. The steel plant, a once giant complex of churning molten ore and spewing smoke stacks that employed 35,000 people in its heyday, was now an abandoned husk on the waterfront. The closing of the steel plant devastated not only Lackawanna but the entire western New York region for decades. Boarded-up buildings and shut-down taverns lined the same streets that were once thriving, put down with the irreplaceable loss of the steel workers and their paychecks.

In the middle of Lackawanna, close to its city hall, sat its other famous landmark: Father Baker's Our Lady of Victory Basilica. A shining white marble and stone masterpiece, it looked out of place in the post-industrial landscape. A humble priest and a Civil War veteran who saw action at Gettysburg, Father Baker built his monument to the Blessed Mother, along with an infant home, a hospital, a school, and an orphanage, with little more than his faith. Charlie Daley's cemetery was located just down the road from the Basilica.

"Have you ever been inside?" Lauren asked as they approached the huge church.

"Took a field trip there once when I was in grade school. The only thing I remember is a bedroom they had roped off that the guide said was Father Baker's. I remember wondering why they would rope off someone's bedroom. It seemed very strange to me at the time."

"Father Baker is close to becoming a saint," Lauren told him, looking up at the angel statues that flanked the entrance. Legend had it, the angels would rise up and fly to heaven on the last day. As a little girl riding in her parents' car, she'd always look up to make sure the statues were still there.

They got caught at the light directly in front of the Basilica. A group of tourists came marching up the sidewalk, trouping after a guide energetically waving an umbrella over his head. They looked both ways, crossed, and followed their leader to the impressive white steps, where he halted, continuing his history speech before they would move on.

"How does that work?" The light was taking forever. Another tour group exited a bus parked farther up the street. She wondered if the church controlled this particular stoplight so it could cater to all the visitors. The holiday season was particularly busy, she knew, as everyone wanted to see the church decked out in its Christmas glory.

"He needs his miracles to be recognized by the Vatican. It's just a matter of time."

"Do you believe in that stuff?" Reese asked.

"Look around you. He built all this from nothing; the church, the hospital, saved hundreds of kids in his infant home and orphanage.

The fact that all this survived after the Bethlehem Steel plant closed..."
She gestured toward the school and hospital, which had become a
long-term care facility. "That has to be some kind of miracle in itself."

The light turned, and they made their way toward the cemetery.

"My cousin got married there because it was her husband's parish."
Lauren gave a laugh. "Talk about a lavish wedding."

"Not like yours, huh?" Reese asked.

"My first wedding lasted three minutes at the clerk's office in City
Hall. My mom cried the entire time. My second wedding was on the
back steps of the Albright-Knox Art Gallery with a reception at the
Buffalo Club and a honeymoon in Paris. The whole thing cost more
than my house."

"The first time for love, the second time for money," Reese joked,
pulling to a stop behind a school bus. Kids streamed off as a tired-
looking bus aid shepherded them across the road, so unlike the dy-
namic tour guide.

"In my case, it was the first time I was knocked up, second time he
loved his money more than me."

"You think Mark Hathaway didn't love you? Or that he still doesn't?
I hear the messages on your landline when you play them at night."
Reese gave her the side eye. She had to remember to lower the vol-
ume now that she had a houseguest.

The bus retracted its flashing stop sign and they started forward
again. "He loves himself more than anything. And he hates to lose."

"Is this it?" Reese nodded toward a pair of rusty gates that opened
into a garden of gravestones. Just inside the gates, to their immediate
left, was a modest two-story wood house with a small porch. The sign
hanging from a post out front declared it was the OFFICE. Reese
turned in toward the house, parking half on the road, half on the

grass. There were no parking spaces. Both the cemetery and house had been built long before cars were invented.

In the house's front window, dividing the white lace curtains in two, was a hand-printed sign that read: *Open*.

Gravestones lined the road and the front lawn of the house, almost as if the dwelling had been an afterthought, plunked down in the cemetery after it was full. Maybe it had been. This close to Ridge Road would be the oldest part of the cemetery. Some of the tombstones were unreadable, the engraving washed away by weather and time. The few Lauren could make out as she picked her way through to the front door were mostly Polish names: Baranski, Stanieschewski, Pliscka. She carefully stepped around a tilting monument to Helen Matcheviez, born 1862, died in 1888. Wondering if anyone ever came to visit Helen anymore, if anyone even knew Helen was here, Lauren walked up the sagging wooden steps and waited for Reese to join her.

He had taken the long way, careful not to step on any of the graves, no matter how close they were. "Did I ever tell you I hate cemeteries?" he said when he finally managed to maneuver onto the porch.

"I'm well aware of your phobia."

"It's not a phobia." He looked around the vast graveyard that stretched in front of them. "It's just creepy as hell."

"Try to be brave." She rang the doorbell, which bonged in a gentle singsong way. Very soothing for the bereaved.

They heard the office manager's approach, probably from the moment she stood up from her desk. *This whole house must creak,* Lauren thought as footsteps and sound of groaning wood got closer. *I would have thought "like my grandmother's knees," but now like mine.*

"Creepy," Reese whispered as the door opened.

The manager was a very pleasant-looking, matronly woman of about sixty. She wore a tasteful pastel pink dress with a floral scarf knotted around her neck. Her frosted blond hair was pinned up and sprayed, as though she had just come from the hairdresser's that morning. "Hello," she said, holding the door wide. "Are you interested in buying a plot?"

No need to beat around the bush. "Actually, we were hoping to see Charles Daley," Lauren said. "Is he here, by any chance?"

"You're friends of Charlie? Come in, come in. I'll call him. He's out doing some maintenance. You can have a seat in the living room, if you like." She gestured to an area remodeled to look like your grandmother's front sitting room, complete with Tiffany-style shaded lamps and embroidered throw pillows on the brocade settee.

The owners of the cemetery must have spent a fortune on renovating the interior of the old house while leaving the outside to blend with the grounds, Lauren thought, looking around. *Business must be booming.* Lauren and Reese sat themselves side by side on the sofa, a little squished despite Lauren's small frame. Reese inched his butt to the edge to give her more room.

"Who should I say is stopping by?"

"Tell him Lauren Riley." Her hand wrapped itself around her wound again as she stifled a cough. Her voice was still scratchy and raw, like she was getting over a bad cold. She had blown off physical therapy again. The department would never let her come back if she kept that up.

"Perfect." The lady clasped her hands together in front of her. "Can I get either of you any tea, coffee?"

"No, thank you," they said in unison.

Watching the sweet lady's face pinch up, Lauren knew what was coming next. "Do I know you, dear? You look so familiar to me."

"I don't think so," she deflected with as pleasant a smile as she could muster. "I get that sometimes. I think I have one of those faces."

"Maybe," she conceded, still studying her face. "My name is Nell, and if you need anything, I'm right through there." She pointed to a pair of pocket doors adorned with another OFFICE sign. "I'll get Charlie on the radio right away."

The polished hardwood floor groaned her entire way to the office. *You can dress up an old house, but it's still an old house*, Lauren thought as Nell slid the pocket doors closed behind her.

"I hate cemeteries," Reese whispered out of the side of his mouth. "Did I ever tell you I hate cemeteries?"

"It's come up once or twice." Cemeteries were great places to meet with informants. Very little chance of running into someone the snitch would know at midnight in the middle of a graveyard. But Reese always white-knuckled it through those meetings. He had told Lauren as a kid his friends had dared him to go into a graveyard by his house and steal a flower from a certain grave they said was haunted. When he got to the grave, an old man in a ratty trench coat with no teeth was standing there putting carnations on the ground. He saw Reese and yelled something unintelligible at him. He ran back to his friends, tripped over a headstone, and broke his wrist. Adding insult to injury, everyone had heard the old man yelling and were gone, leaving him to walk home in the dark alone, cradling his broken wrist to his chest.

"I think they're peaceful." Lauren gazed out the picture window to the rows of stone memorials, some decorated with flowers, other with small American flags stuck in the ground next to them.

"When I bite it, I want someone to scatter my ashes someplace cool, like Iceland."

"You've never been to Iceland," Lauren pointed out.

"If you scatter my ashes there, I will be. And it will be even cooler."

"I'll be sure to inform the future Mrs. Shane Reese of your last wishes. You do realize that Iceland has a crapload of active volcanos?"

"Thank you for the warning, partner. But no cemeteries. If that happens, I will definitely be coming back to haunt you."

She was just about to tell him he already haunted her when the rumble of a loud engine filled the air. They both turned to the picture window to see what was coming.

Motoring down the road was a gas-powered Cushman utility vehicle. It was overloaded with landscaping tools: a shovel, a rake, a wide broom with leaves caught in the bristles, all sticking up from the back. Stuffed in front of the steering wheel was a mountain of a man. All six-feet three, two-hundred and ninety pounds of Charlie Daley overflowed the front seat.

Lauren watched as he lumbered out of the cart, brushing off the front of his coveralls, and made his way through the plots to the front steps. Flinging open the front door, Charlie had to work his way through the narrow frame. "Lauren Riley," his voice was as loud and booming as the golf cart, "come over here, girl, and let me hug you."

Lauren had barely risen from the couch when he swept her up into a bear hug. "Easy," she laughed. "I'm not completely healed."

He put her down and held her at arm's length, his mop of white hair falling over his forehead into his eyes. "I saw you on the news. They said someone tried to kill you."

She nodded, his giant hands still holding her by the shoulders. "That's why we're here. I need your help, Charlie."

"And who might you be?" he asked, stepping back to look at Reese. "I'm Charlie Daley." He stuck his huge hand out and engulfed Reese's. "Lauren has always been rude like that, not introducing people."

"I'm Lauren's partner, Shane Reese. Nice to meet you."

"Come upstairs to my apartment and we can talk." Letting go of Reese's hand, he motioned to a narrow staircase off to the right of the office and walked past them. Riley and Reese followed the big man. It seemed impossible that a person his size could squeeze through such a tiny opening, but Charlie stooped and bent his way up the stairs to his door. Pulling an enormous key ring from his back pocket, he selected an old-fashioned black key and turned it in the lock. Bowing again, he ducked his way inside, holding the door for Riley and Reese to enter. "This house wasn't built for gentlemen of my size," he said. "It's a bit of a tight squeeze."

The renovations to the house hadn't exactly reached the upstairs apartment. While it wasn't 1800s décor, it was definitely 1970s, complete with a scuffed linoleum floor and a Formica kitchen table. "Sit. I'd say you look great, but you know I'd be lying. So I'll put the coffee on instead. Still take it black?"

"Yes. Thanks."

The apartment was freezing cold. Lauren noticed the kitchen window was opened a crack, sucking the corner of a yellow curtain out with the breeze. She knew Charlie was the type that never felt a chill. He used to walk around on the coldest winter days without a jacket, mocking her because she was bundled up like she lived in Antarctica. Half smiling at the memory, she wrapped her arms around her herself to keep warm and said nothing.

"How about you?" he asked Reese. "You look like a double cream and sugar guy to me."

Reese cracked a smile. "I like sugar on top of my sugar."

Charlie laughed. "Good man. Just like me. Have a seat, both of you."

Riley and Reese took a spot on either side of the table, facing each other. Even the chairs were dated, bent metal frames with cracked, red plastic seats. At the head of the table was a wide, sturdy wooden chair. *That one must be Charlie's,* Lauren thought. *The ones we're sitting on would crumple like paper flowers under his weight.*

"I can't believe you work in a graveyard," Lauren said as she watched him carefully measure out the coffee.

"This is the best job I've ever had," he told her, pouring water into the machine. "I make my own hours. The work is mindless. The residents don't complain." He turned back with a grin. "And the shit I see and hear? It's better than the police department. Women confessing to cheating on their husbands over their graves. Couples coming to make whoopie in the middle of the night. Brothers fist-fighting over who gets dad's cheap-ass watch. I tell you, it's the greatest show on earth."

"Do you dig the graves?" Reese asked, looking a little green at the thought of it.

"Naw. They sub-contract that out to a construction firm with a little backhoe. Used to be the maintenance men did, but that was a long time ago. Sometimes I neaten up the plots when they're done. Clean up the mess. I got it down to a science, so it's no bother."

Charlie opened his refrigerator, pulled out a carton of creamer, and set it in the middle of the table next to a sugar bowl with a spoon sticking out of it. "I'm going to stay until it's my turn to be planted here."

He dug around his cabinet, hooking three mugs with his pinky, and sat down in his chair. "My coffee machine takes a while, but man, does it make good java. Here." He passed the mismatched mugs to Riley and Reese. His looked like a child's teacup in his big paw.

"Thanks," Lauren turned the empty mug over and over in her hands. It was time to get down to business. "You know I got attacked. The reason we're here is we think you might be able to help."

"Me? I haven't been back to that filthy police building in fifteen years. How could I help?"

106

Riley explained the mystery messages to Charlie, who nodded along as he reached back without getting up, grabbed the coffeepot, and poured them all a cup. Setting the pot directly on the already-burned Formica table, he asked, "You got the tape?"

Tape, Lauren marveled. *There hasn't been actual tape in years.* "Reese copied it onto his cell phone. Listen to this and tell me if you recognize the voice."

Reese pulled his phone out of his jacket pocket, opened the recorder app, turned the volume all the way up, then hit Play. Charlie bent forward, elbows on the table, forehead creased in worry lines as he listened to the recording.

"I'll be damned," he said, half to himself as he took a sip of coffee.

The last message hadn't even played yet. "Do you know the voice?" Reese asked.

Charlie nodded. "That's Peaches, all right. One of my best informants. I'm telling you, I dealt with that woman for three years until I had to cut her off. She started taking buy money, going into dope houses, getting the shit and coming out and telling me they were charging her twice as much. She didn't leave me a choice."

"You're sure?" Lauren asked, but the look on his face was confirmation enough.

Leaning back in his chair, which groaned in protest, he told them more: "She called me ten times a day, every day, for three years straight. It may have been years ago, but I can still hear that woman's voice in my sleep. They said she cried when she found out I retired. Hell, I'm the one that gave her the nickname Peaches. I gave all my informants fake names. That way I could call them and they could call me without using their real ones."

"Who is she?" Reese asked, cutting the audio.

"Rita Walton. AKA Rita Williams. AKA Monique Jones. AKA Peaches. Hooker, crack head, informant extraordinaire. If she says she's got information, I'd bet my life it's good. Are these tapes current? I can't believe she's still alive after all these years."

Reese stuffed his cell back in his pocket. "Do you know where we can find her?"

Charlie turned his watery gray eyes on him. "You're the one still on the job, right? Get on your fancy computer and do your job. She shouldn't be hard to find. Had a rap sheet forty pages long."

"I never should've doubted you'd know whose voice that was," Lauren told him, cold fingers wrapped around the hot coffee mug. "You knew everyone on the street."

"I was on the street for a long time," he said. "Wouldn't know any of the players now. All their grandparents, maybe."

"You think she'll talk to us?" Reese asked.

Charlie shrugged. "It's been so many years, I can't say what she'd do. Back in the day, she was funny about who she'd talk to in person. But I will tell you this: she sounded afraid on that recorder. And that woman has seen a lot of shit. So whatever scared her, scared her big time."

"The DA's office had the cell phone tracked to a tower over on the West Side," Lauren told him. "Does she have people there?"

"She had people everywhere. That's what made her such a good informant. I can't believe she's still alive, that one. She lived hard."

"About how old would she be?" Reese slipped in. Lauren could tell he didn't want to get chewed out for not doing his own homework again.

"She was around my age. I used to tell the guys she was my senior prom date. That always got a laugh, especially from her. I turned sixty-eight in September."

108

He's sixty eight and still built like a locomotive, Lauren thought. *I'm thirty-nine and can't walk up my stairs without getting winded right now.* "I'm going to give you my cell phone number, Charlie. If she won't talk to us, would you be willing to come out of retirement and help me out?"

"For you, Lauren, of course I will." He pulled out his cell and handed it to her so she could punch her number into his contacts list.

"Thanks, Charlie," she said, squinting at the phone. She had forgotten to bring her readers along.

"And that prick you used to go out with, that Wheeler guy? You know for sure he's not the one who ambushed you?" She couldn't believe Charlie remembered she was with Joe when she hooked for him. They didn't break up until after her undercover detail was over.

"He has a solid alibi." Joy and Ben had assured her of that before she left the hospital. She returned Charlie's cell, complete with her number stored in it. "Why would you ask about Joe Wheeler, of all people?"

He gripped the phone and started scrolling across the screen with his index finger before handing it right back to her. "Because he made the paper today."

There on the screen was the *Buffalo News* app. The headline of the local section read: Injured Officer's Alleged Harasser to Keep Police Job. *Arbitrator Rules 30-Day Unpaid Suspension Punishment Enough for Harassment and Trespass Charges.*

The article went on to say that Joe Wheeler had pled guilty in Buffalo City Court to two violations, but the arbitrator in the disciplinary case sided with his union lawyers, saying the violations did not meet the standards for Conduct Unbecoming an Officer. The Garden Valley town supervisor stated they would appeal the decision. Police Chief Bernard Ritz was also quoted, saying that, "Detective Joseph Wheeler will not only return to active duty but will also be entitled to the eleven months' worth of back pay lost while on suspension."

"That snaky bastard." Lauren gave the phone to Reese, who quickly scanned the article.

"How can his department do this?" Reese asked, voice raising a notch. "You caught the guy in your backyard with a loaded gun."

"Which he was allowed to have because he's a cop. And it's not a domestic because we haven't been in a relationship in years. And him punching me in the mouth only constitutes harassment because I wasn't seriously injured." Lauren's face flushed red with anger. "He's not the guy who stabbed me, just the guy who gets away with hitting and threatening me."

"Some bastards know all the loopholes. Sorry to be the bearer of bad news, kid." Charlie took his phone back, setting it on the table.

"We should go. Call my cell so I have your number." Lauren stood up and gave Charlie a one-armed hug. She was trying to suppress the rage that was building up in her chest, already causing her pain every time she took a breath. "It was great to see you again, Charlie. Thanks for your help with the phone calls."

"You always had rotten luck with men. I remember you going out with Wheeler when you did the prostitution detail for me. I thought he was a nasty weasel even then. I always knew you were too good for him."

"I wish you would have said something at the time," Lauren said.

"You were young and in love. Would you have listened?" Charlie asked, but Lauren didn't answer. She picked up her and Reese's coffee mugs, setting them in the sink for Charlie. The ice maker in his refrigerator rumbled loudly while it deposited a load of cubes into its internal bucket.

"Probably not. Anyway," she switched the subject, "we'll be seeing you."

"I have a feeling I'll be seeing you sooner rather than later." Charlie winked at her but didn't get up.

She cracked a smile for his sake. "I think you're probably right."

"It was good meeting you." Reese stuck out his hand and Charlie gave it a pump.

"You too, boss," he replied, not bothering to show them out. Charlie reached back, grabbed the coffeepot, and gave himself a warm up as they closed the door behind them.

Lauren could still feel the heat that had risen to her face as they made their way down the narrow staircase, the burning feeling raw in her chest. Joe Wheeler succeeded in sticking it to her again. Would it ever stop? Would she ever be done with him?

I should have pulled the trigger, she thought, as Reese held the front door open for her, *when I caught him in my backyard and had the barrel of the gun pressed against his temple. It would have been far more merciful than whatever he had planned for me.*

"Sorry about Wheeler," Reese said when they got back into the car.

"Why be sorry?" She shook her head in bitter resignation. "Why *wouldn't* his department give him back his gun and reward him with back pay? I'm the stupid one for thinking anything different would happen."

Reese pulled out, heading toward the cemetery gates. "Let me get you home. We shouldn't have come here today. I should have taken you home to rest after the meeting with the DA. You've had enough."

"Don't start that crap with me," she snapped. "We have a solid lead on someone who may know who attacked me. I'll just add Joe to the list of guys who want to kill me."

"Don't you start with your bullshit," Reese shot back. "Everything is not about you. You got stabbed because you were in the office. It wasn't personal. If I had stayed late instead of you, it would have been me. You're a cop. Your job is dangerous. I can rattle off the names of ten guys I've put away over the years who'd love to put a bullet in my brain first chance they got. Remember, I got a fake tooth and a screw in my finger from getting beaten with a two-by-four in a backyard. That guy screamed at his sentencing that he should have finished me off. Don't start boo-hooing at me."

"It just seems like everyone I associate with is a psychopath."

"That's bullshit too. You don't associate with anybody but cops, lawyers, and criminals," he pointed out. "Who else is going to make your life miserable? Besides Dayla, you have no non-law-enforcement friends. It's a numbers game. If every person who crosses your path is an apple, all the bad apples are going to come along too. You just keep biting into the worms."

"Why—"

"Stop, okay? You're a good-looking woman. You probably used to be totally hot, when you were younger. But not every guy is obsessed with you. In case you haven't noticed, I've been busting my ass trying to figure out who stole that Murder Book and why. Every day since it happened. Because I know if I can figure out who wanted to steal that book, I'll figure out who attacked you. Get over yourself already." He took the next turn a little too hard. "And you're welcome, by the way."

Lauren crossed her arms over her chest and stared out the passenger-side window. He was right. She wasn't the only cop to ever have been attacked on the job, man or woman. Reese had still been on patrol when he caught a robbery suspect in a backyard. They had wrestled over Reese's gun, which had become jammed in the fight. The suspect grabbed the nearest thing he could, a piece of wood, and bashed Reese with it repeatedly until his backup found him, bloody and half conscious, but still holding onto his useless gun. The guy got sentenced to fifteen years in jail; the DA's office had asked for twenty-five. Every cop knew what it was like to be on the losing side of a court battle.

"Should we call Ben and Joy? Let them know about Rita?" she asked, trying to change the subject.

He glanced at the time on the dash display. "They're probably gone for the day. Tomorrow I'm going to find Rita Walton. One way or another."

"Just keep them in the loop. Don't go all lone wolfy." Which was rich, coming from her.

"I really think this is the break in your case we've been looking for," he said. "I'm not going to do anything to jeopardize it. Believe me, I'll fight fair."

If I expected everything to be fair, I shouldn't have become a cop, she told herself as they passed by the Basilica again.

20

Later that evening Reese picked up Lauren's parents from the airport. The only flight Erin could catch brought her in at eleven that night, so she Ubered it to Lauren's house. Dayla came over, making drinks and telling funny stories while Watson charmed everyone he could. Dayla's two sons and their families were taking her and her husband to dinner at the Roycroft Inn in East Aurora for Thanksgiving dinner the next evening.

Both of Dayla's sons lived out of state, but somehow she seemed much better at the whole empty nest thing than Lauren. Lauren suspected that might be the cause of Dayla's plastic surgery addiction, along with the fact that she refused to offer up that she was a grandmother to two toddlers. She called herself their "Mimi" instead. Anything to avoid admitting she was middle-aged.

Lauren hadn't really thought much about being middle-aged until she got herself laid up in the hospital. Now it was something she clung to late at night in bed. She was still alive. That felt like no small accomplishment to her in the wake of her near-death experience.

Someone, probably her dad, had put a recorded football game on the big flat-screen TV over the fireplace. Looking around her full living room—Reese sitting on the carpet trying to wrestle Watson away from Erin, her parents sitting together on her floral couch, Dayla gesturing grandly as she regaled them with one of her wild tales—it occurred to Lauren that almost getting murdered had brought her family closer than it had been in years.

Lauren's mom and Dayla began making plans to take Erin and Lindsey Black Friday shopping at three in the morning. "I'll drive," Dayla told Erin. "We'll go to the outlets in Niagara Falls. My Escalade can hold oh-so many bags," she squealed.

"I want to get a new ski jacket," Erin said. "The stuffing is literally coming out of mine."

"I can't believe you guys would get up at three in the morning to fight those crowds just to go shopping," Lauren said from her seat on the side chair near the front picture window.

"It's like going hunting," Dayla said. "You have to strategize and plan to get the best deals. You have to know the layouts of the stores, where the best stuff is located, and be ready once those doors open up."

"It sounds like too much work just to buy Christmas gifts," Lauren said.

"If I were you," her mother piped up, "I'd skip the Christmas presents and update your wardrobe."

"What's wrong with my clothes?" Lauren demanded, looking around at all the heads nodding in agreement.

"Nothing," Dayla said into her drink, "if you like looking like you're wearing a potato sack all the time."

Ohh, Lauren thought. *She going to try to shame me into shopping.*

"Yeah, Mom. Let me pick out some clothes for you," Erin joined in. "You're too pretty to look so frumpy all the time."

Reese snorted a laugh from the other side of the room. She glared at him for a second, then turned back to the rest her attackers. "I have a closet full of clothes upstairs—"

"From the year 2000," Dayla finished.

"I like the way I dress. I'm not interested in high fashion." Being thin and almost five-nine meant that most pants were short on her, so every purchase involved a trip to her seventy-year-old Italian seamstress to have the waist taken in and the hem let out. It seemed like so much time and effort, especially since Lauren had put a moratorium on dating when she broke off her affair with her ex-husband a year ago. Now that she had a beautifully puckered and angry-looking chest-tube scar, she definitely wasn't trying to impress anyone.

"Clearly." It was Dayla again with the shot.

Lauren smoothed down her favorite gray sweatshirt self-consciously. "I'm not going shopping at three in the morning," she said. "You ladies have fun. It's not like I can buy off the rack, anyway," she added, but she wasn't sure anyone was listening.

"I'm going with them," Reese added jovially. Lauren's dad clapped him on the shoulder. *They're all ganging up on me,* she thought. *Thank God I'm here for them to do it.*

"Like I said, you ladies have fun." Between the DA's office, headquarters, and Charlie's graveyard, it had been a long day and it was past midnight. Lauren struggled against the exhaustion that had been creeping in. Seeing her family and friends together was well worth it, but she could barely keep her eyes open. "I hate to leave the party," Lauren announced, rising from her chair, "but I've got to get some rest. Doctor's orders."

Erin bounced up from the floor, giving her mother a careful hug. "Goodnight, Mom." Her voice was light and happy.

She kissed her cheek. "See you in the morning."

"I'll clean up down here, don't worry," her mom called to her. She had bought a twenty-two-pound turkey and left it in Lauren's fridge to thaw before she had gone back to Florida the week before. Lauren knew her mom would be up at the crack of dawn no matter what, puttering around the kitchen, apron on, cooking for the family.

"Lock the door when you leave, Dayla," Lauren reminded her. Dayla was famous for exiting and leaving the door wide open in her wake.

Patting her thighs as she stood at the foot of the stairs, Lauren expected Watson to come running. Instead he was lying across Reese, letting him scratch his belly while his back leg kicked with every stroke. "Sorry." Reese shrugged. "There's no loyalty when it comes to belly rubs."

Walking up the stairs to her second floor, looking forward to coffee with her family in the morning. Lauren tried to keep the positive vibes going. Ever since their return from Lackawanna, Lauren kept hearing the sounds of the three phone calls play over and over in her head. There was a feeling from them that she just couldn't shake.

Lying in her bed, staring at the ceiling, the woman's voice from the phone call flooded her brain. *Where are you, Rita?* Lauren thought. *And what did you see?*

21

"**M**om, you look good!" Lindsey wrapped her arms around Lauren's neck carefully, the enthusiasm in her voice at being with her mom unmistakable. A cold rain had started to fall outside and Lindsey's coat was damp against Lauren's cheek. As if to combat the precursor to snow, turkey smells from the oven permeated the entire house even at ten in the morning, giving it a warm, cozy feeling. Lauren's mother had dug out all of Lauren's fanciest dinnerware—her wedding-to-Mark china and her crystal wine goblets—setting the table for an extra special feast. With her oldest daughter home in her arms, it really felt like Thanksgiving to Lauren.

"You're lying, but I don't care." Lauren hugged her back as much as she could muster. "I'm just glad we're all together."

"I'm sorry Aunt Jill couldn't come," Lindsey said, rolling her pink suitcase into the middle of the living room, the wheels leaving two thin, wet trails behind. Watson sniffed it carefully, decided it wasn't something he could eat, and moved on.

"It would have cost her and her family a fortune to fly to Buffalo over a holiday, plus she was just here last week." Lauren resisted the urge to smooth a stray piece of blond hair out of Lindsey's eye, the way her mother had always done to her growing up. *I guess we all really do turn into our mothers in the end,* she reflected.

"I get it. But we're doing Christmas at their place this year, right?" That was another thing the family had apparently arranged while Lauren was hospitalized: a trip to the Pacific Northwest. Who knew what other adventures they had planned while she was unconscious? "Why not? I'd love to see Seattle at Christmas time."

"Is Shane going to come too?" Lindsey asked coyly.

Lauren knew she was trying to needle her. "No. Reese has his own family. The only reason he's with us today is because his parents are on a cruise to Mexico."

"Hey, big sister." Erin ran out from the kitchen and caught her sibling around the shoulders in a bear hug. "I've missed you so much since last week."

"Get off me! Get off me!" Lindsey grappled with her younger sister on the carpet while Watson jumped up and down, barking in approval. Lindsey's and Erin's favorite mode of greeting was still Roman-Greco style wrestling. Rolling around, Lauren's mind flashed to them at eleven and twelve, each trying to overpower the other. Lindsey was stronger, but Erin was quicker. Their bouts almost always ended in a draw. Lauren knew they'd outgrow it soon, but she hoped not too soon, not just yet.

"What's all the racket?" Reese stuck his head in the living room. With the rain imminent, he and Lauren's father had been trying to fix the gutter on the back of the house all morning. Giving up and coming inside, a wet leaf was stuck to the side of Reese's navy-blue baseball

119

cap. Mr. Healy, equally rain-spattered, wandered into the living room after him.

"I'm here!" Lindsey announced from the floor, where Watson was energetically licking her face. "Me and Watson."

Lauren reached down, scooping up the Westie. "That's enough, Watson." He turned his attention to Lauren's cheek and commenced licking her full-force. She looked around her living room, suddenly overcome with gratitude for the people she loved.

I am thankful to be here, she thought, handing the dog over to her dad, *really and truly and utterly thankful. It only took a knife to the lung and a kick in the head to appreciate it.*

22

It was dark outside when the doorbell rang the Sunday after Thanksgiving. Because of their extended stays when she was in the hospital, both her girls and her parents had left Saturday during the day. The four days of chaos of having her family staying with her had been wonderful but exhausting for Lauren. She had gone to bed well before midnight, ready to sleep in Sunday morning, with no physical therapy and no other appointments. She fell asleep looking forward to the empty day that awaited her.

BONG.

BONG.

Watson's head jerked and he let out a concerned *woof*, waking Lauren from a deep, dreamless sleep. Lauren sat up, blearily wondering what time it was, if she was hearing things.

The bell rang again.

Without bothering to grab a robe, Lauren made her way down the stairs with Watson at her heels. A sleepy-eyed Reese appeared in the hallway in a Bills tee shirt and boxer shorts, his little black Beretta in his right hand.

Lauren approached the front door from the side. It was solid wood, and Lauren had made the mistake of not putting a peephole in when she had it installed. She could hear rain splattering against the roof in a pounding rhythm. "Who is it?"

"Lauren, it's Garcia and Thorenson. Could you open up?" Craig Garcia's grating voice was unmistakable. *What the hell are they doing here?* Hesitating for half a second, Lauren twisted the deadbolt and threw open the front door.

Outside the weather was trying to decide if it wanted to flip into winter mode. The temperature had dropped once the sun went down, and now a freezing rain was coming down in sheets on the two cops standing on her front steps.

Craig Garcia was wearing the stupid old-fashioned fedora he always sported because he wanted to make himself look like a 1940s flatfoot. It was just another of the many reasons Lauren disliked her fellow Homicide detective. Rain dripped off the brim into her doorway. "We got a situation. You and Reese need to get dressed and come down to headquarters with us."

Watson growled. Reese reached down, sweeping him up before the little dog pounced on the two soaked detectives. "What's going on, guys? It's five in the morning."

Tim Thorenson shook his head, scattering droplets from his thick blonde hair. "We'll get into it in the car. Can we come in? I'm getting drenched out here."

Lauren stepped back, letting them into her hallway. "What happened?" she demanded. Something was very wrong, and she wasn't going anywhere until she knew what the deal was.

It was Garcia who answered. "Joe Wheeler is dead. Murdered. And you both need to come downtown with us. Now."

23

Detectives Thorenson and Garcia were kind enough to wait while Lauren changed into a sweatshirt and jeans. Reese pulled on an old pair of sweatpants and put Watson in his crate. As she walked out to Garcia's car, she noticed Thorenson leaning over, looking into the back-passenger side of Reese's car. Snapping up when he saw her notice, he walked over and opened his police car door for her. She sat shivering in her seat. The sweatshirt she had just put on was soaked through. Reese slid in next to Lauren without a word, equally drenched from the short walk. The rain ran down the window glass in rivulets as Lauren stared out into the night, the streetlights blurred into foggy halos by the downpour.

The car stunk like the cheap cologne that Mario Aquino was known for; enough to make her eyes water. He must have had the vehicle before Garcia.

Garcia and Thorenson got in. Thorenson spoke up first. "Listen—"

Reese cut him off. "Save it until we get downtown. I can't hear you over the weather."

"Reese, come on." Thorenson turned in his seat to look at him.

Reese shook his head. "Downtown."

It was a quiet ride to headquarters. The police car was the last place Lauren wanted to talk about what happened to Joe Wheeler. She was glad Reese had stopped the conversation before it started. She didn't trust Garcia. And she trusted anything he had to say to her even less.

Days after Lauren had been thinking she should have blown Joe Wheeler's brains out when she had the chance, she was sitting in her own Homicide office with Chief Bernard Ritz of the Garden Valley Police looking at pictures of Joe Wheeler's dead body.

Thorenson and Garcia had separated her and Reese once they got them to Buffalo police headquarters. She was in the big interview room with Tim Thorenson and Chief Ritz, like the cracker, giving a statement about her whereabouts that night.

Joe Wheeler had been Garden Valley's only detective, so Lauren wasn't surprised their chief was handling this personally. She had seen another Garden Valley officer in the Homicide office when they brought her and Reese in, looking pale and shaky. A cop's death was difficult to deal with on any department. A cop's murder was devastating.

The Buffalo brass had called its entire squad in on overtime to assist Garden Valley PD. Lauren pictured half the Homicide squad watching her on one monitor in the viewing room, the other half watching Reese's interview on the second monitor, their heads bouncing from screen to screen like spectators at a tennis match.

"Can you give me a detailed account of where you've been the last twenty-four hours?" Ritz asked. This wasn't how Lauren would have started an interview. She would have started with some feeler questions, like *How are you doing? Can I get you something to drink? Do you know why you're here?* On the other hand, she supposed Ritz wasn't going to be looking for any critiques when he was finished.

"My daughters both left this morning—yesterday morning," Lauren corrected herself. This morning was currently the one in progress. "We dropped my parents off at the airport around six in the evening. I made a frozen pizza, walked the dog around the block, took my medicine, and went to bed," she summed up. It was pretty straightforward, she could have answered those questions at her house. But Lauren knew if they wanted her downtown, there was a lot more they wanted to get out of her.

"What time did you go to bed?" Ritz asked. A muscular man of about fifty-five, he was the type of guy who stood ramrod straight, as if always at attention. His white hair was buzz-cut into a perfect box, his face shaved smooth, not a hint of five o'clock shadow, even though it was literally five o'clock. In the morning, but still. His hazel eyes bored into Lauren's, as if every word that ever came out of her mouth was bound to be a lie and needed to be questioned. Ritz hadn't been happy when David Spencer was acquitted of Garden Valley's only homicide in the last twenty years and even less happy when Lauren had filed charges and lodged a formal complaint against Joe Wheeler. Now he was outright hostile.

"I was tired. I was in bed around nine thirty. My pills usually put me out pretty quick."

"What time did Shane Reese come to bed?" Ritz asked.

"I don't know. Reese sleeps in the guest room downstairs." She tried not to sound defensive. Ritz didn't have a clue about her and

126

Reese's relationship, or lack thereof. She would probably assume they were in a romantic relationship as well, if she were Ritz.

"You didn't hear Reese leave?" Thorenson asked. Tim Thorenson was a nice guy with twenty years on the job. He was no ball of fire when it came to homicide investigations; he typically did somewhere around the bare minimum to get by. The captain had paired him with Garcia, who was so abrasive he'd gone through five or six partners by the time Lauren had gotten to Homicide. While Lauren liked Tim personally, she couldn't stand Craig Garcia and avoided him at work at all costs. She was glad that Garcia was talking with Reese. Thorenson she could at least stomach.

"I don't know that Reese left at all. I didn't hear anything."

"He did. At ten thirty. The guard at the gate took down the plate and the time." Thorenson looked at the notes he had written on a legal pad. "Came back at three thirty-six."

Trying not to look shocked, Lauren said nothing. Reese hadn't mentioned to her that he'd planned to go anywhere last night.

Chief Ritz tapped a picture on the desk in front of her. It was black-and-white and blurry, from a security camera, and an old one at that. "This was taken by Joe Wheeler's neighbor across the street. Apparently, the elderly gentleman believed someone was putting trash in his garbage cans so he set up surveillance. One of my uniforms recorded the footage on his cell phone before taking the video tape for evidence. The quality is shit but it gives us the gist of what happened." Ritz opened up the laptop that had been resting flat on the table. He hit a few keys and flipped it around so she could see the screen. "We printed the stills from this. There's no sound."

A grainy black-and-white video played.

The camera was trained directly at the two garbage totes on the curb, but Joe Wheeler's driveway was in full view in the background.

She recognized the residence right away from the knotty old tree to the right of the mailbox; it had been Joe's dad's house. She remembered going there when they were a couple. Joe must have moved in after his father died.

For ten seconds the scene was still. The image danced a little, probably from the officer's shaky hand. Then a dark-colored car pulled into the driveway. From behind, you could make out movement in the vehicle, either Joe gathering up some things or putting them away. The driver's door opened and Joe stepped out. Almost immediately a figure stepped into the frame from the right. Lauren watched as Joe's head turned in that direction.

The figure wore dark clothes, a hood pulled up around his face, with something long in his right hand. *A tire iron*, Lauren thought. *It looks like a tire iron.*

The person closed the distance between them quickly. Joe's hand went for his waistband and the left hand of the person came up with the iron and brought it crashing down on Joe's arm. Joe went to his knees, grabbing his forearm, looking up at the attacker.

As Lauren watched in horror, the assailant rained vicious blows down on his head, even after he was face down on the ground. Even after it was clear he wouldn't be getting up again.

In her mind she knew the dull, cracking noise those strikes were making:

THUNK!

THUNK!

THUNK!

With each contact, Joe's body convulsed, and even though she couldn't hear the sound, parts of Lauren's body jerked in reaction.

With one last devastating smash to the head, the attacker backed up for a moment, surveying Joe's lifeless body. With one foot he kicked Joe over, flat on his back. In the grass, a few feet from Joe, was the gun he'd tried to pull from its holster. The attacker looked at the corpse of Joe Wheeler for a second, then turned and walked back the way he'd come, still holding the tire iron as if nothing at all had just happened.

Joe's body lay on the concrete, absolutely still. Lauren felt her throat constrict, cutting off the air in the room. Seconds went by, maybe a minute. Still Joe lay there, splayed out, a dark pool spreading around his head.

Finally, a car came by. It passed Joe's house, then abruptly stopped and backed up. Two men jumped out and ran up the driveway. Both of them stopped short. The driver, who already had a cell phone in his hand, stood stone still while he dialed. The other man turned away and promptly threw up on the grass.

Ritz closed the laptop with a *snap.*

Lauren looked down. Fanned out in front of her were fifteen black-and-white stills from the neighbor's camera.

"That's a tire iron," the chief confirmed. "Here Joe Wheeler sees the person and tries to draw his weapon." He tapped another photo. "Here the assailant smashes the tire iron into Wheeler's arm, breaking it and sending Wheeler's gun flying. Here the attacker proceeds to beat my officer to death. The time on the video says it's one twenty-seven a.m. In case you weren't counting, Joe took a total of twelve hits. Twelve. The gun was recovered in the grass six feet from his body."

Now Ritz pulled a large color 8-by-10 out of a folder on the desk and dropped it in front of Lauren. It was not a grainy black-and-white picture taken from a video. It was a high-resolution crime scene photo that captured the carnage in shocking detail. There was Joe Wheeler, face unrecognizable, head smashed open like a pumpkin, lying on his back in his driveway.

"Did Shane Reese do this?" Ritz asked.

She picked up the picture and stared at it. Joe's right forearm was bent at a grotesque angle, away from his elbow, hand empty and palm up. Blood pooled around the back of what was left of his head, dark and thick-looking on the driveway. *His nose*, she thought as she tried to keep her hand from shaking, *it's next to his ear.*

"No. Shane Reese did not do that." Lauren's voice choked. It was one thing to think about revenge, it was another to see it, guts and all. She felt a wave of nausea pass over her. No matter what Joe Wheeler had done to her in the past, no one deserved to die like that.

"Joe Wheeler gets his job back and within days, someone takes a tire iron to his head," the chief said, his shirt white and crisp, even at that early hour. He was on his feet, standing over her as she sat in her chair. "You take a knife to the back and a foot to the head a few weeks ago. What's the connecting factor here? Shane Reese. I don't believe in coincidences, do you, Detective?"

Lauren shook her head. "That would mean Reese stabbed me and stole our Murder Book. He had no reason to do that. That makes no sense."

"Unless he wanted to look like a hero. He came back and saved you, then killed your abuser."

"Oh, please." She dropped the photo. Her hand was shaking so badly she stuck it under her leg. "Reese does not have a hero complex. He didn't stab me, and he didn't kill Joe Wheeler."

"Can you offer me a better explanation?" Ritz was up in her face now, his coffee breath bouncing off her lips. She choked back a gag, craning her head back from his.

She wanted to repeat what Reese had told her, to tell Ritz that being a cop was dangerous and that not everything was about her. She wanted to tell him that Joe Wheeler, if he was still alive, could probably name ten guys who wanted to see him dead, because he did his job and that was what happened. She wanted to say Reese was her partner, and while she had no doubt he'd take a bullet for her, he would not kill for her. But saying those things wouldn't help Reese, so she did the smart thing and said nothing at all.

"How would you feel if another cop knew something about the guy who attacked you and sat here and stonewalled?" Ritz pressed. He was trying to piss her off and he was succeeding. A dull throb began behind her right eye. She knew the game Ritz was playing, because she played it better than anyone, but to win you had to have the facts on your side. She decided to let Ritz in on a few of the ones she knew.

"There's nothing to say." She tried to keep her voice in check. "Reese didn't kill Joe. Look." She grabbed one of the black-and-white photos off the table. "I can tell this is Joe Wheeler, not because of his face, but because I know Joe Wheeler. I know the way he stands and his body posture and the way he moves. I can't make out his face in this picture, but I know this is him. And this other guy? I know it's not Reese. Reese is shorter than Joe Wheeler. The attacker is clearly taller than him. And he's holding the tire iron in his left hand. Reese is a righty. He plays baseball, he bats right. See here?" She pointed to the still shot of the strike to Wheeler's arm. "That's a lefty. That's not Reese."

The door to the interview room opened. A tiny, dark-haired woman in a navy-blue pants suit with a wrinkled white blouse stepped in. "Not another word, Lauren." She turned to Ritz, sticking out her hand. "Amelia Jones-Cortez. I'm the Buffalo Police Union's lawyer. I don't believe I've had the pleasure."

Ritz looked down at her outstretched hand, straightened up, but didn't shake it. "Detective Riley didn't ask for a lawyer."

"It's too early for me," she said with a smile to Lauren, stepping in front of Ritz. "Let's me, you, and Detective Reese go get a coffee. You're done here."

Chief Ritz tried to take back control of the room. "I have a dead police officer—"

"And this one's recovering from a murder attempt." Literally half his size, Amelia turned and faced Ritz. "She's in no condition to give you any kind of statement. Are you charging Shane Reese with murder?"

Ritz's lips mashed together as he towered over the tiny lawyer, whose smile never faltered. "I'll take that as a no. Then he's done too. Let's go, Lauren." She slipped her arm through Lauren's, helping her up.

Trying to catch her breath, Lauren wobbled for a second. Amelia's eyes flashed at Ritz and Thorenson. "If she suffers a medical setback because you tried to question her about a murder she has no knowledge of, you'll both be hearing from me. You"—she turned directly to Tim Thorenson—"go get Detective Reese for me, right now. We'll be waiting in the hallway."

They left the police chief standing in the interview room and made their way slowly out to the hall. Lauren was holding onto the shorter woman, the throb becoming a full-blown pounding to her skull. She watched Thorenson dip into the other interview room, say a few words, then hold the door open for Reese as he exited. Thorenson mouthed the words *I'm sorry* to Lauren, but she was in too much pain to care. Her heart was thumping in her chest.

"You're not okay," Amelia said, touching Lauren's forehead with two cool fingers.

"I just need—to breathe—" She bent over in a spasm of coughing.

"Riley." Reese sounded a million miles away as Lauren sensed his hands grab onto her arms and her vision began fading into a gray fog.

Amelia yelled, "Someone call an ambulance!" Lauren felt herself sliding to the floor as the fog swallowed her up.

24

Lauren woke to the familiar brightness of a hospital room. The beeping monitors, the same nasty disinfectant smell. "Son of a bitch," she swore, examining the IV stuck in her arm. The roar in her skull had dulled to a low ache. On the wall, directly in front of her, the whiteboard announced in neat capitals: YOUR NURSE TODAY IS ROSE in green ink. It was déjà vu all over again.

Instead of Reese stretched out in the hospital chair, it was Dayla. She looked up from scrolling through her phone messages. "You're awake."

"What happened this time?" Lauren struggled to sit up. Someone had tilted her hospital bed so far, she had slid almost flat.

"They thought you threw a blood clot at first. Which would have been very, very bad. But it turns out that you're dehydrated and exhausted. I wonder how that happened?"

"Where's Reese?"

Dayla unfurled herself, dropping her phone into her enormous black designer bag, and approached Lauren's bed. "I sent him home before he ended up in the bed next to you for, you know, dehydration and exhaustion. You two have a very unhealthy codependent nonsexual relationship. All of the heartache, none of the fun."

"Joe Wheeler is dead." Lauren said it aloud more to confirm it to herself than anything else.

"I know." Dayla's voice became sympathetic. "It's all over the news. Awful. I'm so sorry, Lauren."

Lauren squeezed her eyes tight to block out the image of Joe's crushed skull. "Are my parents on the way? Do my daughters know?" she asked, trying to keep her breathing under control.

"Relax." Dayla waved a dismissive hand. "You only got admitted four hours ago. They're pumping you full of fluids. You'll be out tomorrow morning. They're just keeping you for observation so they can cover their asses."

Lauren opened her eyes and took as deep a breath as she could manage. "They think Reese killed Joe Wheeler."

Dayla actually laughed out loud. "Not anymore. He has an alibi. Airtight."

Lauren's ears pricked up. "What is it?"

She flashed a wicked grin at Lauren. "I'm going to let him tell you."

25

"Anna? My nurse? The one who wiped my ass and changed my tubes?"

"It wasn't a steady thing, you know? She'd call me, I'd call her, we'd get together—"

Lauren was disgusted. "You were on a booty call with my nurse when Joe Wheeler was beat to death?"

Reese was parked on the edge of her hospital bed, baseball hat turned backward, looking a little shamefaced. Dayla was back in the chair, listening in amusement. "When you put it that way, it sounds so dirty."

"Leaving my house without telling me almost made you a murder suspect."

He ticked off the list of unincriminating factors on his fingers for her. "The guy who killed him was taller than Joe, who was six feet, while I am five-eleven. I'm a righty, while the assailant was clearly a lefty. And I was engaged in consensual amorous acts with a lovely young woman at the time of the homicide, which was documented—"

Lauren held up her hand, cutting him off. "Stop. I don't want to know."

"Not to speak ill of the dead," said Reese, about to speak ill of the dead, "but Wheeler was a known douche bag. If he used to beat you up, I'm sure he left a string of brothers, dads, and boyfriends who wanted to kick his ass."

"Kicking his ass is not the same as bashing his brains out."

"His chief went after the most obvious suspect, in his mind. Now, at least, I'm eliminated, and they can concentrate on the real killer. Wheeler was still a cop. His friends on the job are hurting, including Chief Ritz. After seeing those pictures, I would love to find myself in a dark alley with the bastard who thinks he can execute a cop like that."

Lauren mulled that over for a second. "Do they really think my attack was related to his?"

Reese shrugged. "It's hard to ignore that angle. You're only alive because I found you in time. Our department is cooperating with Garden Valley in the investigation, treating them as if they're related."

"Joy and Ben are investigating Joe Wheeler's murder too?" She wondered if Reese had told them about Rita Walton yet. She wanted to ask, but not in front of Dayla, so she bit her tongue.

"And Thorenson and Garcia, now. You should thank Tim Thorenson, by the way," Reese added. "He's the one who called the union as soon as he was ordered to go pick us up."

"I should have known. Tim is a standup guy. But I still don't trust Garcia."

Reese turned his Yankees hat around on his head so it faced front, another of his nervous habits: rearranging his baseball cap. "Garcia is the least of our worries. He couldn't find a haystack in a pile of needles.

He won't add anything to the investigation and he's too lazy to mess it up, either."

"I still can't believe Joe's dead." Lauren's voice came out almost in a whisper. As bad as it had become between them, she still remembered the man she had once loved. He hadn't been the best-looking guy in their police academy class, but he had been the most confident. He had encouraged her, helped her study, ran with her, and supported her when she thought she was about to give up. He didn't show his ugly side until later, after he was on the street.

She had been young, with two daughters she was sure needed a father figure and starting a new job she wasn't sure she could handle. He played on her fears and turned his possessiveness and jealously into faults she thought she needed to correct. He manipulated her into forgiving the beatings because they were somehow, always, her doing. It had been a very dark time in her life, brought back to reality last year when they worked on opposite sides of the Katherine Vine homicide.

The old blame came bubbling up. Joe whispering in her ear that it was all her fault, she had caused this, if she were a better person, if she had only done what she was supposed to do, none of this would have happened.

Then Lauren pushed all of those thoughts aside. She remembered the beatings and the lies and the false promises he gave her while they were together. This time was always the last time, until the next time. The day she had finally thrown Joe Wheeler out the door, she swore she would never let him make her feel that way again.

Then last year he had punched her in that parking lot and she had done nothing. He took it to mean that she was still the same old Lauren. Still ripe for his brand of tough love.

When she had cornered him in her backyard and pressed her gun to his temple, part of Lauren had wanted to pull the trigger, but part of her had wanted to let him live. She wanted him to live and see how he couldn't affect her life anymore. She wouldn't allow it. She was the one in control now.

She had allowed him walk away that night.

So why was she upset now? Because he hadn't lived long enough to see her happy? Or because someone else had done what the darkest part of her had wanted to do?

"Lauren?" The concern in Dayla's voice brought her back.

She shook her head to clear the ghosts from it. "Sorry. I zoned out for a second. Maybe I do need to sleep."

"I'll call the nurse and have them give you something." Reese punched the call button above her bed with his finger. She knew she had done more than zone out a little by the look on his face.

"Okay," she agreed, but she didn't close her eyes. She was afraid that the image of Joe sprawled on the ground would come back. Of his forearm, twisted and broken. Of brains and blood on the concrete. She was too exhausted to deal with it just now.

No, she'd wait for the pill and hope for a dreamless sleep.

26

With the promise to Dr. Patel that she would take better care of herself and let someone else do the detecting for a while, Lauren was home the next day. Dr. Patel didn't bat an eye at the boldfaced lies she gave him; what else was she going to do but leave there and try to figure things out? He wasn't a moron. She knew all he could hope for was for her not to overwork herself. Again.

She'd use the sleeping pills he prescribed her. They actually worked and chased away most of her nightmares. Not all of them, but most.

Dayla picked her up from the hospital without any fanfare and brought her home. Lauren told her she was drained and going to bed so she could get rid of her. "You promise you'll call if you need anything?" Dayla asked, standing in the morning sunshine on Lauren's front walk.

"I promise. Thank you for everything."

Dayla waved and flounced up the sidewalk toward her own house. "Just be good, okay?" she called back. "Reese will kill me if anything happens to you."

Reese had already left for work. He had gone out with Joy trying to locate the elusive Rita, who had fallen completely off the grid eight years ago. Not an arrest, not a complaint, no applications for social services or apartments. It was as if she'd totally disappeared.

Except for her voice on that answering machine.

Reese was good, but Rita was an artifact from a time on the street that was foreign to him.

"I need to get back in the game," she told Watson as he sat wagging his tail, watching her get dressed. "What your daddy doesn't know won't hurt him."

The media had gone nuts when word of Joe Wheeler's murder got out. They were eating up the idea that a madman might be trying to murder local cops. Somehow, her private cell number had gotten out—possibly from the same leak that had been plaguing the Homicide squad—and she had to change her number. Which meant Charlie Daley had no way to contact her. Which meant she was going to see him because she needed him.

Her stitches were itching, but all in all, she felt okay enough to drive. She'd been careful to eat something and drink an entire glass of orange juice before getting into her car. *Hydrate*, she reminded herself, *or you'll end up back in the hospital*. Cranking the music up as she drove to Lackawanna, she decided she really did feel better. Or at least useful. Working was better than lying in bed doing nothing.

Joe's face kept swimming before her eyes. She'd seen hundreds of bodies over the years, in person and in crime scene photos, killed in every way imaginable. But to see someone you used to share a bed with, someone you once loved, no matter how warped it may have become, murdered like that shook Lauren to her core. What had been done to her was brutal; what had been done to Joe was downright evil.

Lauren had to separate his case from hers, or she'd freeze up. She had to compartmentalize and concentrate on finding Rita Walton, trust that the Garden Valley cops would bring the state police in if Buffalo wasn't enough. *I have to let them handle Joe's case,* she thought as she pulled into the cemetery. *I'm no good to them right now. Unless I can find out who attacked me and link the two crimes somehow.*

Charlie was surprised to see her coming up the porch steps. He had dirt smeared all over his face and coveralls as he held the door open for her. "I had to tidy up after the gravediggers. Slobs, they all are. No respect."

"We've seen each other look worse." She stepped into the magically modern sitting room. Nell, hearing someone come in, stuck her head out of the pocket doors, but Charlie waved her away. She gave Lauren a cheerful smile and closed herself back into the main office.

"That we have," he agreed. "Terrible what happened to Joe Wheeler. I know that he—"

She held out her hand, cutting him off. They had to focus on his old informant. "I need to find Rita, Charlie. Reese has been searching for her and it's like she never existed. I need your help."

He scratched his white bristly chin. "No one's going to find Rita unless she wants to be found. She hasn't lived this long because she's stupid."

"But can *you* find her?"

He looked past her, into the graveyard. "Maybe. But it's been a long time since I was on the streets. Most of the people I knew are probably dead."

"Then this won't be different from any other day for you."

He let out a snort. "Always quick with the comebacks. Give me a minute to change and clean up. I know a couple places we could stop and inquire."

She sank down onto the floral sofa. "I'll wait here."

"You got a gun on you?" he asked, pausing at the staircase leading to his apartment.

"I got two. My Glock and my Smith and Wesson."

"She swallows a peanut, you can see it sticking out of her stomach. But two frigging cannons she can hide without a wrinkle," he muttered, creaking his way up the stairs.

27

The lower West Side had changed since Charlie Daley patrolled those streets. The Feds had RICO'd the entire 10th Street Gang eight years before, rounding up the worst of the worst and setting the stage for urban renewal. Location was everything, and with the neighborhood being so close to Downtown, Canalside, and the Elmwood Village, people had started snapping up the cheap real estate and began renovating. It was nothing to see a brand-new house that would have been on the market for hundreds of thousands in the suburbs sitting next to a derelict building. Millennials loved the funky urban vibe, being close to the arts scene, and the affordable prices.

Still, there were pockets of streets that hadn't been revitalized yet, where the poor and old were isolated and the drugs and violence were kept contained. That's where Lauren had found one of her witnesses from a stabbing last year, in the upper of a rundown house whose neighbors were gangbangers, addicts, and drunks. The woman had cooperated, despite what that meant on the streets, and was key in her friend's murderer going to jail. As she and Daley rolled through the neighborhood, Lauren vaguely wondered where her witness was now. Whether she had stayed in Buffalo, or if she'd had gone back to Puerto Rico. Either way, Lauren would never know now because the cell number that she'd had for ten years as a detective had been changed. She didn't want to think of all the calls going to her voicemail that would never be answered.

Charlie was wedged into the passenger seat of her Ford Escape. *Even SUVs aren't meant for guys his size,* she thought, watching him squirm beneath the seat belt that threatened to strangle him. He had wanted to ride without wearing it until Lauren reminded him the car would angrily beep every thirty seconds until he was strapped in.

"I can't even breathe wearing this Goddamn thing," he griped, pulling the strap away from his chest as far as it would go.

"I couldn't breathe when I had a knife in my lung," she countered. "Stop being such a baby."

"You always have to one-up me," he said, then pointed. "Turn here. Go slow by the green house with the porch."

She let up on the gas, coasting by the old flop house. At some point there had been a fire on the second floor; black scorch marks rose from the upper glassless windows. The house number, 453, was spray painted in red across the lower front, signaling it was marked for city demolition.

"I guess Sadie don't live there no more," Charlie said as they passed.

Lauren continued on, letting Charlie take the lead.

"Turn down Pennsylvania Street. There's a place I want to check out." The window was down, his arm hanging out, despite the cold that had crept in during the night, turning late November from brisk to chilly in hours. Charlie had changed out of his coveralls into a Buffalo

Bills sweatshirt and jeans. He had the cuffs stuffed down into his tan work boots, like he used to do when he was on the job. It kept the critters off your legs, he used to tell her; the roaches will climb right up into your underwear if you don't cut them off at the pass.

"Shouldn't your partner be doing this with you?" he asked.

"He's trying, but I'm still a control freak. I can't just sit home and do nothing," she replied, slowing down to look at some older women standing on the corner, all holding plastic shopping bags. They noticed and turned toward the SUV to stare back.

Charlie snickered. "It's not like we don't stick out in this Ford, not in this neighborhood, being this color. And you're staring at them."

"I probably look like a heroin hype out trying to score some drugs with her old sugar daddy."

"I don't like skinny broads. I'd have to fatten you up before I became your sugar daddy."

"Duly noted." Lauren smiled as they passed a middle-aged man pushing a shopping cart full of groceries down the sidewalk. Stalks of celery stuck out of one of the plastic bags as his head nodded in time to the music only he could hear coming from his earbuds.

"Pull over up here," Charlie pointed to a spot at the curb. "We'll just wait."

Lauren did as she was told, pulling up in front of a vacant lot. She put the car in park, leaving it running. "What are we doing?"

He looked over at the houses a little farther up the block and repeated, "Just wait."

Looking straight ahead, arm still hanging out the window, he sat watching the neighborhood foot traffic. Most people ignored them, a few gave them curious glances as they passed. Lauren looked at the digital clock on her dash: it was one thirty in the afternoon.

"How long are we going to sit here?" she asked.

"Wait for it," he said patiently.

After another minute or so, Lauren watched a young woman with braids carefully pull apart an umbrella stroller on the porch of a double two houses up. She set it down on the sidewalk, then retreated into the house and came out with a toddler, who she protectively buckled in, tugging on the nylon straps to make sure they were secure. Walking with a look of dignified purpose, she pushed the stroller their way. Lauren could see the baby, a little girl dressed in a puffy pink coat, looking all around as her mother pushed her right up to the car.

"Hello," the woman said to Charlie, her eyebrows knit together in a sort of determined resolve. She was in her early twenties, dark-skinned and beautiful, with high cheekbones. She was what Lauren's mother would have called "big-boned"—broad in the shoulders and hips. She wore a long yellow dress with a fleece-lined denim jacket over it, and a thin gold chain hanging around her throat with a single letter done in script: *S*.

"This is my neighborhood," she began in a calm, steady voice, "and I don't know what you're looking for, but you need to leave my street right now. There are children here." She glanced down at her little girl who was staring at Lauren and Charlie like they were aliens. "And they don't need to see addicts come to buy their drugs."

Charlie didn't smile but said in a tone of respect and deference, "We apologize for alarming you, but we're not looking for drugs. Do you know where I can find Jackson Morgan?"

Her eyes narrowed. "How do you know Mr. Morgan?"

"We're old friends. If you could point me in the right direction, I'd appreciate it. It's important."

"You? Friends with Mr. Morgan?"

Charlie nodded.

The woman looked Charlie and Lauren up and down, trying to determine if she should get involved. Charlie gave his best grin at the little girl in the stroller and waggled his fingers at her. She giggled and gave him a clumsy wave with her chubby hand.

"What's your name?" the woman with the braids asked.

"Charlie Daley."

"Charlie Daley" she repeated, to get it right. "Hold on." The woman held one manicured finger up and pushed the stroller past the car. She stopped at the edge of the vacant lot and pulled a cell phone out of a maroon-colored shoulder bag. Lauren watched in the rear-view mirror as she spoke to someone, her other arm crossed around her waist, her left foot rocking the stroller gently back and forth while she spoke. When she was done, she pushed the stroller back to Charlie's side.

"Stay here," was all she said, then continued with her walk down the street, her sunny yellow skirt swishing back and forth until she hit the corner and turned out of sight.

"Now what?" Lauren asked.

Charlie slipped a Glock 19 out of the inside of his jacket and rested it next to his enormous thigh. "Now we wait again. Just be ready."

Lauren put her hand on the small gun in her jacket pocket but didn't take it out. "Who's Jackson Morgan?"

"Someone who knows things. He owes me a favor."

"Do I want to know for what?"

He shook his head. "Probably not."

Charlie began to hum the theme song from *The Love Boat* as they waited. Lauren only recognized it because during her home confinement this last week she'd taken up watching old TV shows during the day. *The Love Boat* had come on right after *Bonanza*.

The minutes ticked by. First a half hour, then forty-five minutes. All the while Charlie hummed television theme songs. Just when Lauren was about to suggest they call it a day, a black BMW came around the corner and slowly rolled up to the car.

Sleek, shiny, with intricate chrome rims, the vehicle purred like a cat as it idled next to Lauren's. The passenger side window, tinted well past the legal limit, slid down. A thin black man about Charlie's age wearing thick black-rimmed glasses peered into Lauren's car, past her and on to Charlie. One of his eyes strayed off to the side, watery and pale. "Daley, is that really you? I heard you were dead."

"Not dead, just retired," Charlie said. "Which makes me good as dead."

Giving a knowing chuckle, the other man smiled. "I consider myself retired, too, but I still have to look after the neighborhood. Make sure everyone is doing what they're supposed to be doing. I got a call you needed to talk to me. I was concerned. It's been a long time, Daley. A long time."

"Seems like we've been talking on this same street corner since horse and buggies."

"It does seem that way," Jackson Morgan agreed. "It's nice to know someone else remembers how things used to be."

There was a moment where the two of them just regarded each other. *Old soldiers*, Lauren thought. *Old soldiers who fought on different sides.*

It was Charlie who broke the silence. "Can I talk to you alone?"

"Sure thing, Daley." He turned to his driver. "Pull up."

The driver, a young guy with the word HONEST tattooed across his neck, pulled the BMW in front of Lauren's Ford and parked. Charlie slid Lauren his gun and told her, "Wait here. This will only take a second."

"Charlie, wait—" She tried to slow his roll, but he was out of her SUV, meeting up with Morgan on the sidewalk. Slipping out of the driver's seat, the neck-tattooed friend of Morgan's leaned against the car, watching the two men carefully. She couldn't see the telltale bulge of a gun on him, but she knew if she got out he wouldn't see hers either. She could see he was tense, like a coiled spring, and that made her nervous. No one knew they were here. And he could take Charlie out before she could get a shot off.

She turned her attention to the two old men. Lauren knew she was skinny, but Morgan looked like he might blow away if Charlie exhaled too hard. There was a toughness about him though, a calm certainty that said Morgan was a dangerous man. In all her years as a cop, she'd never seen or heard of Jackson Morgan. Now she watched as the two men, both approaching seventy, stood on the street corner, their white-haired heads almost touching as they discussed their business. Charlie in his working man's jeans and Morgan in a neat gray pinstripe suit.

She gripped the gun at her side, ready in case things went bad. Lauren realized her heart was pounding in her chest; the adrenaline of the job was flooding back into her system.

After what seemed like an eternity, they shook hands, Charlie slipping something into Morgan's, and they clapped each other on the back. Charlie walked back to the SUV, hands stuffed in his pockets. Morgan got in his own ride, waited until Charlie got into Lauren's vehicle, then had his driver back up alongside of Lauren again.

"Thanks for your help, Morgan," Charlie told him.

"Young lady," he said addressing Lauren for the first time. "This here is one of the most honorable men I've ever had the pleasure of doing my business against. Daley, good luck. But don't you come back here, okay?"

"You've been more than gracious. Take care of yourself."

"I always do," he laughed, sliding the glass back up. "I always do."

The luxury car pulled off in a squeal of tires.

"Who was that?" Lauren demanded, finally letting go of the gun.

Reaching over, Charlie stashed his Glock in his waistband, fluffing his shirt over it. "Just drive and I'll tell you."

She pulled out, turning the opposite way Jackson Morgan's car had gone.

"Morgan ran the numbers for the entire city in the seventies and eighties. He was over on the East Side back when the numbers were huge money. Lots of payoffs to police and politicians. Morgan kept a low profile, always smart enough to stay one step ahead. The few times he did get arrested, the charges never stuck. He had his hand in everything back then. I remember chasing his guys around when I was a rookie cop."

"And now?"

Charlie shrugged. "He keeps his toe in the water. The numbers are still around, a lot of the older folks still play, but not like they used to; now that there's a lotto machine in every street corner deli. He still gets his cut from the gang bangers on drugs, guns, and prostitution, I'm sure."

"How have I never heard of him?"

"When everything went to shit during the crack wars in the early nineties, he went underground, let the drug runners shoot it out, played from the sidelines. But us old-timers, we knew who was calling the shots from afar."

"Does he know where Rita is?"

"He'll find out. I gave him my cell number. He'll call, but you might as well take me home now. He's in no rush, and my back is screaming from all the shoveling I did today." He reached down and massaged his lower spine. "You gonna tell that partner of yours what we're up to?"

"I'll wait. What if she's dead or he can't find her? Besides, it sounds like she'll talk to you. Maybe not Reese and his new temporary partner, Joy Walsh. I don't want to distract them with a wild-goose chase."

She made a left and headed for Niagara Street. The traffic was picking up, more so toward the Peace Bridge, which was backed up. She could see the line of cars stopped on the bridge on their way to Canada in her rearview mirror. "You really think Morgan will call?"

He nodded with a grim certainty. "Yup. He'll call. I'll clear my grave-cleaning schedule. Tomorrow you're going to meet my old friend, Rita Walton."

28

"You sure this is the place?" Lauren looked up at the senior apartment complex on Elmwood Avenue, smack in the middle of the trendy Elmwood Village, with its boutique shops and martini bars. A U-shaped construction, it boasted a sad, narrow courtyard between the two main buildings. A fuzzy-haired octogenarian in a puffy coat slowly pushed a walker toward a wooden bench at the far end, plastic shopping bags filled with God-knows-what hanging from each hand grip. The lady gave them a suspicious look as Lauren and Charlie came up the sidewalk, then sat down and began fiddling with her goods.

"That's what Morgan's message said. Apartment 202."

The weather had turned overnight, coating Lauren's front lawn with frost. She had watched Reese scrape his windshield that morning, then head to work. She hadn't said a thing about yesterday's excursion with Charlie. It wasn't that she didn't trust Reese; she just couldn't be a hundred percent sure Ben Lema or Joy Walsh weren't the leaks. If word hit the street that Rita Walton was trying to snitch on someone, that would be akin to signing her death warrant. The fact that the police couldn't find Rita, and Charlie had to resort to using Mr. Morgan, meant she'd already been hiding from something or someone.

After all, it could be nothing.

The outer door to the south-facing building was open. Walking into the lobby, Lauren noticed a fat, twenty-something security guard eating nacho chips and playing on his phone. He didn't look up as they crossed the filthy carpeted floor to the elevator. Benches were pushed up against the walls, filled with the residents who took no notice of them. They sat with coffee mugs or holding onto their walkers with one hand as they spoke in loud voices to be heard over the television set mounted above the security guard station, currently airing a daytime talk show.

One older gentleman looked up at them as they waited for the elevator car to come. "You got a smoke I could borrow?"

"Sorry, boss," Charlie told him, "I quit when I was sixty."

"Yeah?" He laughed, showing off a lifetime's worth of tobacco-stained teeth. "So did I, but it didn't stick." He burst into a fit of hacking coughs, drawing dirty looks from the lady next to him.

"Have a good one," Charlie said as he and Lauren got on the elevator. When the door shut, he turned to her. "Don't you ever let me end up in a place like this."

"What?" She stared up at the floor numbers. "This place is heaven compared to some of the nursing homes I've been in."

Stepping off onto the second floor, the smells of greasy home cooking flooded Lauren's nostrils. She'd been in these apartments a few times before and she knew they each had little kitchenettes. Just big enough to cook for one. An enormous orange cat sat on the window sill at the end of the hallway, watching them with yellow eyes as he soaked up the afternoon sun.

"201." Charlie's finger pointed to the brass number on the door to their left, then changed course, across the hall. "202," he declared.

Positioning himself in front of the door, Charlie took his oversized thumb and put it over the peephole, an old street copper's trick, before he knocked. Lauren stood off to the side, watching his huge fist pound three times on the door. From inside, they could hear the sound of a person shuffling around, some swearing, and a very loud television.

"Ellie, if that's you, I ain't got no money you can borrow—" The door swung inward to reveal a heavy-set black woman around Charlie's age with her hair in pink plastic curlers. A pair of huge gold hoops hung from each lobe as she stood dumbstruck in the doorway, clutching her blue and white house dress together at the chest.

"Hey, Rita," Charlie said. "Long time no see."

"Am I dead? Am I seeing a ghost? Oh Lord, you come right in here!" She stepped back, waving her arm frantically for them to come inside. "Did anyone see you?"

Lauren followed Charlie into the tiny but neat apartment. A huge flat-screen TV was blaring from its place on the floor, the box it came in propped against the wall next to it. Charlie seemed to take up the entire space of the living room; Lauren would bet if he held out his arms he could touch each side wall. Poor Rita was throwing the deadbolt and fastening the chain behind them, mumbling to herself, "I knew it. I knew it. I knew I shoulda minded my own business."

"You're not in trouble, Rita," Charlie told her when she was finished with the door.

She turned to face him, her meaty hands propped on each hip. "If Charlie Daley is at my door, I'm in trouble. And don't call me Rita, unless you *want* me to get my ass kicked out of here."

Framed family photos took up almost every inch of space on the walls, some in color, some in black-and-white, interspersed with embroidered Bible quotes and colorful inspirational prints. It made the small room feel even more claustrophobic now that there were three of them inside.

"So who are you now?" he asked in amusement as she shuffled by him to her kitchenette to turn off the burner under a whistling tea kettle.

"Virginia Robinson, my older sister. She died in North Carolina six years ago when I was staying with her. I needed to come back home to be near my babies, but I got too much negativity because of my previous lifestyle. I'm clean and sober now, seven years, and I ain't been in *no* trouble. You know that, Daley." She held up the kettle and looked at Lauren. "You want some tea? It's Earl Grey."

Lauren shook her head. "No thanks."

Rita squinted at her. "I ain't got my glasses on, but you look familiar. Who are you?"

"My name's Lauren Riley. I'm a cop who used to work with Charlie."

Reaching over the stovetop, Rita extracted a chipped teacup from a shelf. "So now you bound to him for life? Because that's what it feels like for me. Charlie's like a bad penny, he always turns up."

Charlie gave a little snort of laughter.

"Actually, Rita, he's helping me, and I hope you can help me too."

"I ain't rude, I just know Charlie don't drink no tea." She poured herself a steaming cup, dipping the tea bag up and down in the hot water. Lauren watched as she poured sugar from a glass container, exactly like the ones they had in restaurants, into her teacup. She vaguely wondered if Rita had slipped it into her purse the same way her own grandmother used to do every time they ate out. Every Sunday night there'd be a new set of salt and pepper shakers at Grandma Healy's.

"Rita." Charlie's voice was low, like he was in business mode now. "Did you make some phone calls to the old Snitch Board?"

"Ain't this a bitch?" she asked, leaning back against her countertop, tea in hand. "I ain't seen you in a million years. I'm living a law-abiding life and you still wondering if I'm in the mix?"

"Law-abiding except for the identity theft?"

"She's dead. She don't need it no more," Rita protested, taking a long slurp from her cup.

"Rita—"

"Shhhh, shhhhh, shhhhh!" she snapped. "It's Miss Robinson now."

"Rita," Charlie said, a little more sternly now. "Quit playing games. Did you call the Snitch Board or not?"

Rita crossed her arms over her ample chest, earrings swinging, a couple of tea drops flying out of her cup. "Not."

Feeling around in her jacket pocket, Lauren produced the slim black digital voice recorder. Without a word she held it out and hit Play.

Rita's lined face fell as her voice filled the small space. She put the teacup on the counter, shoulders slumping along with the sound of her own voice. Lauren let all three calls play through before she spoke again. "Did you call the Homicide office that day?"

"Damn you, Charlie Daley," Rita said. "I'm almost seventy years old. I can't be involved in this shit no more." She seemed to sink in on herself, like a great burden had just been replaced where she'd managed to shake it off.

"I know you don't want to." Lauren took a step forward. "But something made you call. You said you saw a murder."

157

"That was a long time ago." Her voice was barely a whisper. "Years and years ago."

Lauren caught Rita's eyes with hers. "If you have information about a murder, it must be weighing on you after all this time to leave those messages. Something made you call."

Rita wiped her nose with the back of her hand, taking a deep breath. She had her other hand on the counter behind her, almost holding her up. Rita's eyes went to Charlie's. "When you cut me loose, I was in a bad way. Worst I ever been. You wouldn't return my calls. I got busted a few times. Then I picked a john's wallet, and he punched me, so I pulled a knife on him. I got arrested for robbery third. Didn't show up to court, because I knew I was gonna do time." Her voice got stronger as she continued to stare at Charlie. "You remember how it was. What I was into."

"You were out of control, Rita." Charlie's voice was gentler now. "I couldn't have you stealing half the drugs you bought for me."

Nodding to herself, one of the pink plastic curlers unfurled a little, sending it spiraling alongside her face. "I know. Crack was like a demon. I had to have it, had to have it all the time. You let me go in the fall of 1991; I remember that because I got the robbery charge around Halloween. I was trying to get enough money to get down to my sister's in Raleigh. But I smoked up every twenty dollars I made."

She itched around the cheap lace of her housecoat collar and Lauren saw a puckered, jagged scar that ran down the side of her neck. Unconsciously, Lauren's hand snaked to her side. Rita noticed her noticing. "Some bitch with a razor blade cut me. Twenty-seven stitches I got that time."

"I didn't mean to stare."

Snapping her fingers, she pointed at Lauren's face. "That's where I know you. You the lady detective that's been all over the news. You got stabbed in the back or something."

"That's why I need your help. You called the district attorney's office the afternoon I got attacked. I need to know if you called the Homicide office and who you talked to."

"Aw, shit. This is worse than I thought." Her round brown eyes turned back to Charlie's face. "You ain't a cop no more. You can't protect me. These guys will kill me."

"I never let anybody hurt you when we worked together, and no one's going to hurt you now."

Waving him off, she walked over to her sad, tired-looking blue sofa and sat down. "That's just words, Daley. This is for real. They stabbed *her*"—she pointed at Lauren—"and she's a cop! What do you think they'd do to an old junkie hooker like me?"

"You keep saying 'they'," Lauren interrupted. "Who do you mean by 'they'?"

"I never took care of that robbery warrant," Rita said. "I can't go to jail for no felony now, not at my age. That's why I left this town in the first place."

"The statute of limitations is long over for a robbery third," Charlie pointed out. "They probably pulled that warrant years ago and you've been living like a spy all this time for no reason."

"Do I look like a lawyer to you?" she demanded, the pink curler flopping around. "How would I know that shit?"

"You know it now." Lauren tried the gentle voice again. "Tell us what happened."

Rita sat, looking back and forth between Riley and Charlie, as if that would make them leave, her mouth working from side to side like she was practicing what she was going to say. The noise of the TV seemed deafening to Lauren as she waited for Rita.

"Listen to me now." Rita put a hand over her heart like she was about to recite the Pledge of Allegiance. "Because I'm only going to tell this once and only to you two right now, right here. I was trying to save money to get to my sister's, so I was working a lot. East Side, West Side, wherever I was, I'd find me a corner to stand on. There's always a guy to pull over. It was in late January and it was cold as hell out. I remember standing in front of the liquor store at ... let me think. Allen and Wadsworth? You know the one?"

Charlie nodded. "I know it."

"I was smoking my last cigarette, hoping some drunk would stumble out of one of the bars so I could lift his wallet."

Lauren watched as her face hardened, the lines etched around her mouth becoming more prominent, as she steeled herself to tell her secret. "I was watching Culligan's Bar, but it was dead that night. Had to be around midnight and nothing was going on. If I had somewhere to go, I would have called it a night," she sighed at her own memory, "but I had gotten thrown out of my grandmother's earlier because she caught me stealing from her purse. Anyway, I see Spider creeping around. He was a neighborhood kid, Somalian. His mama spoke almost no English and he was a pistol, always boosting anything that wasn't nailed down. But he wasn't a good thief because he was always getting himself caught. If something turned up missing in Allentown, the coppers would go knocking on his mama's door and she'd hand over the stuff. They couldn't charge him because he always ran and they never caught him dirty."

"I remember this," Charlie said.

"I'm sure you do," she shot back at him. "You was there that night, but later, after it all went down. When every cop in the city showed up. Anyway, I see Spider—never knew his real name—and he's poking around, looking into car windows, trying door handles. I tell him to go home to his mama, but he just says she knows he's out. He had a very thick accent. A real skinny kid, all arms and legs. He was never nasty, just couldn't stay out of trouble. And he was a runner. That child could run so fast and hop a fence so quick, you'd think it was just a blur.

"So I'm watching him case the cars and he finds one unlocked. He opens the passenger door and crawls his skinny ass halfway in, trying to scoop all the change out of the center console. Next thing I know, there's this young cop I ain't never seen before, holding a nightstick in one hand, trying to grab Spider out of the car with the other. Spider got startled, you see; he wasn't expecting no cop to walk up on him. They always came in cars and by twos. He starts trying to squirm his way out of the copper's hands, but the cop's not letting him go. Then Spider hits the cop—accidently or on purpose, I don't know—and now there's a real struggle. The cop drops his nightstick. They're rolling around on the sidewalk. I see the cop's radio mic has come off his shoulder and is flying around. He can't call for no backup. Then Spider breaks free and he starts running down Allen Street toward me. That cop pulls his gun and right there in front of me he shoots Spider in the back." She paused to let the words sink in. Rita's eyes welled with tears.

"I was so scared, I pressed myself into the alley, so the cop couldn't see me. I was trapped. That young cop, he freaked out. He swore and stamped up to Spider and looked over that boy's body. Then he looked up and down the street, threw his gun under the car next to Spider, and ran around the corner, down South Elmwood." She paused, closed her eyes for a second, then took a deep breath.

"The people in the bars must have heard the gunshot because two guys trickled out and looked around. They saw Spider on the ground and ran back in to call the police. I was still trapped in the brick alley, freezing my ass off, scared to death. Then the police cars started showing up. First one, then two, then it seemed like every copper in the city was there. I saw you Narco guys pull up. I couldn't let you see me, Daley. I still had that robbery warrant on me. I needed to get out of there. I pushed a metal garbage can to the back wall of the alley and threw myself over onto the next street. Then I ran like hell."

"I remember that night," Charlie pinched his nose between his fingers. "It was cold, like you said, and we were surveilling a house a couple blocks over when the shots-fired call came out. Everybody knew Spider. The thought was that someone tried to stop him from breaking into cars and shot him, but not a cop. No one ever suspected a cop."

"So it's a cold case?" Lauren asked.

With a grim look on his face, Charlie nodded. "Never solved. The Homicide squad put a lot of work into it, because the victim was just a kid. Spider had just turned eighteen but was still in the tenth grade because of the language barrier, if I'm remembering it right. It was Ricky Schultz's case. He worked it hard."

Lauren knew that name. "Ricky retired five years ago. His other brother, Vince, is still on the job, on patrol. He must have at least thirty years on."

"Ricky was a hell of a detective," Charlie said.

"I bet he was." Rita pulled open a drawer in the small table next to her couch. She ruffled through some papers, then withdrew a shiny campaign mailing. She threw it down on her scratched glass coffee table. "The young cop I saw shoot Spider was this guy in the middle."

She tapped the photo. "And it says that the guy standing next to him is his brother, Richard."

The picture on the front of the glossy flyer showed three men who all resembled each other, standing in front of the County Court building. A man in his late fifties on the left side was wearing a police uniform, the younger man in the middle had on a three-piece suit and was smiling confidently into the camera, while the third man sported a solid blue golf shirt. The tagline above the photo read in bold black letters: HE USED TO PUT CRIMINALS AWAY WITH HIS BROTHERS BEFORE HE BECAME A LAWYER. NOW HE'LL PROSECUTE THEM. ELECT SAM SCHULTZ FOR ERIE COUNTY DISTRICT ATTORNEY THIS NOVEMBER!!!

"This here is why I called the Snitch Board. I ain't done a lot of things right in my life, but I never hurt no one that didn't hurt me first. I didn't know who that cop was. I ran because I was scared. I'm still scared. I thought I'd just make a phone call, tell someone what I knew and that'd be the end of it. The police would do their job, leave me out. Anonymous, ain't that what it's supposed to be?"

Lauren's throat closed up so tight, she thought she'd suffocate. The Schultzes were a prominent police family. Their father had been police commissioner in the late 1960s. The brothers had juice, as cops would say, connections that went all the way to City Hall and beyond. Lauren knew what kind of favors it took back in the day to get appointed police commissioner, and patronage was often handed out like candy before entrance and promotional exams were given.

She quickly picked her brain for what she knew about the brothers. Sam Schultz had been on the job for less than a year when he left to go to law school in the early 1990s. She'd worked briefly as a detective with Ricky right before he retired a few years ago, but she'd been in Sex Offenses. The middle brother, Vince, was one of those

163

old-timers everyone was convinced would die on the job, still in patrol humping calls.

She couldn't tear her eyes away from the mailer. Pain seeped up from her chest as her heart began to race. That pockmarked face, that barrel-shaped chest. There was no mistaking him: Vince Schultz had been in the Homicide office the afternoon she was stabbed.

"You're sure, Rita? This is the guy who shot Spider in the back?" Charlie picked up the picture, snapping Lauren's attention back to the reluctant informant, who was now nervously pulling at the foam seeping from a rip in her couch cushion.

Dropping little tallow bits by her pink house shoes, Rita nodded. "I know that was a bad time for me, but I ain't never forgot that man's face. I thought I knew everyone in old Precinct Three, but I never saw him before, or since, until now."

"He left the job for law school, wasn't on but a couple months," Charlie told her. "Probably because of this."

"I have to get to the file room." Lauren's voice was tinged in panic. "If Vince manages to get back in the Homicide office and gets his hand on the original file, whatever Rita saw won't matter."

Starting to charge toward the door, Charlie swept her up in one of his huge arms. "Easy, Lauren. You're going to end up in the hospital. Your face is as red as a baboon's ass. We'll call that partner of yours—"

"No. I have to get that file. Get it out of there. Make copies of it, right now." She was breathing so hard, she was panting. Charlie eased her down onto the couch next to Rita. He knew how to use his size, and Lauren was no match for him in the state she was in.

"You're going to sit, and I'm going to call Reese, and we're going to figure this out."

"No more cops," Rita wailed. "They'll kill me for sure. Look what they done to her. And she *is* a cop. You can't do this to me, Daley."

Charlie turned to Lauren. "We gotta get that file, and you gotta start working the case, however you do these cold cases now, without anyone knowing about Rita. At least until you've enough to make an arrest."

Practicing the breathing techniques her physical therapist had taught her, Lauren managed to get herself under control. Her stitches throbbed under her shirt. She pressed her hand against them, doubling over a little. "No one in Homicide will know. Not even Joy Walsh, who's been working with Reese since I've been laid up. There's a leak in our office."

Rita threw her arms up, sending the hanging pink curler across the room. "A leak, she says! No way am I saying nothing to nobody. I never seen either of you before. My name's Virginia Robinson and I've lived here in this apartment for six years without any trouble. Now you two get the fuck out."

"You listen to me, Rita." Charlie leaned down, hands on his knees, causing Rita to lean back into the cushions away from his face. His nose was almost touching hers. "If I found you, don't you think they can too? What did you say when you called the office, anyway?"

She swallowed hard, and Charlie backed off an inch or two. "The man said, 'Homicide.' And I said I needed to speak to a detective. He asked what for, and I said I knew about a murder of a young man people called Spider. I said I seen it happen back in '92 on Allen Street. Then he got quiet and I thought he hung up on me. I asked, was he still there? And he asked me, real serious, real quiet like, where was I now? He could come and pick me up right then. I got scared. Something wasn't right, you know? I hung up and threw my phone in the nearest garbage tote. Then I went on with my life, until you two showed up."

Charlie gave Rita a pat on the shoulder as he straightened up. "You did good, Rita. And I ain't letting no one hurt you. You just need to lay low, stay here and don't open the door for no one that ain't me or her." He jerked a thumb at Lauren.

Pulling herself to her feet, Lauren held onto her side as she stood next to Charlie. "I'm good. Ready to go," she assured Dailey. She turned toward Rita, who was wringing her wrinkled hands in front of her. "Thank you. I want you to call me if anything seems suspicious. And I mean anything." Lauren extracted her business card from the back pocket of her jeans, putting it on the coffee table. "Day or night."

Charlie flipped a bunch of twenty-dollar bills down on top of Lauren's card. "Don't leave town."

Snatching up the money and the card, Rita quickly tucked it all down the front of her housedress. "I can't believe we back in business, Daley."

Looking over his shoulder at Rita as he turned the doorknob to leave, Lauren heard the catch in his voice as he agreed. "Neither can I, Rita. Neither can I."

29

Back in Lauren's Ford, she clenched the wheel with both hands as they sat in their parking space. Shoppers, hip stay-at-home moms, and artsy types filed past the SUV. Elmwood Avenue was alive with people crowding the sidewalks on both sides of the street. The shops were in full Christmas swing. Lauren watched a woman on a rickety step ladder three shops up from their parking meter hanging another string of lights around her candle shop. "I'm calling Reese," she told Charlie as he tried to arrange himself in her seat.

"You two can't let anyone know about Rita yet," he reminded her, finally getting the seat belt to click.

"Call Reese," she said out loud to her dashboard.

In a pleasant, canned English accent, her car replied, "Calling Reese."

"Does this car wipe your ass too?" Charlie asked in skeptical amazement. He shunned technology as much as living in the modern world would allow.

The display on the dash showed Reese's cell number while the speakers amplified the ring tone throughout the car. After two rings Reese picked up. "Yeah?"

"Reese? It's Riley. You're on speaker. I need to meet you at headquarters, but not right now; after shift change. Can you wait there for me?"

"Sure I can. What's up? Do you need Joy to stay too?"

"No." She hoped that didn't come out as harsh. "I'll meet you there at six thirty." She glanced at the time on the dash display. It was just after noon. "I think I got something on my case. You can't tell anyone, not even Joy, and I can't talk about it over the phone."

There was a long pause, then: "You sure? Just me?"

"Positive. Just you. I'll see you at six thirty. Meet me at the police memorial."

The Fallen Officers Memorial was just south of headquarters on Franklin Street, past St. Joseph Cathedral. A ladder of stone guided water down and into a round pool. Engraved in black lettering around the gray granite encircling the pool were the names of every police officer who had lost his or her life in the line of duty while serving on the Buffalo Police Department. At six thirty on a Tuesday, after rush hour, that end of Franklin Street would be deserted.

"Are you okay? Is everything all right?" Concern tinged Reese's voice.

"I'm fine. I'll explain everything. See you at the memorial." As she clicked off, it occurred to her just how close she had come to becoming one of the names on that memorial less than a month ago.

Turning to Charlie, she put the car into drive. "I'll drop you off. After I get into the file room, I'll let you know what we've got."

His voice was grave. "Keep me in the loop on this. I'm not kidding. Those guys? The Schultzes? They're old-school. Family always comes first. Rita ain't nothing to them."

Lauren waited for a break in traffic to pull out. "Neither was I," she reminded him and headed south on Elmwood toward the Skyway.

30

"Okay, Mata Hari, what's so important we have to have a clandestine meeting in the dark away from the office?"

Reese had his heavy navy-blue peacoat on. The wind off the lake had been wicked all day, and the temperature had plummeted as soon as the sun went down. After dropping Charlie at the cemetery, Lauren had turned around and gone home to get a heavier jacket. She had grabbed her gray wool waist-length coat to keep the chill at bay, thinking that would do. Now she stood with her hands stuffed into the pockets, collar up, trying to keep her back to the wind. "Is everyone still up in the office?"

"Only a couple of people. Vatasha. Major. A few other guys, probably. Why?"

"I need to get into the file room and I don't want anyone to see me."

Reese scratched his five o'clock shadow. "That's going to be tough, considering they just installed a new camera on the door to get into the Homicide wing. And then there's the camera inside the file room itself."

"No one is going to be sitting watching those monitors 24/7. I don't care if I'm taped. I just need you to run interference so I can grab a file and get out without anyone seeing right away, since we still don't have a clue who the leak is."

"Okay. I'll swipe in. If the hallway is clear, I'll give you a wave. Have your key ready and pop into the file room. I'll hang around outside until you're done. You going to tell me exactly what you're looking for?"

She braced for the full force of the wind on her face. "Let's walk and talk. This is a long story."

They both bent their heads into the wind as they walked toward the ancient brick building that currently housed headquarters. The wind off the lake whipped down the sidewalk, carrying the day's refuse with it: plastic bags, a newspaper, an empty Styrofoam cup that bounced off Lauren's shoe and kept skipping down toward the Canalside entertainment complex.

When she was finished, Lauren said, "We have to protect Rita until we can make a case." As they reached the back door, Lauren saw that most of the windows on the upper floors were dark. That was a good thing, it would help her to focus. *Let me see what Vince Schultz saw right before he attacked me,* she half prayed. *Let me find what he wanted to find.*

Reese let out a low whistle. "When I was a rookie, me and Vince Schultz worked in D-District together. No one wanted to ride with Vince, so he became the training officer for a while. He was a miserable prick, but he knew all the shortcuts: where to go to get free coffee, what pizzeria would give you a whole pie, how to blow off calls and let other cars do the work for you. I spent six weeks on pins and needles thinking this guy was going to get me fired."

"It looks like he's graduated from free donuts to attempted murder. And possibly premeditated murder, if he killed Joe Wheeler."

Reese swiped the outer door open to a darkened hallway. "Why would he kill Wheeler?"

Slipping inside the building and out of the wind, Lauren shook her head. "I don't know. Misdirection? *Look over at Joe while I frame you?*"

"Seems a little extreme."

Taking the staircase instead of the elevator, Lauren was huffing by the second landing. "So is covering up the murder your brother committed so he can become district attorney twenty-five years later."

She couldn't see it because she was in front of him, but she knew he had his sarcastic smile on when he agreed with her. "Right."

They stopped on the third-floor landing, Reese sticking his head out into the corridor to be sure they were alone. When he gave her the thumbs-up, they walked to the main Homicide door, not bothering to creep because of the newly installed cameras. She waited as he swiped himself in, took a look around the hallway, then waved her inside.

She went right for the file room door, key in hand. On the door near the latch were deep grooves where Vince had tried to pry it open when the keys hadn't worked. She slipped hers in, and the lock turned easily.

The room was black as India ink. The RTs had the windows covered to keep direct sunlight from damaging the fragile paper files. Lauren fumbled her fingers along the wall until they hit the light switch, the familiar smell of stale paper and dust filling her nostrils.

The first thing her eyes focused on was the camera aimed directly at her. If someone was in the captain's office, they'd see her face filling up the monitor. Thankfully the Invisible Man was gone by six like clockwork, and no one went into his office if they could help it.

What year did Rita say? Lauren stepped into the file room, looking at the rows of metal cabinets: was it 1991 or 1992? Winter, for sure, but sometimes people's sense of time was distorted, especially if they were cracked out. Lauren moved to the cabinet with 1991 written on a white piece of copy paper taped to the front of the drawer and opened it.

The fronts of the folders were all printed the same, with spaces for the victim's name, age, gender, date of birth, address, and place of death along the top. Beginning with September she pulled the files one by one, read the information and replaced them: too old, too young, too female, strangled, drowned.

She got to December 31st and shut the drawer. It was disheartening, downright depressing, that there were this many unsolved homicides. A lot of them were gang-related drive-bys, the hardest to solve. The early nineties were the height of the crack epidemic and with no clear cut head of distribution, thirty separate small street gangs fought each other relentlessly for turf and money.

Lauren moved to the next olive-green cabinet, pulling open the drawer. On January 1st, 1992, the detectives logged the first homicide of the new year at 12:16 a.m. Harry Cranston was shot in the chest on Zenner Street. She scanned for a name added to the arrest information. There was nothing. Another unsolved. *I'll get back to you,* she thought as she tucked the file back in. *I promise.*

As she continued to tick through the drawer, a file thicker than the ones around it caught her eye. She kept checking each file before it, but somehow she knew that was going to be the one she wanted. The January files ended. February started slow, until she hit the big file:

February 24th, 1992. Sure enough, file 92-035 belonged to Gabriel Mohamed, age 18, from 1801 Wadsworth Avenue.

Lauren carefully pulled the file the rest of the way out, then checked to make sure there weren't any supplemental files in the drawer connected to the case. Pulling back the elastic tie, she made certain the crime scene photos were intact. It would have held things up if she had to order them from Andy Knowles over in Photography.

Satisfied she had everything, Lauren went back to the outer door with its frosted glass window and listened for a second. If Reese was engaged in a loud boisterous conversation, she'd have to wait it out. Technically, she was violating departmental policy by removing the file. *Not technically,* she thought, *actually and totally.* The only place those original files were supposed to go was the DA's office and court.

If I'm going to get suspended, I might as well make it count. She turned the knob, holding the folder under her right arm.

Reese was waiting by the door. "Got it?" he asked in a quiet voice.

Just as she nodded her head, Garcia came walking from the main Homicide office into the hallway. Lauren handed the folder off to Reese, who cradled it in front of him, as if he'd had it the whole time. Garcia didn't notice. "Hey," he said strolling toward them. "What are you doing here, Riley? I thought you were still out injured. Stab wound healed already?"

"You find out who killed Joe Wheeler yet?" she asked.

Garcia shrugged his shoulders. "Not my case. Joy and your boy here are all over it. Ain't that right, Reese?"

Reese's face pulled back into a tight smile, his voice cold and hard. "Call me a boy one more time. Let's see what happens."

Garcia held up both hands. "No offense, buddy," his words stumbled out. "I didn't mean it like that."

Without answering, Reese hit the exit bar for the door with his hip and Riley slipped through. He let it slam behind them, cutting off Garcia's nervous laughter.

"Let's go," Reese said, handing her back the folder.

31

Lauren's basement office didn't have a mess table to spread the file out, like in the Cold Case office, so they had to improvise. Combine that with a very enthusiastic and known-paper-chewing West Highland Terrier and it was a hectic first few minutes of set up.

Lauren wrestled the card table out of the back storage closet while Reese carried two folding chairs with one arm and Watson with the other, who was licking Reese's face like it was a bacon ice cream cone.

"Should I put him in his crate?" Watson wriggled around in his arms to get at the unlicked side of his face.

"No, he'll just bark and cry until we let him out." Lauren arranged the chairs and deposited the folder onto the brown padded surface. She retrieved a couple of pens from a cup holder on her computer desk. Sitting down, she realized she hadn't used this table or these chairs since she and the girls used to play games of scat on Friday nights. They'd both been in grammar school then. Lauren ran one hand over the cracked faux leather top. How many nights had she and the girls spent laughing and drinking soda over that table?

"You're spoiling him." Reese let Watson down. He promptly ran over and tried to crawl onto Lauren's lap. She held him off with one hand.

"There's a rawhide bone over on the shelf. Go grab it."

Reese pulled the knotted bone off the shelf and tossed it to Watson. Catching it easily, he settled at Lauren's feet and began to gnaw on it. "Why do you have bones hidden around your house for my dog?" he asked, putting his hands on his hips like Lauren's mom used to do when she got caught doing something she shouldn't.

"I got him a couple of treats and toys when I was at the store." She feigned innocence. "What's so bad about that?"

"It's going to break his heart when we leave," Reese reminded her, taking his seat at the card table.

Lauren ignored that comment; they could argue about custody another time. She pulled the elastic off the fat file folder. For larger files, the Homicide squad used extra-large accordion folders that could expand to about seven inches before they had to add another. This one was stuffed to maximum capacity, a lot of room taken up by the crime scene photos. Slipping those out first, Lauren put them aside. She then divided the paperwork into witness statements, police activity reports, and physical evidence articles. Smattered about the file were handwritten notes, messages, and phone numbers. Those she separated into their own pile and pushed them to the corner. They'd get to those last.

"I'll go over the crime scene reports, the integrity sheet, and 911 print outs," Reese said, gathering up those particular documents.

Lauren reached across the table to her computer desk, grabbed a legal pad, and passed it over to him. "I'll start with the evidence reports." Plucking her readers off the top of her head, she put them on, adjusting them until she could read the fine print on the old paperwork. "That gun had to be collected by someone."

Spending the next hour poring over the paperwork, Reese and Riley managed to fill three pages of notes each. Every so often Lauren would say, "Paper," and Reese would tear a sheet from the back of the pad and hand it to her without looking up. The only sound in the room was the scratching of their pens and the chewing of Watson, who had turned one end of his bone into mush.

"Son of a bitch," Reese said, holding up a two-page crime scene integrity report. It was the job of the first officer on the scene to record every single person who came into the crime scene, at what time, and what their assignment was. "Right here on page one, it says the first Homicide car to show up was Richard Schultz and his partner, Walter Lindhydt. Four minutes later Vince Schultz and his car partner in 3-South One get logged in." He flipped the page. "Here, twenty minutes later, baby brother Samuel Schultz is logged onto the scene as walking the beat that night."

That made sense. They still made cops walk the beat in Buffalo, only now they parked their patrol car and walked in the entertainment districts, like Canalside or Chippewa Street. Back then, another car crew would dump you off, usually a lone rookie, and pick you up when your watch was over. You were supposed to learn the neighborhood, check the businesses, and get to know the usual suspects.

"Do you see Charlie Daley's name on there anywhere?"

Reese ran a finger down along the column on the second page. "It looks like three Narcotics cars came to the scene to help out. Yeah, he's there, but he doesn't show up until after all three of the Schultz brothers. A lot of cars came over; must have been a cold, boring night in February."

He handed the integrity sheet to Lauren. She scanned it with a practiced eye. "All those cops coming to the scene, now it makes sense why no one saw the shooter running away."

Reese finished her thought. "Sam Schultz probably scooted down one of the side streets and doubled back."

Sifting through the crime scene photos, Lauren noticed a picture of the gun sticking out from beneath a beat-up four-door sedan. When the car had been parked, the heat from the engine caused the snow under it to melt, leaving a dry patch on the pavement. "At least we got lucky, and he didn't toss the gun in a snow bank."

Reese's brow furrowed as he looked at the picture. "That's a five-shot revolver. It's not city-issue."

"The second gun old-timers used to carry," Lauren told him. "Now you have to qualify with every weapon you carry and make sure it's on your C-Form down at the range. Back then, guys would take a gun off a guy, stick it in an ankle holster, and it became their backup gun."

"Could you even imagine doing that today?" Reese asked.

Lauren examined the rest of the scene photos. The young victim looked like a broken doll, crumpled face-down on the icy sidewalk. Cop cars ringed the scene, crime scene tape stretched from light pole to light pole. Officers milled around the perimeter, jacket collars turned up against the cold.

Someone had stapled the victim's school ID card to the inside edge of the file flap. Gabriel Mohamed, date of birth January 5th, 1974. He had just turned eighteen. From under the yellowing laminated plastic, a handsome dark skinned young man grinned up at her. The card proclaimed he was in the 10th grade at Hutch Technical High School on South Elmwood Avenue. Heat crept across Lauren's cheeks as anger flooded over her. His mother had escaped famine and poverty in Somalia just to have her son gunned down on the sidewalk for stealing change out of a car.

"The good old days definitely had their dark side." She tried to push the disgust for what the three brothers had done to the side for now. She needed to be clinical and precise, not emotional. For Gabriel's sake. "One of Sam's brothers probably gave that gun to him. Told Sam that was how things were done." Putting the photo back in its pile, Lauren picked up another piece of paper, dangling it in front of Reese. "We have a problem, though. The gun was put into evidence at the Erie County Lab that night. It was test-fired and sent back to Property. There it sat until 2006, when a cold case DNA initiative from the state gave out grants to test evidence from old homicide cases. The gun was tested, and DNA was recovered from the trigger area, the grip, and the barrel."

"That's good news," Reese said. "Where's the problem?"

"The lab sent the results to the detective in charge of the case: Ricky Schultz." She slid the DNA report across the card table. "What do you want to bet if we go down to the Evidence unit, Ricky checked that gun out and it never came back?"

Engrossed with the data on the DNA report, Reese didn't look up. "Doesn't matter. The actual samples are on file at the lab. All we need is Sam Schultz's DNA and they can still match it."

"I'm sure he's just going to open up his mouth and let me swab him." Lauren sat back in her chair, which creaked in protest.

"Then we'll have to get creative. If Rita won't go in front of a judge for a search warrant, we'll have to get an abandoned sample." Reese's green eyes flashed as they met hers, thinking of how they could swipe one of Sam's used Tim Hortons coffee cups or a discarded toothpick. "We're going to get these guys, Riley. We're going to get Sam for murdering that kid, Ricky for covering it up, and Vince for stabbing you."

"If my memory is correct, I was a detective working on the Sex Offense Squad when Ricky retired. I remember not being able to go to his retirement party because I had a call out on a rape. I was at the hospital, holding this woman's hand thinking I needed to put a transfer in."

"I could never handle Sex Offense cases," Reese admitted. "Too hard."

She nodded. "It was, especially with two daughters at home. It wears you down. But I learned a lot. I just remember feeling guilty that I was mad at missing a party when this poor girl was so horribly abused. I knew I needed to leave the squad before I lost my mind."

"You did." Knowing when it was time to put the witty banter aside, he told her, "You never stop fighting for the victims. You taught me that."

"It's funny the way you remember things. I should have no idea when Ricky retired. But it's etched in my brain because it's attached to that poor woman's suffering. And now it's attached to Gabriel Mohamed." She put her pen and paper on the table.

The images of Joe Wheeler and Gabriel Mohamed, both lifeless, left for dead on the street, mixed in her mind. Bending forward, she pinched the bridge of her nose, taking as deep a breath as she could manage.

Reese laid a hand on Lauren's shoulder, gripping it. "You okay?"

"All these years these guys have been covering up this murder. They're still covering it up." She touched her hand to her side where her scars were throbbing. "And Sam has the audacity to run for Erie County District Attorney. It's a sick joke, really."

Picking up the crime scene photos and talking while he examined them, Reese tried to get her to refocus. "The Schultz brothers have always stuck together, right? Daddy was the old police commissioner. I bet they thought they could do no wrong."

Pushing away from the table, Lauren stood up. "I'm making myself a drink. Do you want one?"

"I'll have a whiskey on the rocks. The good stuff. Not the girly crap you drink with Dayla." Reese continued to leaf through the paperwork spread out in front of him. "Too sweet." Watson dropped his bone and stood up with her, tail wagging a mile a minute.

Lauren marched up the basement steps into her kitchen with Watson at her heels. A dozen thoughts rolled through her mind at once. Vince Schultz had stabbed her and stomped her. To get his hands on the Gabriel Mohamed file. Because his little brother had shot Gabriel. And his older brother, Ricky, covered it up. Reaching into the top shelf over her stove, she produced a bottle of Jameson Irish whiskey. Reese might have assumed she drank "girly" drinks—and she did, on occasion—but at times when her head was about to explode, she always pulled out the Jameson.

She put ice into two plastic tumblers and let the whiskey slosh over the cubes liberally. Stopping to give Watson one of his squeaky toys— a little rubber chicken wearing a bow tie—Lauren made her way back down the basement steps.

Reese was sitting straight up in his chair, holding a single photo, clamped between his finger and thumb.

"What's that one?" she asked, careful to put the sweating tumbler on the desk next to him and not on the table with the fragile papers.

"This, my friend, is a picture of the scene, from Wadsworth, facing east on Allen Street. Examine closely the unmarked car in the upper-left corner. Sure looks to me like Ricky Schultz is sitting in the back-seat talking to Sam Schultz, who doesn't appear to be very happy."

Snatching the picture out of his hand so fast it made her spill a couple drops of whiskey on her Berber carpeting, she squinted at the picture. Sure enough, there was a young Ricky Schultz in his winter detective gear sitting in the backseat of a Lumina talking to Sam Schultz. Sam, whose mouth was set in a hard line, looked like he was intently trying to absorb whatever his brother was telling him. "Ricky knew right from the beginning. That night. At the scene. And all of this"—she waved her hands over the piles of paperwork—"was just to cover up for his little brother."

Reese took a hard slug from his plastic cup. "I'll have to get the original property sheet for the gun tomorrow. If Ricky did sign out the evidence, that signature is the nail in Sam's coffin."

"He'll have sent Vince to get it. He's not dumb. He's been on top of this thing for over twenty-five years."

"Vince is a patrol guy. He'd need a detective to sign for it. I wonder if anyone has tried. It might raise a few red flags if a patrol officer came out of the blue wanting an original property sheet for a case he didn't work on." Reese tipped the cup back so that the ice came rat-tling forward against his teeth.

"It would be interesting to see who tried to get it for him, though." She swirled the ice cubes around in her glass. Reese set down his empty cup. "I should have brought the whole bottle."

"You aren't supposed to be drinking anyway." Reese deftly swiped the drink out of her hand, taking a sip before Lauren could protest. "Go to bed. You look like hell. I'll go and check on the property sheet tomorrow and make sure the samples are at the lab."

"Nope. I'm coming with you. We can't trust anyone with this."

"You're supposed to be off duty with your injuries. Recovering, you know?" Reese drained the whiskey from her stolen tumbler. "But I'm not going to argue. Not tonight."

"Good." Scooping Watson in her arms and ignoring the pain in her side, Lauren headed back up the stairs.

"Where is that whiskey bottle anyway?" Reese called after her.

"Above the stove."

"Think Dayla is awake?"

Lauren turned and looked at him standing at the bottom of the stairs. "Yes. But don't even think of calling her. You'll wake her husband."

"Does Dayla really have a husband? I mean, I've never actually seen the guy."

"Yes, Dayla has a husband. The plastic surgeon with all the billboards on the thruway? He works a lot, kind of like cops are supposed to."

Reese snapped his fingers in recognition. "Now that you mention it, she does look a little more perky now than she did this time last year. Maybe you should pay him a visit. Get him to do something about that twelve-year-old boy's body you're walking around in."

She wanted to throw something back at him about getting his own breast-reduction surgery, but she was too tired to start down that road. "Go to bed. We've got work to do in the morning."

She thought she heard him mumble something about being a party pooper. She ignored it. *This party is just getting started,* Lauren thought as she made her way to the staircase to the second floor. *And I'm the one who's doing the conspiring now.*

32

She was back on the floor of the Cold Case office, the scratchy, stiff pile of the carpet biting into her cheek. The taste of blood was flooding her mouth. All around her there were sounds of people; people walking and talking, laughing, a few coughing. Lauren tried to call out to them, tried to get their attention somehow, but all she could do was wheeze and gasp for air.

I can't breathe.

She tried to reach out to something just on the edge of her field of vision, some dark shape that maybe she could grasp, get someone's attention with it. Using every bit of strength she had, she snagged the object and pulled it toward her.

If I could just signal someone…

It was hard and cold. It took her a second to realize it was metal. When she finally pulled it into view, she choked on the gore in her mouth from fright.

It was a tire iron covered in gray brain matter.

Lauren shot up from bed like a bullet, drenched in sweat, gasping for air. Watson bounced awake next to her, scared at her panic, and began to bark.

I can't breathe, I can't breathe. Her hands went to her throat. *I'm going to die.*

Watson finally broke through her terror, licking frantically at the tears that were running down her cheeks. Her eyes darted around the darkened area, taking in the familiar landmarks of her bedroom, the horror slowly draining away.

"I'm all right," she whispered out loud, grabbing onto Watson and holding him close. He still licked at her face as she rocked with him in bed, back and forth. "I'm all right. It was just a dream."

33

One good thing about going to headquarters at ten o'clock on a Thursday was that you could blend in with the crowd on the first floor where the property room was located. After morning arraignments, the arrestees from the night before lined up on the Church Street side of headquarters to retrieve their property. That day people were bunched around the side door, waiting for their turn at the Property Department's window. Riley and Reese breezed past them into the main hallway, past the elevator, to the back of the building, and up to the door where the coppers who worked Property came and went.

The door was old, as old as the building, having never been replaced. The word PROPERTY was painted in red across the frosted glass. It had no swipe; you either had a key to get in, or you didn't. Not even the commissioner could get inside after the personnel assigned there went home for the day. Reese gave the heavy wooden door a good double knock, so the RTs up front at the window would hear it.

Helen Downey, who'd been with the department for fifty years, opened the door a crack and pecked out.

"Shane!" She threw the door open wide. Helen was straight off the boat from Dublin and made no secret of her crush on Reese. "What brings you to see me today?" It came out more like: *Wha brings ya ta see ma to-da?* Lauren didn't care why she let them in. *Whatever works,* she thought, giving Helen a huge smile.

"And Lauren, how are you feeling, love?" Helen leaned in and gave her a hug. In her white shirt, navy-blue pleated pants, and tastefully tinted red hair, Helen resembled an aging airline stewardess; all she needed was the tiny scarf tied around her neck.

"I'll live," Lauren replied, still smiling. "Thanks for asking."

"Of course you'll live! You got the Irish in you, Miss Riley. We're hard to kill. Just ask the British." She gave Lauren a wink and backed farther into the Property room to let them all the way in, the door falling locked behind them.

"We need your help with something, Helen," Reese told her, lowering his voice. "We have to ask you a few questions, but it cannot leave this room."

"What do you need, darlin'?" she whispered back, eyes glancing over to Sadie Covington, who was helping a sad-looking man at the window. Sadie was a notorious gossip.

Pulling a copy of the property sheet from his back pocket, he put it in her hand. "I need you to see if the property on this form, especially the gun, is still here. And we need to know if anyone else has come looking for it lately."

Helen perused the sheet. "It's a homicide case. Everything should still be here. No statute of limitations on murder."

Reese nodded along with her. "Exactly. Can you get the chain of custody sheet so we can look at it?"

"For you, Shane? Anything. Be back in a jiff." She walked toward the side room where the files were kept, disappearing behind another heavy door.

"Laying it on pretty thick, weren't we?" Lauren asked, leaning up against one of the desks.

"What? My attraction to women knows no age limits. Real men know mature women are sexy as hell. That's good news for you; you're getting a little long in the tooth."

"I'm thirty-nine."

"Soon to be forty, according to my calculations." He shook his head. "You have officially passed into straight-up cougar range. You should embrace it. Get a younger man in your life."

"I have a younger man in my life, and he drives me crazy," she pointed out.

"Only because we have a strictly platonic relationship. Believe me, if you were getting a piece of this"—he motioned grandly from his head all the way down to his toes—"you'd be one happy lady."

"I think I'll just stay single, thank you very much." After her disastrous affair with her ex-husband the year before, Lauren had put a moratorium on her sex life. Not that there was ever any danger of her and Reese crossing any lines.

"Plenty of cats available at the shelter this time of year," he told her. "No better time to start your brood than now."

Frowning, Helen appeared in the doorway holding two pieces of paper. "This is odd," she said, smoothing a yellowing sheet on the desk in front of her. It was the original of the form Reese had handed to her, except that as the evidence moved from the lab back to Property and out again, various handwritten notations had been added to the back page.

"It says here the gun went to the lab the night of the homicide. Came back in March of 1992." Her knobby finger traced its way down the page. "Here, in April of 2006, the lab checked the gun back out. It was returned in August. On September 5th of 2006, that same gun was checked out by the lead detective, Richard Schultz. It doesn't show it was ever checked back in."

"Did Schultz actually sign for the gun?"

She turned the paper around and pointed out the signature. "Right here."

"I knew it," Lauren said.

"Has anyone else asked to see this evidence or the property sheet? Recently, I mean. Last two weeks maybe?" Reese pressed.

Helen shrugged. "Not that I know of. But if they did, they didn't leave with it, did they?"

"Ok, Helen, now this is important." Reese leaned across the desk, palms down, fingers splayed over the blotter. "I want you to make a copy, put it in the file, and give me the original with the signature. Don't worry, we'll get it back to you when we're done. You won't get in any trouble."

"I can't give you the original property slip," she protested. "They don't ever leave here."

"This slip itself is important. It's evidence in a homicide investigation. That's why I need it. And it's important that you don't tell anyone about this. I promise when we're done you'll get it back. Have I ever lied to you before?"

Her watery blue eyes softened. "No."

"Please make a copy, put that in the file, and call me if anyone else wants to see it."

Helen gathered up her paperwork and disappeared into the side room. Coming out four minutes later, she handed Reese a manila envelope. "No one's come asking about it, as far as I could tell. Just you two. Don't let anything happen to this."

"You know I won't," he said, taking it from her. He gave her one of his dazzling smiles, but Helen still looked distressed at breaching her sworn duties to protect the property sheets.

Lauren tried to sound reassuring as she told her, "I promise we'll take the blame if anything blows back on you. We wouldn't have asked if it wasn't really, really important."

"I trust you two. Never done me wrong, yet. But I don't want it getting around I do this sort of thing."

Chucking her gently under her double chin, Reese said, "It's our secret, Helen. See you soon."

They left the poor woman wringing her hands near the door, still unsure if she made the right call or not. Lauren felt bad for putting Helen in that position, but Ricky's signature on that document proved he tampered with, and probably destroyed, evidence in a homicide case. That piece of paper was a crucial bit of evidence.

"You wait here. I'm going up to the Homicide office to check in with Joy, tell her I'm taking off the next couple of days." Still holding the envelope, Reese hit the button for the elevator.

"I'll just wait here for you here with my thumb up my ass," Lauren told him as the doors opened.

"Better take the stick out first," he advised as the doors shut in front of him.

Cocky, immature, unprofessional—

Lauren's thoughts were interrupted by a tap on the shoulder.

Swiveling around, she found herself face to face with Vince Schultz. Her hand reflexively went to her gun at the small of her back. Vince took a step back with his hands up. "Whoa! I didn't mean to startle you, Lauren. I just wanted to say hi and see how you're doing."

Struck dumb for a second, Lauren stared at the man who had shoved a knife between her ribs. His pockmarked face, his graying dark hair, his blue uniform shirt stretched over his broad chest. Somewhere, in the back of her mind, the rational part of her brain was telling her, *Smile, right now. Don't let on that you know anything.*

It took every ounce of undercover police training she had to keep herself together.

"I'm sorry." She managed what she hoped was a smile. "I'm a little jumpy these days."

"Yeah," he laughed, hitching his thumbs in his gun belt. "I get that. I'm glad you're doing all right. Do they have any leads on who hurt you?"

She noted he said *hurt*, not *attacked*, or *stabbed*, or *tried to kill. Hurt*, like he had hurt her feelings, not left her to die on a dirty carpet in her own office. She shook her head. "Right now, they have nothing." Lauren was not going to give anything away to this piece of garbage.

"And your old boyfriend? Do they think it's connected?"

Realizing as she stood in front of him that he was taller than Joe, like the killer had been, she took a step back. The dream from the night before came rushing in, the brain and blood on the tire iron, the copper taste in her mouth. She blinked hard twice, trying to keep her focus.

"They're looking at all the angles," she replied in the most neutral tone she could muster. Standing so close, Lauren could smell Vince's bad breath. Her eyes fixed on the gold chain around his neck and the way his white chest hair curled around it. *Can he hear my heart? The one he tried to stab?* Her mind raced as she tried to control the panic rising up in her. *It's about to beat out of my chest.*

"I think it's pretty sick, that someone is running around ..."

His voice trailed off in her ears as her eyes slid down to his black city-issue boots. Pant legs stuffed inside, laced up high. *Those have my blood on them.* Her pulse raced. *Soaked in the laces or stuck in the cracks of the leather from when he stomped on my head. Or from when he walked through the blood pooling on the carpet next to me or spatter from Joe's crushed head. He washed them, I know he washed them, but there's always a trace …*

"What's going on here?" Reese's voice cut through her thoughts, bringing her back to the dirty hallway in front of the elevator whose car just deposited Reese next to her.

Head reeling from the images embedded in it, Lauren said, "Vince just stopped to ask how I'm doing. I think you were right, Reese. I shouldn't have come here. Not with all the medications I'm on. Not yet."

Reaching past her, Vince stuck out his hand to Reese, who shook it without hesitation. "Good to see you," Vince told her partner.

Reese answered with his normal, pleasant, friendly tone. "You too, man. Let me get my partner out of this place. I told her not to come."

"Yeah. It takes a long time to recover from those kind of injuries," Vince said. "Don't overdo it."

Reese held up the manila envelope Helen had given him. Nothing was written on it. It could have contained anything, but Reese waved it in Vince's face. "Sorry, Vince, but we've got to go. I got what I came here for, and we're running late."

Vince's eyes ran over the folder, possibly trying to figure out if it was something for Lauren's case or totally unrelated. Lauren could sense he wanted to linger, to fish for more information. Him coming up to her in the hall was not a coincidence, she was sure, but something of a calculated risk. He wanted to gauge what they knew.

"No problem." Vince stepped back as he spoke. "I hope you feel better, Lauren."

I hope someone straps you to an ant hill and pours syrup on you. "Bye, Vince. And thank you." *For letting me know you're a remorseless piece of shit who covers up an eighteen-year-old kid's murder.*

Lauren and Reese left Vince Schultz standing in the hallway. Waiting until they were in the confines of the car, Reese let out a long breath. "It took everything I had not to throttle him."

"My first instinct was to shoot him," Lauren said bitterly. "It's my only instinct, actually."

Sliding the manila folder onto the dash, Reese threw the car into drive. "I called the lab. The samples are still there. All we need is a comparison, and it's game over."

"We could have gotten one from Vince just now. Punched him in the nose, gathered some of the blood. The tests would show the familial link."

Reese dismissed that idea. "While that would have been fun, then it would be all subpoenas and hearings and lawyers. They could get to Rita. No, we're going for the straight-up abandoned sample from Vince's little brother, Sam. I don't want a family tree. I want Sam Schultz's direct match."

"And how are we going to get that?" Lauren was trying to bring her heart rate down, breathing in deeply, then exhaling slowly. "I think he'll notice a tall blonde and a biracial guy following him around all day trying to recover his used Kleenex."

Reese fished around in his back pocket, eyes never leaving the road, until he produced another glossy piece of paper. He passed it over to Lauren. "These were on everyone's desks today. I snagged one when I was in the office."

It was a fancy invitation to Sam Schultz's campaign kick-off party that coming Saturday night, December 1st, at the new Strand Hotel. Formal attire required, only two hundred dollars a person.

194

"You want to crash his party?" Lauren cocked an eyebrow.

He shrugged. "Why not? I look good in a suit."

"Because Vince and Ricky both know me and know I'd never go to a political fundraiser in a million years."

"We know for sure where our suspect is going to be Saturday night. We know he won't be expecting us." Reese hit the horn on a man turning without using his signal in front of them. "You need to call your ex-husband and have him buy two tickets under his name."

Mark Hathaway had always been a big donor to political campaigns. Lauren used to hate when he'd drag her out in a sequined dress to some function or other. She'd cringe in a corner most of the night, nursing a drink, making awkward small talk with other donors' wives while her husband schmoozed and worked the crowd. Reese was right, Mark buying tickets wouldn't raise any eyebrows.

"Since when do you make the operational plans?" Lauren asked, reluctant to revisit that portion of her life with Mark.

"Since you got put on injured reserve," he shot back. "Let's do this. We get the sample, call the DA, tell him what's up. Carl Church gets the lab to rush it through. We get a match, all the brothers go to jail."

"Sam's DNA on the gun doesn't prove Vince attacked me," she pointed out.

"It's enough for us to get search warrants for his apartment, his car, his work locker. Vince Schultz is a slob. He's probably wearing the same crusty uniform he had on the night he stabbed you. You know those are the same boots; he's too cheap to buy new ones. The knife is probably on the all-purpose tool on his belt. He has no idea we're on to him or his brothers. If we're lucky, we can nail them for you and for Gabriel without exposing Rita. I'm telling you, this is the best plan."

She thought back to the way Vince had stood there, as if it was nothing that she had been hurt. Like she'd fallen down the stairs or got rear-ended in the parking lot. He had stabbed her from behind and then mercilessly cracked her in the head. He hadn't been trying to *hurt* her, he'd been trying to *destroy* her. The way Joe had been destroyed by a tire iron. The way Gabriel Mohamed had been destroyed by a bullet. She fingered the metal clasp on the back of the envelope.

Well, she thought as she watched pedestrians cross in front of the car at a red light, her bitterness turning to anger, *it's my turn now.*

34

Lauren spent the rest of her Thursday night at home, dreading seeing her ex-husband in the morning. She'd changed into her pajamas almost as soon as she and Reese came in the door, stomach still in knots over running into Vince Schultz. She sat with Watson in the kitchen, watching Reese take abuse from his latest lady friend on his cell phone.

"I'm sorry, I've just been really busy. I know. I know. I know." He looked over at Lauren who was smirking, then turned his back to her. "I'll be right there," he assured the woman on the phone. "I'm leaving now. Goodbye."

"My nurse Anna giving you a hard time?" Lauren asked, slightly amused and grateful at the distraction that Reese's love life provided for her.

"What? No. Anna and me are taking a break. The whole Wheeler thing freaked her out. That was my friend Ebony. Remember her? We dated two years ago?"

"Didn't she dump you when you wouldn't move in with her?"

"It was a mutual break-up," he corrected, adjusting his baseball cap. "Anyway, I have to meet her over at Carlin's bar. You going to be okay on your own?"

Lauren nudged the sleeping Watson with her foot, who responded with a furious wag of the tail but didn't look up. "I've got my guard dog here. I'll be fine."

He grabbed his keys off the kitchen counter. "Don't wait up."

Giving him a two-finger salute as he left, she called, "I never do. And it gets us in trouble."

The back door banged shut behind him. Lauren had cranked the heat, but she was still freezing. She wrapped her hands around her mug of decaf coffee to warm them. She had given in to Reese's demand that she drink decaf after six because the sound of her walking around upstairs all night kept him awake. She wanted to try to explain it wasn't the caffeine that caused her to wake up every two hours, it was nightmares. Switching to decaf seemed easier. But it didn't help her sleep.

Alone at last at her kitchen table, she propped her iPad up on the little stand that folded out of the cover of its case, slipped her readers on, and brought up the sign-in page for Facebook.

Lauren Riley officially had seven Facebook friends: Erin, Lindsey, Reese, Dayla, her mom, her sister, and a girl she had gone to high school with named Marie Butkiss, who she had found while scrolling around. She loved the fact that she was reconnected with Marie, who had been her best friend and now lived in Michigan. Reese had shown Lauren how to put pictures of her daughters on her account and share them with Marie so no one else could see them. Marie responded with pictures of her son and daughter, only thirteen and seven. Lauren slipped a couple shots of Watson in too. She would have felt like a bad mom if she hadn't.

Lauren had spent the night before on her sister's page, going through photos of her nephews, snapshots of Jill and her husband posing in front of their rustic, cabin-like house in the Pacific Northwest, and reading posts Jill had written over the last five years. Lauren had no idea how much she'd missed of her sister's life by being so disconnected. Her stubbornness against technology had backfired on her. When Lauren's sister instant messaged her because she saw she was online, they spent an hour typing back and forth until Lauren absolutely had to get offline and go to bed.

Tonight, Lauren wanted to stalk her daughters. She clicked on Lindsey's page, liking a couple of things she posted, leaving a comment under a selfie of her and her roommate at a concert: *Looks like fun!!* Adding a smile emoji for good measure. *I'm getting good at this social media stuff,* she told herself.

Pouring herself the inky bottom of the coffeepot, she sat back down and opened Erin's homepage. Her youngest daughter's beautiful, pixie-like face filled her screen. *My baby,* she thought, paging through her photos. *When did you get so grown up?*

There was Erin striking a pose in front of the funky Shark Girl sculpture at Canalside. Here was another one of her making a duck face with her sister on Thanksgiving. Her heart skipped a beat at a picture of them at the beach last summer when Lauren had managed to get both girls home the same weekend. The summer before they'd both stayed at school, and she'd only gotten to see them separately, making her miss them even more. Lauren clicked on the picture to make it bigger. All three were sitting on a blanket. A nice older gentleman had offered to take the picture after a five-minute struggle to selfie it with the sunlight blinding them. He'd directed them, telling them to get closer, smile, now hold it, as he stood there in his long shorts and black socks with sandals. The result was a close-up of all three smiling straight into the camera, the sunlight just right on their faces, radiant in the joy of the moment.

Underneath the photo, little "thumbs up" and heart icons indicated how many people liked or loved the picture. Fifty-one likes and two hundred and seventeen hearts. Lauren clicked on the heart to see who loved their photo.

David Spencer was first on the list.

Furiously trying to remember the steps, Lauren clicked back to Erin's friends list and opened it up. She had 1,167 friends. Lauren typed David's name into the search bar and sure enough, there he was. David Spencer had friended Erin. Or Erin had friended him.

Next she clicked on David's name and went to his page. His banner was a spectacular orange and red sunset shining through two mountains. His profile picture was cropped and whoever had been in the photo with him had been cut out. But it was him. David was showing off his dyed blonde spikey hair and killer smile. *Literally a killer smile.* Lauren clicked on the "About" icon, but it didn't yield much. Only that he was a criminal justice student and the high school he'd graduated from. Nothing about a job. Under relationship status: "It's complicated."

Complicated. Lauren wondered what shiny Melissa thought about that statement.

He had over a thousand friends as well. *I don't even know a thousand people.* Lauren scrolled through his friends list, which consisted of mostly young, very attractive females. *And I thought Facebook was just for old people.*

Still staring at his homepage, Lauren took her cell phone out of her pocket and called Erin. Simultaneously filled with fury and fright, Lauren tried to calm herself.

Erin answered right away. "What's wrong?" The panic in Erin's voice was unmistakable.

"A lot actually." Lauren's protective mother instinct was now in overdrive. "Why are you friends with David Spencer on Facebook?"

"Who?" She sounded confused.

"David Spencer. I was on your page and I saw that he liked one of your pictures, and I see that the two of you are friends."

There was a pause. "I don't even know who David Spencer is. Wait—isn't he the guy you helped get off from that murder last year?"

"Yes." Lauren tried to control the anger in her voice. "Why are you two Facebook friends?"

"I don't know. He probably sent me a friend request and I accepted it. I don't know every single person I'm Facebook friends with."

"How can you accept a friend request from someone you don't even know? Has he tried to communicate with you? Sent you any messages?"

"Mom." She drew out the *mom* so that it sounded more like *maaaammm.* "That's not how Facebook works. People friend you and you friend them back. You want to have a lot of followers."

"Why?"

"I don't know why, you just do. So people know you aren't a loser, I guess."

"You're going to be a loser and unfriend him and block him, or erase him, or whatever you have to do. Do you understand?"

"Okay, Mom. Chill. I'm doing it now." Lauren waited, listening to the soft rustling sounds of Erin manipulating her smart phone. From somewhere in the background another female voice called out, "What's wrong?"

"Nothing. Nothing," she muttered to the voice. "It's just my mom."

"Is that your dormmate?" Lauren asked.

"Yes." There was another pause. "Okay. I've unfriended and blocked David Spencer."

"But he already knows where you go to school, who your friends are, and where you hang out, right?"

Erin sighed into the phone. "I guess."

Lauren took a deep breath. "It's not safe to have all those people have access to so much information about you."

"Mom." Erin sounded like she was trying to not lose her patience with Lauren. "Things are different from when you were my age. This is how things are."

Yeah, killers can track you or your family over the Internet. Stalk you, toy with you, torture you with fear. Lauren bit her tongue on those thoughts but told Erin, "I know. I get that. I'm just trying to protect you."

Erin's voice softened. "I appreciate it, Mom. I do. But I'm far away from David Spencer. I think I'm safe here."

Lauren didn't say it, but in her gut, she wasn't so sure.

She hung up with Erin and immediately punched in Frank Violanti's cell phone number. It rang and rang, and then just when she was sure it was going to go to voicemail, a whispered voice said, "Hello?"

"Frank, it's Riley. We need to talk. David Spencer friended my daughter on Facebook."

In the background Lauren could hear a screaming baby. She'd forgotten Violanti and his wife had gotten pregnant right before the start of David's trial last year. "You woke up my son to tell me that?"

"You don't think it's odd," she demanded over the baby's wails, "that David Spencer went out of his way to find and friend my daughter?"

Lauren could hear him fumbling, probably trying to make a bottle and hold the phone at the same time. In exasperation he told her, "They're the same age, doing what young people their age do, but we don't understand what that is because we're old. It's harmless. All the kids are on social media constantly."

Lauren wasn't buying that excuse. "I want you to call him and put a stop to all this. Coming to the hospital, trying to get close to my daughters. I'm warning you—"

He cut her off. "Stop right there. I'll call him, okay? But not to-night. My hands are full right now. I've got to go." He hung up on her.

What if it was your child? she wanted to ask Violanti, staring at her phone, *and you couldn't protect him? What would you do?*

35

"**S**eriously, Lauren? I've been trying to contact you since you got *stabbed*, you don't so much as send me a text saying you're all right, and now you show up at my office asking me to buy you fundraiser tickets for tomorrow night? You're unbelievable."

Lauren edged her way around the front of Mark Hathaway's desk. Her ex-husband hadn't gotten up when his secretary had buzzed her in, he'd just sat there with his hands folded in front of him, scolding her. She'd spent half the night scouring David Spencer's Facebook account, looking at every picture, analyzing every post, every "like," looking for clues into his intent for friending Erin. Even now, with Mark in front of her, she had to push her concern with David to the side and concentrate on the matter at hand.

Lauren knew she deserved Mark's anger. Some of it, anyway. After all, the last time she'd asked Mark for a favor, they'd ended up in bed and—eventually—ended his second marriage. Then she had dumped him. But Mark had divorced her first, ten years before, leaving her shocked and devastated.

I should have a timeline with me to keep track of all my disastrous, train-wreck relationships, Lauren thought. *I can barely keep them straight in my own head: Baby daddy, Joe Wheeler, Mark Hathaway, self-enforced celibacy, Mark Hathaway, back to celibacy. I could write a manual of what not to do in romantic relationships.*

"I'm sorry. About everything. And I appreciate the flowers and the robe and the slippers—"

"It's not about a robe, flowers, and slippers. It's about us and you damn well know it."

Lauren drank in his curly, near-black hair, his stormy blue eyes, and felt her resolve weaken. This was why she had cut him completely out of her life. She couldn't trust herself with him. He got to her in ways that no other man ever had, and it broke her heart when she thought of how everything had turned out between them. She put a hand on his desktop to steady herself. "I know it is. I know you're right. But I need you to do this for me. You know I wouldn't ask you—"

"If you could get this from someone else?"

The anger in his voice toward her was foreign. During their entire relationship, brief as it was, they'd never had a real fight, not even when he'd up and left her. Or more precisely, when she threw him out after he had sat her down and told her he'd knocked up his secretary. Lauren had been more devastatingly sad than angry, telling him through her tears to pack his things and leave. He left her with a huge house, mortgage-free, a cash payout that ensured her daughters' college tuitions would be paid, and a broken heart that had never healed. Which was what led to their grievous affair last year.

She leaned a hip into the desk, suddenly feeling tired. "It wouldn't have been fair to you. To drag you in again. Because if we talk, we meet for drinks. We meet for drinks, we end up in bed."

"Because that's who I am, right? I can't control myself. I'm a womanizer. You'd end up with a lying, cheating scumbag of a lawyer husband again."

Yes, that's exactly right. "No," she lied. "I just needed time to think things through."

"A year is an awfully long time. Not one text, not one phone call. Nothing. When I took the girls to dinner on Friday night, Erin asked me straight out why you weren't talking to me. You know what I had to tell her? That I don't know."

When Erin had told Lauren that Mark had texted her and was taking her and Lindsey to a new restaurant at Canalside the day after Thanksgiving, she hadn't been surprised. Mark had always maintained his relationship with her two girls, even after he married the knocked-up secretary. They called him Dad, and Lauren had no objection to that. Their biological father was dead and had never even seen Erin, much less parented her. Mark had come into their lives when the girls were eight and nine, and he was more of a dad than a lot of biological fathers she knew, never forgetting a birthday or missing a special event. Blood doesn't make family, Mark used to say, love does. It wasn't love that Mark lacked; it was the ability to stop spreading it around.

"I just thought it might be better to maintain radio silence while you were going through your divorce with Amanda. I know you were worried about little Mark, and you needed to be there for him."

At that he seemed to soften a little. "He took it harder than I expected. He started acting out, his grades dropped. We have him in counseling now." He glanced at a framed picture on the wall of the two of them in a canoe. "I'm in counseling, too, with him."

Mark agreeing to go to counseling surprised Lauren. He was one of those macho guys who had always claimed that counseling was all bullshit, for weak people who couldn't handle their own problems. "I know I keep saying it," Lauren told him, "but I am sorry."

Letting go of his anger, Mark finally took a good look at Lauren. She knew the circles under her eyes, the limp hair, the pallor of her skin gave away just how injured she really had been. And how she still needed time to recover. "Sit down before you fall down, please." Rising from his seat, he motioned to the chair in front of him. "What really happened? And not the newspaper version."

Lauren took the seat. "Someone snuck into my office and stabbed me from behind. Collapsed my lung, kicked me in the head to give me a nice little concussion, then left me for dead."

"That's unreal," he said as Lauren tried to get comfortable in the heavy wooden chair positioned directly in front of his desk. "Was it Joe Wheeler?"

Shaking her head, she saw the image that immediately popped into her brain at the mention of his name: Joe on his back with his nose next to his ear. Brain and hair and bone. Bright red blood and broken teeth. "It definitely wasn't Joe."

"Did you have anything to do with it?"

Her eyes went wide at the accusation. "You think I murdered Joe?"

"I read online that they questioned you and your partner the night he was killed. It's a fair question, after everything that happened."

Damn that leak. She gripped the sides of the chair until her knuckles went white.

"And now that you and your partner are living together ..." Mark said it like it made perfect sense, that she and her partner would conspire together to kill her ex-fiancé right after she got stabbed by some un-known cop. One of her daughters must have told him about the living arrangement at dinner.

Lauren held up a hand, cutting him off. "Stop right there. Reese and I are not in a romantic relationship. He's staying with me until I'm strong enough to come back to work. That's all."

"So Reese didn't exact revenge for you?" He didn't sound con-vinced.

"No," she countered. "He was actually banging one of my nurses when Joe was murdered. You should be satisfied, after everything that's happened, that Reese and I don't have anything between us. And we never will."

Now Mark laughed out loud. "I really thought when my secretary buzzed me that you were here, you wanted me to help set up your defense."

"You think I could kill Joe like that? Or have someone do it for me?"

He shrugged. "Anyone is capable of murder under the right cir-cumstances."

I taught you that, she wanted to tell him but tried to stay on track. "You handle real estate law. Why would I ever ask you to defend me?"

Leaning back in his seat, the boyish smile Lauren loved crept across his face. "Because I know people. I have connections."

Which brought her full circle back to why she was there. "That's why I need you to buy me these two tickets. It's not like they're a thousand dollars a plate. I'll give you the money."

He waved the idea away as if it were ridiculous. "I don't want your money."

Mark could buy a hundred tickets, probably with the cash he had on hand in his office. He had enough money to buy or sell almost anything in Buffalo. Just not her.

"I know you don't."

He studied her face, looking for something she didn't want him to see. "Does this have to do with you getting attacked in your office?"

"Yes," Lauren told him, trying to stay strong under his gaze. "But I can't tell you more than that."

Pushing back from his desk, he shoved his hands deep in the pockets of his designer suit pants. He looked down at her, his eyes softening. "I'll get two tickets under the firm's name. I'll text you when you can come pick them up. But I want you to know something else."

"What?"

"I'm not going to force you to see me again if you don't want to."

"Mark, that's not it." She lowered her eyes from his gaze, afraid of where it would lead. It was *because* she wanted to see him, to be with him, that she had to turn away. Every nerve in her body was firing, responding with electricity to him being so close to her. It would be so easy for Mark to lean in, kiss her mouth, run a hand along her cheek. So easy to fall back in bed with him. But then so hard when it all fell apart, again, like it surely would. "That's not it at all."

He sighed, resigned that her answer was the best she was going to give him. "I'm just relieved you're okay. I needed to see you in person to make sure, and I have." Stroking her hair back from her face like he used to do every morning before he left for work, he said, "I'll get you your tickets."

Lauren breathed out a sigh of relief, and from deep down, sadness.

Mark bent over and kissed the top of her head. "No strings attached."

36

"**H**ow did it go?" Reese revved the engine of the Dodge Charger he'd plucked from the pool at the police garage earlier.

Lauren slid into the passenger side. The computer that should have been mounted to the dash was gone; an empty bracket faced them. The car rattled, making a knocking sound if the wheel was turned too fast. *That's what happens when you get to the garage late.* Lauren strapped herself in. *All the good ones are taken.* "As well as could be expected."

Reese was parked in front of a fire hydrant directly in front of Mark's office building. A female office worker, smoking a cigarette off to the side of the main doors, was giving them the stink eye. "Can we take off before she makes a complaint?"

"Let's go."

Putting the car in gear, he eased into traffic carefully. "I should make a complaint against her for wearing sneakers with office attire."

"You'll be looking for a new job with those same fashion police if you keep blocking fire hydrants."

Reese changed the subject. "What did Mark say?"

"That he'll do it. He'll get the tickets. But he's not happy with me and I don't blame him."

"I don't blame him, either," Reese said, matter-of-factly. "You're a cold, heartless man-eater."

Lauren fought back the urge to punch him. She might reinjure herself pummeling him.

Her phone vibrated in her pocket. Pulling it out, she saw it was Violanti calling her back. She didn't bother to greet him. "Well?"

"David says he friended her months ago. He tried to friend Lindsey, but she never answered his request, and he would have friended you if he had known you were on Facebook. He says he didn't mean anything by it and he's sorry you're so upset."

"He's sorry I'm upset? He's stalking my daughter and he doesn't think I should be upset?"

"He doesn't think of it like that. In fact, he's unhappy that you're being so hostile toward him."

That was rich, coming from Violanti. "I'm hostile to murderers in general. He shouldn't take it personally."

"David is not a murderer. Just because you changed your mind about that after the trial doesn't mean you get to freak out at every move he makes."

"I changed my mind *during* the trial, but it was already too late. And I will freak out if I think my daughters' safety is compromised in any way."

Violanti sighed into the phone. "He would never hurt you or your daughters. Buffalo is a small place, though. David's path will cross

211

yours at some point. All I can tell you is that he's not sitting home obsessing about it the way you are. Everything is not about you, Lauren."

That pissed her off. "It's not about me. It's about my kids."

"That's a load of shit," he shot back at her. "I don't know if you attract crazy men or you drive them crazy. Maybe you should spend your energy trying to find the guy who broke into your office instead of worrying about what David is doing."

Sharply sucking in her breath, Lauren held back the flood of obscenities she wanted to hurl at Violanti. She managed to squeeze out a tight-lipped, "Thanks for all your help. I can see that this dialogue we've established has been extremely productive."

"One last thing," he said before she could hit the end button. "I really don't know what's going on in your or David's head, but I'm telling you, your mutual fascination with each other is weird, and it ends for me now. Don't call me anymore."

Violanti hung up on her.

She sat for a second, digesting the conversation. They were stopped in traffic on Elmwood Avenue, in view of the Albright-Knox Art Gallery, ironically where she'd married Mark Hathaway.

Giving her a sideways glance, Reese asked, "You okay?"

"You heard that, right?"

He nodded, looking up at the traffic signal. "I did."

"What do you think?"

"Let it go for now. He's right about one thing; you have enough going on trying to put away the Schultz brothers to worry about Spencer."

They were right. She was letting David Spencer sidetrack her when she needed to be focused. "Okay, Reese. What are we going to do about that?"

Reese turned the car southward, almost hitting a city bus as he pulled a U-turn in the middle of traffic. The driver popped the bird at them through the window. Reese didn't bother to send him one back. Instead he told Lauren, "Let's go talk to Charlie in the graveyard. We're going to need him."

37

"You want me to be the getaway driver?" Charlie was back at his kitchen table, dirty coveralls on, sipping coffee so hot that tendrils of steam rose from the rim. They'd all woken up to a hard frost that morning, covering the grass in shards of white, coating the car windows and mirrors in spiderwebs of ice. Winter was coming. There was no denying it. Here in Charlie's graveyard, ominous clouds hung overhead, causing noon to look like twilight.

Charlie was one of those guys who refused to turn his heater on until after the first snow. Lauren pulled her black wool peacoat tighter around her. In Buffalo, everyone had a closet full of coats of varying degrees of thickness to combat the daily, sometimes hourly, changes in weather. Last year, when they'd had an unprecedented heat wave, Lauren's coat closet remained untouched for the longest stretch of time she could remember. This year everything had rolled back to normal, weather-wise, and it was a daily crap shoot to select the right overcoat for the current conditions.

"Unless you want to put a suit on, yes." Lauren blew across the top of her mug to cool her coffee down. Charlie had produced a dented flask from the pocket of his overalls and proceeded to pour a nip into each of their mugs. Normally Lauren would have waved him off, but today, especially after that last conversation with Violanti, she thought she could use a little alcoholic warm-up.

"I, personally, am willing to rock the suit in your stead," Reese offered. "I look really good cleaned up."

Charlie chuckled into his coffee cup. "This is some serious James Bond spy shit you two are into."

"I know, Charlie, I know. But we're trying to protect Rita." Trying to convince him, Lauren laid her hand on his arm. "It's crazy, but we just need an abandoned sample from Sam. A drinking glass. A straw. A fork. Anything that might have his DNA on it. We can't wait around for the valet or park two blocks away in the ramp. We're only going to have one shot at this. We need to grab it and get out of there as fast as we can. Then we call Carl Church, tell him about Rita, get the sample in the lab immediately, and it's goodbye Sam Schultz for the murder of Gabriel Mohamed."

Charlie tipped the flask, adding more whiskey to his coffee, sipped it, and added a little more. "I worked with all three of those guys, even took young Sam along on a couple of raids as a favor to Ricky. Sam was a scared little mouse, that's why no one questioned when he left for law school. He was soft, you know? The bookish type, not a cop."

"Even more reason to protect baby brother," Reese said. "Plus, the fact that daddy was police commissioner at one time. Sam being the county district attorney would restore the Schultz family to political power."

"Listen to me," Charlie said, his voice becoming grave. "Vince is the muscle and Ricky is the brains behind this whole coverup, and that means your assault too. He told Sam to keep his mouth shut while he went through the motions of an investigation, and he's the one who would have known about the files and your Murder Book. I bet Vince's first call after he talked to Rita went straight to Ricky."

"I bet you're right," Lauren agreed.

"Ricky was a bully on the job." Charlie hit the table with his fist to make his point, almost upsetting their coffee mugs. "And he's the one calling the shots now. He told his brother exactly what to do. Vince is too stupid to think of going after the original records himself."

"Does that mean you'll do it?" Lauren asked.

"I've chased down a bank robber, tracked a man through a snowstorm after he killed his entire family, caught a guy by the arm trying to jump from the Peace Bridge, but I ain't never, ever, been the getaway driver for the larceny of food utensils." Charlie turned his whole body around, grabbed the coffeepot off the machine, and gave all three of them another steaming pour. "I'm sixty-eight years old. Why not become an outlaw?"

38

Much later that evening, Lauren excused herself to Reese and Watson, slipping down into the basement with the intention of typing up some notes from an old private investigation she had taken on.

She had done it as a favor to a distant cousin on her mom's side. He had suspected his wife had been cheating on him. And she was. The cousin, Alan, wasn't ready to divorce her—not just yet—he wanted to have all his finances in order, and the photographs Lauren had given him had proved his suspicions beyond a doubt. Cousin Alan's net worth consisted chiefly of an ironworker's pension and a beloved, rundown hunting cabin, but he was determined to keep them both.

Getting attacked had sidetracked Lauren's follow-up and right then seemed as good a time as any to catch up. The daily emails she had been receiving from Alan needed to stop. She could sit upstairs and stew over her meeting with Mark or over her impending covert mission with Reese, or she could sit at her computer and make a few hundred bucks finishing the PI job.

The problem was the distractions she allowed herself.

Even though it was fairly new, and she had sprung for a ton of memory and upgrades, her computer still took a good minute or two to fully come online. Her daughters were constantly telling her to just leave the machine on, but Lauren was convinced that would be a fire risk. From her chair at her desk she could hear the scratching of Watson's claws on her hardwood floor upstairs. She imagined all the little grooves being etched into the wood and thought absently, *I have to find a groomer to take care of that.*

Reese kept saying he was going to get around to having Watson's hair cut and nails trimmed, but as a mom, Lauren knew that even though Reese fed and walked him, he thought all the little extras of caring for a dog took care of themselves. As if the magic doggie shampoo fairy came in the middle of the night and washed muddy white dogs.

Watson appeared at the top of the stairs, tail wagging, and launched himself toward her. She managed to keep him from climbing on her lap by giving him an old green slipper she now kept within arm's reach for just such occasions. He accepted it happily, lying down to gnaw on it.

Watson wasn't the only distraction, though. They were all around her. A picture of her with her daughters ten years ago, the marble ashtray Mark had bought her when she still smoked that now held paper clips, and Frank Violanti's cell number scribbled on a blue Post-it, stuck to the small white board on the wall behind her computer. All of them fought for her attention.

She eyed the Post-it, plucked it up, and crumpled it in her fist. A direct connection to David Spencer had managed to invade her thoughts again.

The past year had been one of deep self-reflection for Lauren. She had questioned her motives for taking on the Spencer case and for wanting to believe in an eighteen-year-old psychopath, for falling back in bed with her ex-husband, and for allowing Joe Wheeler's abuse again and waiting until it was almost too late before she had done anything about it. Although she asked the hard questions, she didn't necessarily like the answers she'd found.

Her usual remedy for confronting bad decisions was withdrawal and immersion in her work, which is exactly what she'd done in regard to Mark. After the trial she broke off all contact with him, even after he sent a copy of his divorce decree to her office. Their affair had shattered her heart all over again, especially because she had finally accepted the fact that they would never end up living happily ever after. Love wasn't the problem; it was trust. Seeing him earlier that day had brought all those feelings of loss and hurt back to the surface. She knew she had to stay strong and resist the urge to give in to the hope that somehow their relationship would finally work out. It wouldn't. Ever. It was past time for her to move on.

Which brought her around to David Spencer. Dealing with him was more problematic for Lauren. David was a different kind of animal. Immersion in work just brought him more into focus for her, since he *was* work.

Over the summer Lauren had attended a homicide seminar the county had sponsored at the Charlotte, a swanky downtown hotel. The main topic was recognizing and identifying different personality subtypes in murderers through crime scene assessment. For four days Lauren sat silently, scribbling notes in her notebook, writing down every word the instructors said. Especially the first lecturer. Every part of his presentation made sense to her. Every point resonated in her brain, connecting David's behaviors to the crimes she knew he had committed.

A line uttered on the second day from the small, pale instructor, a retired criminal psychologist, stuck in her head: "The crime is not over until the perpetrator stops deriving pleasure from the murder." He called this personality subtype Anger Retaliatory, or AR, for short.

As soon as his session ended, Lauren had cornered the owlish little man in the hallway. She launched into her experience with David Spencer and how he was acquitted and did he have any thoughts about the situation? Lauren wanted to know how he would type David Spencer.

Clearly amused, he cocked one eyebrow, offered his arm, and said, "Join me at the hotel bar for a drink and tell me more about your interesting young fellow."

That was at four o'clock in the afternoon. Six hours later, they were still talking.

The psychologist, Dr. Stephen Durand, was a quirky man. He only drank Chardonnay, very good Chardonnay, and only if he witnessed the bottle being opened in front of him. Subsequently, he'd have the server leave the bottle so it was never out of his sight. Lauren was usually pretty good at guessing people's ages, but with Dr. Durand it was difficult. He was surely over sixty, possibly close to eighty, but had such a mischievous way about him, it made him appear much younger. His thick glasses magnified his muddy hazel eyes, and his thinning, sandy brown hair was combed neatly to the side, making the owl comparison even more compelling.

"Your young man has mommy issues," he told her, sipping the contents of bottle number four from his elegant crystal glass. That was another thing he had insisted on. Real crystal, no glass. *It's a good thing this hotel has a five-star restaurant attached to it*, Lauren thought as the bartender sent one of the bar backs to fetch the glasses when they first sat down and ordered. *It's a good thing Dr. Durand drinks hundred-*

dollar bottles of wine. He had told Lauren he'd been in there the night before, so the bartender didn't act put off. *Dr. Durand must also be a very good tipper.*

"His mother was a basketcase the entire time. Not that I blame her. I'd be the same way if my eighteen-year-old son was on trial for murder." Lauren took a small sip, only enough to stay sharp. Dr. Durand was drinking the vast majority of the wine, and even though he was a wisp of a man, it showed no effect on him.

"Ahhh, but you see, he *does* blame her. He blames the mother for everything bad that's happened to him, in one way or another. He can't kill mommy, so he finds a suitable substitute. Maybe his girlfriend laughed at him in bed. Maybe the rich woman turned him down when, in his mind, he thought she was making advances toward him. The fact is, it was a release for him to kill those women and he doesn't feel bad about it. Not at all." He paused for effect. "Quite the contrary. He believes those women deserved it."

Lauren turned that over in her mind for a moment, watching the odd reflection of the two of them in the mirror behind the bar. Her tall, blond, and serious; and him short, bookish, and academic-looking. A mismatched couple if there ever was one. She ran a finger around the rim of the wineglass. "Will he kill again?"

Dr. Durand reclined a little in his high-backed bar chair. "Probably. And I would guess sooner rather than later. His high from killing and getting away with it will only last so long. Then he'll have to find another suitable target, either consciously or subconsciously."

"When he stops deriving pleasure from the other murders," she said, reiterating his classroom statement back to him, "he'll have to kill again."

He pushed his wire rim glasses up his nose with a sly smile. "Precisely."

They went over the other subtypes: Power Reassurance, Anger Retaliatory, Anger Excitation. It was a lot to learn, and a four-day seminar was not going to be enough time. "I'm just the messenger," Dr. Durand admitted as they polished off the last bottle of wine. "If you want an in-depth study, I'd read the Keppel/Walter paper on the subject. It really is fascinating stuff."

Fascinating and useful, especially for re-examining old crime scenes. Lauren looked up the journal where Dr. Durand had told her the article could be found and she'd ordered a copy online the very next day.

She and Dr. Durand developed an odd mentorship-like relationship over the next few days and evenings that extended to emails and phone calls for a few months after the seminar had ended. His validation of her suspicions didn't bring David Spencer any closer to facing justice for what he had done, but she'd become a believer in the offender classification system. Eventually the emails had died off but she had saved every single one in a special folder, in case she ever needed to refer to them, along with all of her notes.

The idea of criminal personality subtypes had fueled her fixation on David Spencer for a while, but like the friendship with Dr. Durand it, too, faded over time as David stayed out of trouble and cold cases stacked up, waiting to be solved. David Spencer was still on her radar when the Murder Book got stolen, but much further back in her brain, in a mental holding pattern. All it would take would be one thing to pull him back into the forefront of her attention.

Like bringing flowers to the hospital.

Absently, she tapped the space bar on her computer with her index finger, sending the curser across the page: *click, click, click.*

She had so much else to be worrying about, like this impending caper with Reese and Charlie.

Click, click, click.

A mother was out there with no answers to her son's murder. Who thought the detective coming to her door was on her side, fighting on her behalf. It'd all been a cruel, sick farce. Gabriel Mohamed and his mother deserved better. Lauren had to do better for them.

Snapping her laptop shut, she startled a snoozing Watson lying at her feet, who had passed out on top of what was left of the slipper. Lauren told the blinking dog, "I'm not going to get anything done tonight."

Standing up and stretching, she looked at a picture of herself with her daughters again. A tightness wound around her throat, that yearning feeling that came with the realization that her girls had flown out of her nest and probably weren't coming back. But also from the urge to protect them from people like David Spencer and the Schultzes: predators who could look like angels.

Maybe I am nuts, she told herself as she started up the basement steps, Watson at her heels. *Maybe I'm the crazy one in this situation and I should have Reese lock me up for my own good. I can't think about David Spencer now. I have to concentrate on Sam Schultz.*

Watson ambled over to his food dish to lap up any remaining morsels he might have missed earlier. The night light in the hood over the stove cast the kitchen in a yellowish tint. Three rooms over, Reese's thundering snores penetrated the walls.

Come tomorrow night, Lauren thought, bending over to scratch Watson's ears as he moved over to slurp from his water dish, *if we go through with this, me and Reese will both be certifiable.*

39

"This tie is cutting off the circulation to my brain," Reese called up the stairs to Lauren, who was touching up her make-up in the upstairs bathroom. "Come fix it before it asphyxiates me."

Blowing out a breath of frustration, Lauren gave herself the once-over in the mirror. Her long black dress hung loosely on her body since she'd lost all that weight from being injured. The last time she'd worn it, to a wedding with Mark thirteen years ago, it had hugged her in all the right places, making her look quite curvy. Now it accentuated her extreme lack of anything that could be remotely called voluptuous. *At least it's floor length and I can wear flats,* she told herself, applying a tad more blush. *I won't look like a flat-chested, fifty-foot woman in heels.*

Lauren had swept her hair up into a chignon, pinning it with the jeweled bobby pins Erin had given her for Christmas last year. She'd noticed her hair growing darker over the past year, the California blond replaced with a honey-colored girl-next-door shade. She had considered getting it lightened back to its original color, then decided to let nature take its course, at least until the grays showed up. Then she'd have to rethink that strategy.

My hair looks nice for once, she consoled herself, *but this is as good as it's going to get.*

She smoothed down the sides of her silky dress and headed for the stairs.

Standing at the bottom, tugging at his cranberry-colored tie, was Reese. He looked up, his green eyes taking Lauren in as she walked down the stairs. He looked strikingly handsome in his new charcoal gray suit and tone-on-tone shirt with polished black shoes.

They locked eyes for a moment, his brilliant green meeting her soft blue. A whisper of a second passed as she stopped on the second stair and he looked up at her, tall and graceful, hand demurely sliding along the railing, a faint smile on her lips. His mouth opened slightly, as if words were about to tumble out he didn't know he had.

Then he shook his head.

"Nope. Nothing."

"What?"

He shrugged his shoulders. "I thought if you got dressed up, and looked super beautiful, which you do, I might find you attractive. But no, nothing."

She put a hand on her hip, a flush rising to her cheeks. "You were afraid if I got dressed up, you might be attracted to me. And?"

"No. I mean yes. And then we couldn't work together anymore. I certainly couldn't stay living here with you. But thankfully"—he let out a sigh of relief—"I'm not attracted to you. At all. Not even a little. Don't get me wrong," he explained quickly, seeing the anger cloud her face, "you're a pretty woman. You just don't do anything for me. Sorry."

"Well, thank God you find me repulsive." She pushed past him, walking into the living room. Picking her jeweled evening bag from the coffee table, she clicked it open looking for a cigarette, remembered she quit smoking years ago, and snapped it shut again.

Following her, Reese tried to rephrase. "You're not repulsive. Far, far from it. You know what I mean."

She let the empty bag slip back down to the table. She didn't know why she had even brought it out, she wasn't going to take it. It went with the dress, she supposed. "I do know. While all these young ladies you like to booty call at one a.m. can't get enough of you, they haven't seen you talk with your mouth full every day or heard you fart so loud it scared your dog awake."

"Hey," he protested. "No need to get personal."

She wasn't mad. She knew what he was so terribly trying to put into words. "We both know if anything was going to happen between us, it would have happened a long time ago. Let's just leave it at that." Lauren turned toward him and yanked at his tie, which he had knotted all wrong. She pulled it out and quickly retied it so he wouldn't pass out from restricted blood flow to the brain.

"Okay," he agreed, thankful that the matter was settled. He wiggled the tie back and forth, testing out how much give it had.

She slapped his hand away from his neck. "Leave it alone."

Reese cleared his throat and rubbed his hand, pretending she'd hurt him. "Are we ready to go pick up Charlie?"

Looking around the living room, she quickly checked her mental list of everything they'd need to pull this stunt off. "Yes."

"You got a gun on you?"

"I have two."

He looked her up and down, much like Charlie had when she'd made the same claim to him. "You gotta teach me that trick."

40

"**S**o what's the plan, Spy Kids?" Charlie asked from the backseat of Lauren's Ford Escape.

"This plan is, we go in, you stay outside with the SUV running." Reese was halfway turned in his seat, looking over his shoulder at Charlie. "The ticket says the cocktail reception starts at six. Champagne toast kicks off at seven. Silent auction at eight. It's"—he glanced at the phone in his hand—"six thirty right now. Lauren and I go and hide in the can until Sam Schultz is done giving his kickoff speech, then Lauren records while I sneak up and steal anything he leaves behind. Then we haul ass out of there, and you drive us straight to the Erie County Lab so we can deposit the evidence in the overnight lockers. Got it?"

"You two are going to hide in the shitter together?" Charlie sounded amused but grim at the same time, as if the danger of what they were about to do barely outweighed the ridiculousness of it.

"Me in the ladies' room, him in the men's," Lauren explained, not taking her eyes off the road as she drove.

"There're going to be lots of cops in there, retired and on duty. We don't want anyone to see us, obviously. I'll hover around the door. When it sounds like Schultz is wrapping up, I'll text her and we'll meet in the reception room. Hopefully all eyes will be on Sam," Reese said.

Charlie smirked. "Ain't technology wonderful? Back in the old days we would have had to synchronize our pocket watches to pull off a heist such as this."

Lauren glared at him in the rearview mirror. "Don't make me regret bringing you."

"Hey," Charlie protested. "I wore my cleanest shirt and a real pair of pants for this. I even slicked back my hair."

"The effort is appreciated, my brother," Reese told him, turning back around.

It hadn't snowed yet, but the sky was dark with clouds just waiting to open up. Lauren could feel the cold creeping into her bones, dry winter air sucking the warmth out of everything in its path. Within the month Buffalo would be white and glittering, like a picture postcard sent from the North Pole. Until then it teetered on that ominous precipice, that plunge into the first real snowstorm where the city would coat itself with ice and slush, freezing itself into its winter state.

The trio headed into the city, down Route 5, coming over the crest of the Skyway bridge. Lauren could see the old grain elevators to her left lit up with blue falling snowflakes, illuminated with lasers. The patterns changed with the seasons: leaves in the fall, flowers in the spring, yellow suns in the summer. It was a beautiful way to embrace the city's abandoned buildings.

The tops of the ships in the Naval and Military Park peeked out above the darkened horizon and Lauren thought about how much the city had changed in the last ten years, trying to reinvent itself through its waterfront. Twenty years ago the city rolled up its sidewalks on Friday nights after all the commuters fled back to the suburbs. With the advent of the new HarborCenter arena, Canalside, and the development of the inner and outer harbors, new life had been breathed into downtown. As she drove straight up Delaware Avenue, the city looked lit and alive. People crowded the Saturday-night sidewalks, rushing to one of the theaters, hopping from bar to bar, or enjoying their favorite restaurant.

She swung around Niagara Square. It was actually a traffic circle, not square, that enclosed a marble obelisk. City Hall, in all of its art deco glory, loomed over them. Offices were randomly lit up throughout the building, even at that late hour. Vaguely, Lauren wondered if the mayor was in his office, watching across the street to the new Strand Hotel and Suites, where the function was being held. Mayor Karnes had yet to announce his endorsement for district attorney, a bad sign for Carl Church, the incumbent.

"Where do you want me to park while I wait?" Charlie asked as Lauren continued around the circle. Warm yellow light radiated from the front of the hotel, decorated with a massive silver wreath under its logo. People in party clothes descended on the hotel from the parking ramps sprinkled around the downtown streets, wearing hats and gloves in preparation for the weather to turn. The trees out front were strung with white twinkling lights.

Pulling into the front reception area, a red-jacketed valet came running up. Waving him off, Lauren pointed Charlie to the front of City Hall. "Wait there. You got your off-duty badge?"

He patted his breast pocket. "Never leave home without it."

"Try to park in front of the cop car there and tell him you're waiting for us," Lauren instructed him. A uniform patrol officer was assigned to sit in front of City Hall at all times. They could see the car's back end peeking out from behind the obelisk. "If he won't let you park, just keep circling the block."

"Like a shark," he groused, opening the back passenger door and easing his bulky frame out. *How ironic*, Lauren thought as she opened the car door, *I can see the old Federal Courthouse, soon to be our new headquarters, from here. If we had already moved, we could have just walked over to carry out this raid.*

Carefully, so as not to step on the hem of her dress, Lauren exited the car, holding the keys out to Charlie. All around them stylish couples were making their way through the massive double glass doors into the brightly lit lobby. Most of the ladies stopped just inside the door at the coat check, shedding their winter weather wraps. Lauren hadn't worn one. She'd be chilly, but picking up a jacket at the coat check on the way out would have slowed them down. Reese made his way around the back of the car and took Lauren's arm.

"By the way, you two look ridiculous," Charlie told them, sliding behind the wheel. Not waiting for a reply, he revved the engine and pulled out into the circle.

"You think we can carry this off?" Reese asked as he beamed his smile at the arriving guests.

Latching her arm more securely around his, she propelled him forward. "Let's just find the bathrooms before someone spots us. I think I just saw Lieutenant Shaffer and his wife pull up."

The boning in the bodice of the dress was digging into her still-healing wounds, itching her like crazy. Fighting the urge to start scratching at herself, she and Reese crossed the threshold into the grand lobby, done up in a White Christmas theme, complete with a two-story ivory tree that twinkled with silvery lights. Piped-in holiday music filled the air. An attractive young lady in a blue evening dress checked their tickets against the list on her clipboard. "Guests of Mark Hathaway," she said warmly, checking them off her list. "Enjoy your evening."

Reese tucked the tickets into his suit coat pocket, then slipped his arm through Lauren's again. A passing waiter paused, handing them each a bubbling glass of champagne from his tray. "The reception is in the ballroom to your right," he informed them before moving on to the next couple.

Standing with a champagne flute directly in front of them, talking to two Asian men and their wives, was Ricky Schultz. Reese spotted him first and whirled Lauren around to face the wall. He huddled close to her, arm around her back, as if they were engrossed in a very private and intimate conversation.

"Smile," he told her, moving closer, "like we're on a date and you actually like me." Reese had her pinned.

"Is he still there?" she asked, trying to get out from under Reese's shoulder.

"It looks like he's wrapping it up. He didn't see us. Just laugh, pretend I'm witty."

She snuck a look at Ricky. Older than she remembered him, the years had not been kind. His barrel chest had ballooned, spilling over into a massive beer gut. He looked like he was stuffed into a suit two sizes too small. His dark hair, now streaked with gray, was too long, too greasy, and halfway combed over a bald spot. A nasty-looking irregular brown spot the size of a quarter marred his left cheek.

Reese tugged her even closer, trying to turn her face back toward his. "Look at me," he hissed. "He'll see your face."

She pressed her cheek against his. "I should have brought some mints."

"Ah." Reese laughed, heaving his shoulders a little for effect. "I should have brought someone who appreciates the rugged scent of a real man." Lauren tried to make a light tittering laugh, but it came out a kind of strangled choke. Feeling her heart start to race, she tried to control her breathing. The last thing Lauren needed was to have a coughing fit.

She peeked over Reese's shoulder. "I think he's gone."

Reese turned, checked the hall, saw that Ricky had moved on, and released her. "That was close. We almost walked right into him."

"Let's just get to the restrooms before we get caught." Lauren plastered her most serene fake smile across her face.

"Good idea." Reese had taken her arm again but was now on the alert for any random Schultz brother who might be hanging around.

"Sam has spared no expense." Lauren took a sip of the sweet champagne, glancing at the faces around her for people she knew.

"I did some research." Reese guided them to the entrance to the ballroom. "Sam Schultz did pretty well for himself as an attorney. Not as well as your ex-husband, but he made a lot of cash in personal injury law after he left the district attorney's office as an ADA years ago. Enough to finance a campaign against Carl Church, who's been considered unbeatable until now."

Her eyes scanned the hallway. "I see the restrooms. Right across from the main door to the ballroom."

"I want to stick my head in there real quick and get the lay of the land. Your phone is charged and ready to record, right?"

She patted the invisible pocket she had sewn into her dress so she wouldn't *have* to carry the silly little beaded purse. Even when she'd been married to Mark, she'd tried to skirt convention at every turn.

"You go powder your nose. I'll check it out, and when I hear the speeches, I'll text you."

Lauren hated letting him take the lead but nodded her head and walked in the direction of the bathroom. She was the planner of things in their partnership. He was the fly-by-the-seat-of-your-pants guy. The role reversal disturbed the delicate balance of power they had established long ago. Sometime soon, they had to get things back to normal. Including his moving back into his own house.

Almost bumping into an elegantly dressed, golden-haired lady, Lauren backed up so she could exit. The lady squinted her eyes after the mutual apologies and asked sweetly, "Have we met? You look so familiar."

Mustering her best bewildered look, Lauren responded, "I don't think so, but my memory isn't what it used to be."

The lady laughed, touching a manicured finger to her temple. "Tell me about it! See you at the party, dear."

The ladies' room was bigger than most studio apartments in the city, complete with a sitting area, a makeup and hair station, multiple stalls, and floor-length mirrors to double check yourself before you exited. She couldn't wait in the designated sitting area; someone might recognize her. Lauren stared at the heavy faux marble doors to the stalls. *I'm really going to have to sit in the can,* she concluded. *Wait until I tell the brass about our glamourous, unapproved, unsanctioned undercover operation in the toilet. If this goes bad, we'll get fired and be humiliated.*

Sucking it up as best she could in her itchy dress, she chose the farthest stall and entered. Thankfully, there were paper seat covers hanging on the wall, and she managed to make a barrier about a half an inch thick before the box ran out. Slipping her cell from the hidden pocket, she perched her butt on the edge of her new paper nest, waiting and listening.

The sounds of flushing, water running, and small talk didn't drown out the music coming from the ballroom. They'd both be able to hear when the organizer—some democratic big wig named Jason Mays—started the speeches. The men's room was located directly next door, so hopefully when they emerged, everyone would be in the ballroom paying attention to the speakers and not the people creeping out of the bathrooms.

"Is someone in here?" An impatient knock brought Lauren back to the situation at hand.

"Occupied," she called out, glad the doors were flush to the stall and there were no gaps like in some restrooms.

"Occupied," she heard the woman say. "They're all occupied. Why can't architects build enough bathrooms for women in the twenty-first century?"

Lauren smiled to herself. *Why indeed?*

She checked the time on her phone. The speeches should start any second. Jason Mays would talk for a while, but they would wait until Sam Schultz actually took the stage. Then all eyes would be on him.

No messages from Charlie. *He must be doing okay or he would have sent a text, or an angry message, or barged into the ladies' room to find me,* she thought, trying to concentrate on the sounds projecting from the ballroom.

Waiting was her weakness. As the minutes ticked by, her anxiety increased. This had to work. If they couldn't get an abandoned sample, they'd have to make Rita go before a judge to get a court order for Sam Schultz's DNA. The word of a retired hooker stealing benefits from her dead sister wouldn't go very far without any corroborating evidence.

Her mouth was dry, Sahara Desert dry, and she wished she'd grabbed another glass of champagne before heading into the stall. Nothing like drinking your problems away on the commode.

Suddenly she was aware that the music had stopped and people were clapping. She looked down at her phone. The program was running a couple minutes late, but it must be Jason Mays on the stage who was thanking everyone and making introductions.

Her phone buzzed. A single line of text appeared across her screen: MEET ME IN THE HALLWAY.

It was game time.

41

Standing in the hallway with his hands folded neatly in front of him, Reese looked every inch the handsome businessman waiting for his trophy wife to exit the bathroom. Except for the vein throbbing ever so slightly in his left temple, no one would ever guess he was under tremendous stress at that moment. Lauren sidled up next to him. "Got everything?"

Pulling so that it only peeked out of his pocket, Reese showed her a plastic evidence bag he had tucked away. "The latex gloves are in my other pocket. I'll try to slip one on as I approach."

Lauren had her cell phone in her hand. "I'm going to start recording now, so watch your mouth."

He gave her his signature grin, but there was a tightness to it. "Let's do this."

Stepping through the door, Lauren marveled at how the investors had taken a ramshackle, broken-down, abandoned building and turned it into an exquisite venue. Three enormous crystal chandeliers lit the expansive ballroom, complete with polished marble floors and enough tables to seat hundreds.

Reese broke away from Lauren. She immediately peeled off to the side, well behind the last table, and into the corner.

Almost everyone inside the ballroom was standing, champagne glasses in hand, listening to Jason Mays explain why Sam Schultz should be the next district attorney of Erie County. Sam stood next to him on the stage, hands clasped in front of him exactly like Reese's had just been, looking handsome in a blue suit with a yellow tie. Sam was built nothing like his brother Vince: he was shorter, slimmer, and he lacked the acne scars that marred Vince's face or the dangerous-looking spot on Ricky's. A high-maintenance blonde stood to Sam's immediate right. His wife, Lauren assumed by the way she was beaming in adoration at Sam. Lauren raised her phone up, mostly to record, but partially to obscure her face. From where she stood, she'd be able to capture everything.

She had a perfect, unobstructed view of Sam as he thanked the host and moved to the lectern to speak.

"When I was approached about running for Erie County District Attorney, my first thought was about my wife and kids. How would this affect them?" Sam Schultz looked over at his wife. "She didn't hesitate. She looked me right in the eye and said to go for it. Caroline's always been my biggest supporter. She's a supermom who takes care of our three kids all day, and then me when I come home at night. Can I get a round of applause for my wife, Caroline?"

Poor thing, Lauren thought with a hint of real pity, as she repositioned her cell slightly as Sam moved, along with countless others in the room, recording the event. *She has no idea what's about to happen to her family.*

From the corner of her eye, she could see Reese slowly making his way toward the front, via the far-right wall. No one noticed or cared; all eyes and cameras were glued to the candidate.

"Also, I'd be a bad brother if I didn't thank two very special men," Sam said, after acknowledging Jason Mays and thanking him and the Erie County Independent Party for hosting the event. Rumor had it Sam was trying to get both the Republican and the Democratic nods as well, effectively stealing the election from Church before the first ballot was even cast. "Vince and Ricky." He turned to his right where his brothers were standing in the front row, raising his glass in their direction.

"I took the Buffalo Police Department's exam all those years ago because I wanted to be like my big brothers. But it was my big brothers who convinced me I should leave the force to go to law school. It was the toughest decision I ever had to make, but they both told me that I needed to follow my heart. And I did. Not everyone can be a hero, but some of us can support our heroes. Vince and Rick, you are my heroes."

You killed a teenager, they covered it for you, and then one of them tried to kill me to keep the scam going. Lauren gripped the phone so hard her knuckles turned white. *Great guys, all three of you.*

Sam raised his champagne flute, waited for everyone else to do the same, amid yells of, "Hear! Hear!" He held his wife's gaze, gave her a playful wink, then took a long sip.

Bingo. Lauren watched the scene unfold on her phone screen. Now Reese just had to snag that glass.

Sam Schultz concluded his speech, shook hands with some random people on the stage, and exited onto the floor with his lovely wife in tow to mingle with the crowd. Lauren stepped back even farther into the corner, lowering her phone, but keeping it trained on the empty champagne flute Sam had left on a small table next to the lectern.

Waiters and waitresses wove in and out among the guests with trays of fresh bubbly. Reese dodged a laughing couple who almost backed into him as he made his way to the steps that led onto the stage. The vast majority of the crowd of about two hundred were gathered near the candidate or were focused in his direction. Even the waitstaff was more concerned with debris left on the tables than on the stage itself. As Lauren recorded, Reese crept up the steps, slipping the latex gloves on as he went.

Holding her breath, she watched as he briskly crossed the stage, snapped up the flute by the stem, turned and walked back the way he came in what seemed like a single fluid motion. With his free hand he fished the plastic evidence bag out of his pants pocket and slid the glass in as he hugged the wall, making a beeline for Lauren, who captured the entire event on her phone.

Out of the corner of her eye Lauren saw Vince spinning away from the woman he was talking to. *Oh shit,* Lauren thought. *He caught Reese's stage show.*

"Let's get out of here," Reese said in the low voice, handing her the bag, then peeling the gloves off, dropping them on the floor. They zigzagged their way through the crowd, getting stopped by a group of women taking a selfie. They managed to maneuver around the photoshoot to get to the door.

"Hey!"

As they stepped out into the hallway, the sound of Vince's voice cut through Lauren. Her head snapped up. Vince was standing in his black suit, chest heaving ten yards down the hall, blocking their exit. Reese's hand went to the small of Lauren's back as he quickly guided her around and they made their way in the opposite direction.

Lauren and Reese followed a stream of workers who were coming and going from a pair of doors off the main hallway.

"In here," Reese told her as they entered the venue's kitchen. "Look for an exit."

He barely had time to get the last word out when a silver serving tray smashed into his head from behind, sending him crashing into Lauren. Her phone, which was still recording, flew out of her hand, skittering across the floor. Lauren fell into a waitress carrying another round of champagne, sending herself, the girl, and the glass flutes crashing to the ground. All around her, stainless-steel appliances gleamed under recessed lights as Vince Schultz advanced on them.

"What the hell were you doing up there?" Vince demanded, grabbing Reese by his coat, swinging him into a wall. Empty bottles fell from a floating shelf onto one of the prep areas, exploding like bombs, showering them both with glass.

Momentarily dazed, Lauren watched as the staff stood stunned, shocked by the melee going on in front of them. Relieved the evidence in her hand was still intact, she looked up to see Vince and Reese locked together in a struggle against the far-right wall. Reese had Vince by the shirt collar pinning him back, while Vince's hand groped the nearest dirty tray table, trying to grab onto something. Butter knives and spoons scattered around his fingers.

"What are you looking for?" Reese hissed as Vince took a wild swing at him with his other hand. "Something to stab me with like you did her? You fucking coward."

"She was an accident," Vince spat back, managing to land a punch on Reese's temple. Reese sailed toward Lauren, who was scrambling on her hands and knees to retrieve her phone. She could see it had come to rest under one of the industrial-sized ovens. Bleeding from what looked like a cut from the broken glass, Reese tumbled on top of her, crushing her down.

"Why are you two here?" Vince demanded again as the kitchen staff scattered, screaming and calling for help. Stomping over to Lauren, he grabbed a handful of hair and yanked her head back, lifting her off Reese. Vince dragged her back, legs kicking as her hands flailed about, reaching for something to stop his momentum.

Backing her onto one of the food prep islands, he braced her against the countertop as he tried to get his other arm around her neck. Lauren grabbed the only thing within reach, clutching it in her fist and plunging it into Vince Schultz's face.

He let out an insane shriek, releasing her hair. As she tumbled away from him, she saw a long silver fork sticking out of his cheek, the tines buried deep into his skin.

Crawling like a crab, somehow still clutching the bag holding the intact champagne glass, Lauren grabbed her phone from under the stove and hooked an arm through Reese's, hauling him up. Sputtering and swearing, Vince yanked the fork out of his face, leaving four distinct blood trails running down his face. Flinging the utensil away, he lunged forward, stepped squarely into a puddle of spilled bubbly and glass shards, and slid into a tower of dessert plates, sending everything crashing down.

"Through here! Here!" Lauren pulled the disoriented Reese through a door marked EMERGENCY EXIT in red letters, setting off a howling alarm.

The wind and snow immediately slapped her in the face as they stumbled out into an alley. Behind them they could hear the commotion still going on in the kitchen. Lauren dragged Reese to the lights at the end of the alley.

Reese was pressing his hand to the side of his head to staunch the blood. "Did you get that? Please tell me you got that."

She looked down at the phone in her hand. The glass was cracked, but it was still lit up. "Yeah. I got that." She stuffed the phone into her hidden pocket and got a better hold on Reese.

The alley opened up to Niagara Square, framing both City Hall in front and the hotel behind them. Scanning the square, Lauren saw no sign of either her SUV or the police car that was supposed to be stationed out front. "Son of a bitch," she whispered, moving Reese onto the sidewalk, away from the kitchen exit and towards City Hall. Curious partygoers stopped dead at the sight of a bloody Reese being hauled along the street by Lauren. One of the valets came running from the front of the hotel, asking if they needed help. "No, we're fine," Lauren called to him, moving Reese farther around the circle.

A door slammed from behind.

Vince Schultz was barreling down the alleyway toward them with a Glock in his hand.

"Get in!"

Charlie was jumping the curb in Lauren's SUV, sending a sheet of slush splashing over the sidewalk. He was yelling through the open passenger-side window. "That cop bastard wouldn't let me park and then he took off. Probably had to go take a dump."

Lauren managed to get the back door open and Reese hauled himself in, with her diving on top of him. Vince ran right up to the car. Charlie managed to hit the window button just in time, closing it in his face. Enraged, Vince slammed the window with the butt of his gun. When it didn't crack, he wound up again, screaming for them to get out of the car.

"Holy shit!" Charlie swore as he hit the gas and sped off around the circle, leaving Vince in the slush. "What the hell just happened?"

"I stuck a fork in Vince Schultz's face." Lauren left Reese bleeding all over her backseat and climbed into the passenger side. A glance into the mirror confirmed what she was afraid of. "I think Vince just commandeered a cab. He's coming after us."

"What?" Charlie grabbed the rearview mirror, adjusting it as Lauren twisted in her seat to get a better view, ignoring her screaming injuries. Sure enough, a yellow cab was barreling around the circle and turning after them. "I thought this was supposed to be a stealth operation," Charlie said, turning the wheel into a hard right. "Vince the psycho brother is chasing us in a cab? Why are there even cabs here? I thought everyone did that Uber thing now?"

Lauren braced against the turn. "We don't have time to discuss the dynamics of cabs and Uber in the city." A pair of headlights bore down on them as they careened around Niagara Square. "Head for the Skyway," she told Charlie. "We'll double back to the county lab once we lose Vince."

A maroon Chevy Silverado cut in front of them, causing Charlie to slam on the breaks. They pitched forward as the Ford slid within inches of the truck's tailgate before jerking to a stop. Charlie hit on the horn and the driver allowed them to pass, but not before Vince managed to get practically on their bumper.

Charlie swung around Perkins Drive to South Elmwood, then onto lower Terrace to the mouth of the Skyway. He floored Lauren's vehicle against the pounding snow. Just as they turned onto the entrance, the entire SUV was jolted, hit from the behind.

"The bastard is ramming us!" Charlie cried, trying to control the SUV on the now icy road.

Lauren wrestled her portable radio out of the center console. "I'm calling this in," she said, keying the mic as her car took a second hit.

Two lanes in each direction, with only a chest-high border, the Skyway was a raised mile-long section of Route 5, 110 feet in the air at its highest point. Lauren knew that ramming them could flip them right off the raised highway and send them crashing to the ground below.

"1279 to radio," Lauren tried to speak over the howling wind as she gave her assignment number.

"1279?" the dispatcher replied right away, her voice questioning why an officer off with an injury would be calling out on the radio.

"Radio, this is 1279. I'm in a blue Ford Escape traveling south over the Skyway, being pursued at a high speed by a yellow Buffalo Nickel City taxi cab."

The irony that she was fleeing in an Escape was not lost on her.

"1279, could you repeat that last transmission? Did you say *you* were being pursued?"

Thunk, thunk.

Two bullets hit the rear hatch of her car but didn't pierce the back window. Lauren crouched down in her seat. Keying the mic on her portable she said, "Radio, we have shots fired. I repeat, shots fired."

"Cap that fucker!" Charlie screamed as he struggled to keep control of the wheel. Snow swirled in the double beams of his headlights, limiting his visibility. Lauren's SUV careened from side to side, trying to find traction on the unplowed pavement.

Lauren pulled her Glock from its hiding place under her dress and peeked her head around the seat, out the back window. The headlights were practically on top of them, blinding her. "I can't. I can't tell if there are cars behind the cab."

The next bullet went through the back window, straight past her face, and exited out the front windshield, leaving a small spidered hole. She sucked in a breath, trying to get a decent visual for a shot. Snow blew across the back window, obscuring the view even more.

The police radio had blown up with chatter. "Where are you now, 1279?"

"Who's shooting, Radio?"

"Is there a police pursuit in progress?"

"Be advised, Radio," Lauren managed as they passed the small boat harbor, still ducked down, "the shooter is a police officer. Vince Schultz is firing on my vehicle. We're approaching the Tifft Street exit now."

A strong, calm voice cut into the wild chatter. "Radio, this Adam District Lieutenant Pearson. Be advised A-District cars will be at the foot of the Skyway at the Tifft Street exit. Any available A-District car, proceed to Tifft Street."

Shirley Pearson's voice continued to direct the A-District cars while Lauren clutched the portable radio in one hand and the evidence bag in the other. From the backseat Reese let out a low moan. "I can't believe that asshole hit me with a serving tray."

"Stay down," Lauren commanded Reese, knowing if he stuck his head up, Vince would blow it off.

Lauren reached back and felt around the floor of the Ford. Her hand caught on the black fleece she kept for weather emergencies. Staying low, she wrapped the jacket around the evidence bag and tucked it quickly under the seat, hoping it would survive what she was sure would happen next.

Up ahead, at the end of the off-ramp to Tifft Street, blue and white flashing lights were converging from three directions. Lauren looked back just in time to see Vince's desperate last-ditch effort. He rammed them full force, twisting and locking metal on metal, causing both vehicles to jam together in a sideways slide heading right at the patrol cars.

"Hold on!" Charlie yelled over the sound of scraping steel, trying to turn into the skid.

Grabbing onto her seat belt with both hands, the momentum pushed Lauren back in her seat. The swirl of lights and snow was dizzying as they spun out, then collided with something solid, causing her to bite down hard on her tongue.

Everything went dark for a second, and the taste of blood filling her mouth transported her back to the floor of her office. She was on the Cold Case carpet, staring at a pair of black boots while blood choked off her airway. Sucking for breath, she startled back to reality and tore at her seat belt.

"Whoa. You're okay! You're okay!" Hands and voices seemed to surround her.

"Where's Reese? Charlie?" She turned toward the driver seat to see several officers carefully helping Charlie Daley out. Someone had opened her door, and hands were gripping under her arm. She turned, and some young cop she'd never seen before was helping to pull her out of the Ford.

"I'm all right," she tried to shake him off. "Reese?"

From outside the vehicle she heard Reese call to her, "I'm fine, Lauren. Get out of the car."

She let the cop help her out and into the blowing snow. It stung her cheeks and eyes as she tried to process the scene around her. At least ten police vehicles with lights and sirens blazing ringed the two connected cars that had been crushed against a light pole. The taxi cab had taken the worst of the hit, striking the pole on the passenger side, caving it in and curving the cab itself around the steel base. The pole was teetering precariously to the left above her, the globe busted from the impact. Wires sparked over the twisted mess.

The tops of the windmills that lined Lake Erie to the south should have been visible, but their white metal frames made them indiscernible in the swirling, heavy lake-effect snow. Even the old grain mill that should be clearly evident to the west was erased by the flakes.

Another siren pierced the commotion.

A fire truck came rumbling up, the firefighters swinging off the rig, peeling left and right to attend to both of the crashed vehicles. The stone overpass that announced SOUTH BUFFALO was just barely detectable in the near whiteout. If the cars had skidded twenty feet in the opposite direction, they'd have been crushed against it.

"Vince Schultz has a gun," Lauren announced, trying to shake off the cops trying to guide her to the firetruck. She was still stunned from the impact, not thinking clearly. "He shot at us."

"Come sit in my car until the ambulance gets here." Lieutenant Pearson cut through the cluster of officers surrounding her. Lauren looked toward the crumpled cab. "Vince is unconscious," Pearson told her, wrapping an arm around her waist. "The firefighters have to get him out." Flakes of snow were caught in the lieutenant's winter uniform hat. Lauren realized she was still wearing her stupid black dress, but one of her shoes was gone.

"Come sit down," Pearson pressed. "Tell me exactly what happened."

"Wait." Lauren ducked back inside what was left of her car and snatched up the fleece with its precious cargo inside. Carefully unwrapping the evidence bag, Lauren was relieved to see it in one piece. Behind her she heard the firefighters firing up the jaws of life, presumably to cut Vince Schultz out of the taxi cab. She held up the unbroken bagged champagne flute for Lieutenant Pearson to see amid the chaos going on around them. "We have to call Carl Church."

42

Lauren shivered against the rough wool of the surplus Army blanket someone had dug up around headquarters for her. The shivering only increased the pain running along her torso, but she couldn't stop. Her tongue throbbed from where she had bitten down on it. Every time she took a sip of hot coffee it was a bittersweet combination of caffeine and pain.

One of the responding South District cops had found her lost shoe on the floor of her SUV, not that it made her any more comfortable; she was still just as cold in her pair of fancy overpriced flats.

Carl Church sat across from her in one of the Homicide interview rooms. She knew they had taken Reese for stitches and that Charlie was in the Homicide squad somewhere, giving his statement about the night's events. Carl Church told her Vince Schultz was in the ninth-floor lockup at the Erie County Medical Center, where they treated prisoners for injuries, with possible internal damage from the crash. Now Church and the Kinger were trying to piece together what they needed for Vince's arraignment on the charges they were laying against him.

Carl rubbed his hand back and forth over his salt-and-pepper hair as he went over an application for a search warrant for Vince's apartment. Church had been in bed when he got the call and had rushed down to police headquarters in a pair of Buffalo Bills sweatpants and a stained tee shirt from a bar that read: *Good Time Chaz's, Memphis, Tennessee.* Rough stubble covered his usually close-shaved chin.

On the table in front of him was Lauren's cracked cell phone. He'd watched the video five times in stunned disbelief, from the snagging of the glass, to the assault in the kitchen, all the way through the car chase and crash. Lauren's smart phone, which she had always hated to be tethered to, had documented the entire incident. She swore to herself she'd never complain about having to carry it again.

The union lawyer, Amelia, was in the room with her, more for moral support than anything else. She sat next to Lauren as she gave her statement, fetched her some coffee, and demanded someone find Lauren a blanket.

"What are you charging him with?" Lauren asked, watching Church and King create more paperwork before her very eyes. The Kinger was busy alternately scribbling notes on a legal pad next to his boss and typing things into an official Erie County District Attorney's office iPad. His red hair seemed especially enflamed, as well as his freckles, with the pressure from Church to get everything right.

Lauren could see by the look on his face he'd rather be going to a hockey tournament for his son at that time of the morning than working on a high-profile case. Kevin King pretended to like the action, but Lauren knew it was all for show. He'd proved that a year ago when a murder suspect had blown his own head off when Lauren and Reese had come to arrest him. King had walked into the crime scene, taken one look around, and walked right back out to his car, leaving Lauren and Reese to piece everything together themselves.

"What aren't we charging him with?" Church asked, looking up from the warrant. "Three counts of attempted murder, criminal use of a weapon, reckless endangerment, assault second on Reese, carjacking…"

"And Gabriel Mohamed?" Lauren pulled the blanket tighter to suppress her shivering. The maintenance staff hadn't gotten around to turning the ancient boiler on in the basement yet and the building was ice cold. "What about his murder case?"

Church gave her an apologetic smile. "Not yet. We'll hold off on that until we serve the warrants. But we have more than enough to hold Vince until we do. The charges for your assault are pending, but I *am* going to charge him. His admission on the recording is clear as a bell. That was a stroke of brilliance to let that phone just keep taping."

She wanted to tell him she forgot to turn it off. After it was knocked out of her hand in the kitchen, she had forgotten it was still recording and just stuffed it into her pocket, but did that really matter? It was all there. Every last sound, every punch, impact, and crash, including the gunshots.

"What about Sam Schultz?"

"Charlie gave us Rita's address and called to let her know officers were coming. We've already moved her to a safe place. We'll be taking formal statements from her as soon as possible, but right now, I have to focus on Vince." Lauren didn't like the sound of that. She and Reese would have to make sure they kept Rita safe. Witnesses had a habit of going back to their old haunts. Rita was no exception. She was older now and that apartment was all she had.

"What about charging Sam Schultz?" Lauren's voice went up a notch. "What about Rick?"

Church deflected the questions again, likely because he knew she wouldn't like the answers. "We need you to put the glass into the lab." He motioned to the perfect champagne flute encased in its clear evidence bag sitting on the desk next to her. "I'll go with you to do that. I'm going to need all the paperwork, and copies of the file, of course. The state attorney general's office will probably take that aspect of the case over from me. Conflict of interest. But brace yourself for a major media shitshow."

"Sam is going to lawyer up right away." Lauren was thinking out loud now, the odds and ends of the case popping out of her mouth as they came into her head. If Church wasn't going to say it, she would.

"He *is* a lawyer," the Kinger pointed out, "and it's safe to say all three brothers won't be cooperating with this investigation."

It was almost dawn and they weren't even close to finishing the paperwork, there was so much to do and search and document. Lauren leaned her head against her hand. "What about Joe Wheeler? Do you think we'll be able to charge Vince with his murder?"

"Don't get ahead of yourself," Amelia told her, wrapping an arm around her shoulder. The little union lawyer was so tiny it felt like one of her daughters giving her a Christmas hug when they were tweens. "Thanks to you, Mr. Church here has weeks' worth of evidence to go through. You know it'll be a while before everything is sorted out."

Lauren did know that. But they'd just stuck it to all three Schultz brothers. There'd finally be justice for Gabriel Mohamed and his family. It was worth a knife in the ribs to bring these scumbags down. *It's taken years*, she told herself, *what does a few more days matter?*

43

The headline scrolling across the front of her iPad read: SHOOTOUT ON SKYWAY ENDS IN CRASH: OFF-DUTY POLICE OFFICER CHARGED. Lauren didn't bother to read the article. She hadn't bothered to go outside and get the newspaper stuffed in her mailbox; it would just be more of the same.

She and Reese had gotten home from headquarters at ten o'clock in the morning and were due back as soon as possible. They'd both gotten three hours of choppy sleep and had to jump right back into the investigation, which would be rolling along without them in their absence. Lauren's OCD ways had to put a stop to that. Whatever happened now, she needed to be sure she was a part of it.

Lauren scrambled to get dressed after she finally gave up on getting a decent nap, kicking the black gown under her bed, hopefully never to be seen again. She came downstairs to find Reese already up and showered, his staples glistening with some antibiotic goop the doctor had spread over them, eating a bowl of cereal in her living room with Watson at his side. Ears pricking up, Watson wagged his tail at her appearance, not even flinching when she tossed the tablet on the couch near him.

"Don't you want to know how it ends?" Reese asked shoveling cereal from the bowl into his mouth. "I was riveted right up to the last paragraph."

She sat down on the couch next to the Westie, careful not to squash her tablet. "I'll wait for the movie."

Watson rolled over onto his back so she could scratch his belly. A Sunday afternoon decorated with the season's first snowfall should have been cause for hot chocolate and cozy slippers. Instead, Reese's head was dotted with twelve staples and every detail of what had gone on the night before had been leaked to the press. Including the fact that Sam Schultz was the suspect in the cold case homicide of Gabriel Mohamed. Carl Church was right when he called it a shitshow. Their whole case had been laid out for the media before they had even stepped in a courtroom.

"I can't believe this." Lauren repositioned herself on the couch to give Watson more room. Every part of her body hurt from the crash, and her tongue was swollen. She was lucky her stitches had all held. Lucky, too, the brass hadn't insisted she go to the hospital. Another night at ECMC and she would have lost what was left of her mind. "Talk about showing your opponents all your cards right off the bat."

"Yeah, well." A piece of yellow Cap'n Crunch hung from Reese's lip for a second, then tumbled off onto her hardwood floor. "At least now we know who the leak is."

"We do?"

Reese nodded, sending another piece of cereal flying. Watson made to jump after it and gobble it up, but Lauren held onto him, not knowing if sugar was bad for dogs.

"I kind of told a lie, accidently on purpose, to someone during my statement last night. Just one detail to just one person. That detail made the paper."

"What did you say?"

Crunching his way across the living room, he picked the tablet up, awkwardly juggling it while still trying to stuff as much cereal in his mouth as he could. After hitting the touchscreen as best he could, he held it out to Lauren. "Right there," he said as she rescanned the article. "Four or five paragraphs down. I gave my full name for the statement. Shane Robert Reese."

Lauren looked up. "Your middle name is Raymond."

"You know that." He winked, that big shit-eating grin spreading across his face as he held the bowl close to his mouth. "But the leak didn't. He only ever saw Shane R. Reese anywhere else. That name in the paper could've only come from the leak. I suspected, but now I know. You should thank me for being so damn brilliant." He then tipped the bowl up to his lips and slurped down the rest of his milk.

44

The Kinger was in tears.

He sat crying in Carl Church's office not three hours later as Riley and Reese flanked Carl Church. King sat in the chair in front of them, blubbering all over his suit coat.

Church had changed out of the bar tee shirt and sweats back into his district attorney power suit. "You put Lauren's assault investigation in jeopardy, you put Rita Walton's life in jeopardy, and you may have gotten Joe Wheeler killed."

Kevin King ran a sleeve across his nose, which was now as red as his hair, spreading a thin line of snot from his wrist to his elbow. "I was just trying to help Sam Schultz's campaign. We've been friends since right out of law school. All I was trying to do was, was"—he took a deep, staggering breath—"show the dysfunction of the district attorney's office. I had no idea that Sam shot a kid, and I *never* suspected Vince stabbed Lauren. I am so sorry, Lauren."

Lauren stood with her arms folded across her chest, in no mood for forgiveness. "You weren't suspicious about their interest in my attack?" she asked, seeing the beads of sweat forming on his forehead along his hairline. "I bet they were asking you about leads. That didn't raise a red flag or two in your twisted little head?"

"No. I swear. Who would think they'd be capable of something like this?"

"A better attorney," Reese snapped. With his silver staples exposed, snaking from the side around the back of his head, he looked downright menacing. Kevin recoiled a little as Reese put both hands on Church's desk and leaned in. "I started to suspect you when my investigation into the Murder Book seemed to stall, when me and Lauren started following up without telling you. If it had been someone in the Homicide office, they would've talked about the bullshit leads Joy and I were tracking, like Patrick Harrington. Because who knew they were dead ends? You knew. And that's why they never made headlines. Seemed like only the really important details got leaked. So I gave you a little test."

"Mr. King." Church rose to his feet, gathering himself to his full height, towering over the crying man. "If it were up to me, not only would you lose your job here as well as your license to practice law in New York State, you'd also be facing jail time. As it stands right now, you are dismissed from this office immediately. I'm turning the case over to the state's attorney general's office for pursuit of further charges. Don't even bother trying to log into our computer system. Not only have you been locked out, your correspondence will be subject to criminal review."

"I have private emails on our server," King protested weakly.

"Nothing is private on my server," Church answered. "Please exit the building immediately. I'll have a court officer escort you out. Your personal property will be sent to you at a later date."

King rose from his chair, looking uncertainly from Riley to Reese, as if he thought one of them were about to attack. When they both maintained their silence, he seemed to muster up some courage to defend himself. "You were no fan of hers last year when she made a fool out of you at David Spencer's trial," he told Church as he backed away from the desk, toward the door. "It took her getting stabbed to get back into your good graces."

Church picked up his phone and called the main desk for an escort. When he was finished, he hung up and looked at King like he was a bug he'd love to squash. "I would never have stooped to impeding an investigation or colluding with possible murderers," Church countered, his voice booming across the room.

"I didn't know about any of that." King tried to sound convincing. "I swear, I had no idea."

Church mirrored Lauren, crossing his muscular arms. "I would advise you that you have the right to remain silent. Anything you say can and will be used against you in a court of law ..."

The Kinger, now dethroned, didn't wait for Carl Church to finish reciting the Miranda Rights. He swung the door open and fled out into the hallway, only to be intercepted by the officer sent to escort him out of the building.

"Good riddance," Church said. He took a deep breath, turning his attention back to Riley and Reese. "That was a damn good bit of police work you pulled off last night, including figuring out that King was the leak," he complimented as he sat back down. "That cell phone audio and video is the nail in Vince Schultz's coffin."

"What about Sam?" Lauren asked, making her way around the desk to sit in the chair King just vacated. She felt like a parrot, asking the same question over and over and getting no crackers.

Church rifled around in his brown leather briefcase for a second before extracting his iPad from it. "Sam sent Lincoln Lewis to represent Vince at his arraignment at noon. I imagine someone from Lewis's firm will be representing both him and Ricky as well. Lewis is a damn good defense attorney, but he's going to have a hell of a time overcoming that recording."

"Lewis will try. He'll probably want me locked up for larceny of a champagne glass and assault for sticking a fork in Vince's face." Lauren knew Lincoln Lewis. She considered him a ruthless gentleman in the courtroom.

Church gave her a reassuring grin. "The fork went right to the bone, by the way."

Lauren ran a hand through her hair and came out with a handful of loose clumps. "I think he was trying to yank my head off." She twittered her fingers over a wastebasket next to her, sending the stray blond hairs into the trash. She had tried to put her hair in a ponytail before she left her house, but it proved to be too painful. *Even my freaking hair hurts,* she thought. *I am really and truly a physical train wreck right now.*

"What's the latest on Vince's condition?" Reese asked.

"Besides the puncture wounds? Three broken ribs. Multiple cuts and bruises. He'll be released from the hospital by the day after tomorrow," Church said. "He'll spend the rest of his recovery in the lovely county lockup."

"Joy Walsh is serving the search warrant at Vince's apartment as we speak," Reese said, glancing at his phone for any messages from her. "Vince is a slob. If we can grab his city-issue boots, I'm sure we'll find something."

"I want the boots, every knife he owns, every pair of uniform pants, gloves. He probably destroyed your Murder Book, but you never know. I want his computer and his phone, and if there's a tire iron in there, I just might throw a party." Church fiddled with the touch screen on the iPad he set up on his desk. Lauren watched him scroll through a hundred emails without opening a single one. "The press is going crazy with information requests. We're going to have to hold a press conference."

"Did your investigators find Gabriel Mohamed's mother?" Lauren asked, trying to change the subject away from press conferences. The tiredness was creeping over her again and she wished she had grabbed a bottle of water out of the soda machine on the way in.

Nodding, Church turned the iPad face-down on the desk. "She still lives on the lower West Side on Grant Street. She's a cook at The Poppy Restaurant on the corner of West Ferry and Niagara. My investigators found her this morning. She's in shock. I sent one of our victims' advocates over to her apartment to help her through what's coming next."

Lauren thought of the long years with no word from the police on who had killed her son, only to learn that the very people she was supposed to trust had been the ones to betray her. She pictured Gabriel's smiling face, his student ID stapled to the inside flap of his Homicide file, yellowing with time.

What's coming next for his case? she wondered. *Do I have to pry it out of Church?* The district attorney's office was constantly being accused by the Buffalo Homicide squad of dragging their feet when it came to charging cases. The DA's office argued they wanted tighter cases from the Buffalo detectives, and the Homicide squad grumbled back that suburban cases got a higher priority. Whether true or just a squad-wide impatience due to the volume of murders they handled, the fear of being blown off had leached into Lauren's head.

"Sir, I'd like to know why you're being evasive about arresting Sam Schultz," she asked Church outright. She was too tired to go around in circles anymore.

Church bristled at her words. "I'm not being evasive. This situation is complicated. Don't make me out to be the bad guy here."

Seeing the frustration on Lauren's face, Reese asked, "How long until you charge Sam Schultz with Gabriel Mohamed's murder?"

Church hesitated a second, obviously not wanting to give a specific time frame. But he was cornered and they wouldn't settle for unanswered questions. "First, we need the lab to process the sample you submitted. Once we have that report in hand and it says the champagne glass is a match to the numbers on the gun, then I'll ask for a court order for Sam's DNA. A week, maybe less, if our lab guys come through quickly."

"A week," Lauren snipped. "Sam gets to walk around building up his defense with Ricky for at least a week. Beautiful."

"We can do it fast, or we can do it right," Church reminded her, growing defensive. "Remember, there are three separate cases here: Gabriel Mohamed's murder, your attack, and Joe Wheeler's murder. Make that four, if we add Vince's psychotic episode last night. We've got a lot to sort out and I will not be rushed."

That was reasonable, Lauren knew. Mistakes could cost you a case. But it still sucked.

Trying to break the tension that had built up in the room, Reese moved toward Lauren and touched her on the shoulder. "Let's get over to the office and see what we can do."

"I want both of you to get some rest," Church's voice raised another octave, sounding like a scolding father to his disobedient children. "You look like Frankenstein, and Lauren looks like she might keel over any second. Go home. Go to bed. I'll call you when I need you."

Wanting to protest but too tired to argue, Lauren rose and exited Church's office in a much more dignified way than Kevin King had.

45

"**H**ey, Lauren? Wake up. You have to see this." Knocking on her door, Reese's voice caused Watson to leap from Lauren's bed. He was now jumping up and down, barking at the closed door, desperate to get to his human. Lauren looked at the digital clock next to her bed on the nightstand. Eight thirty-five on Monday morning, she saw, blinking herself awake. Possibly it could be Tuesday or Wednesday— she had been so exhausted when she had fallen into bed—but she was pretty sure it was Monday.

It had been worth risking Church's wrath by heading to the Homicide squad after leaving his office to see what they had uncovered in the hours since the crash. The search of Vince Schultz's suburban upscale apartment had turned up some interesting evidence. Joy had informed Riley and Reese that Vince lived like a swine in an expensive Amherst townhouse complex. The neighbors had come out when they saw the police cars and told the detectives on scene that Vince was constantly having domestics with his girlfriend, didn't follow any of the complex's rules regarding noise, and was an all-around thorn in their collective side.

Joy told Lauren she assigned a patrol officer to listen to them complain while she conducted the search inside Vince's residence.

Garcia's swipe card was found under Vince's mattress. A pair of city-issue police pants were pulled from the bottom of a hamper in the bathroom and the pant-leg hem tested positive for blood. Even though it was obvious someone had tried to scrub the soles, the laces on his city-issued boots tested positive as well. Things were looking worse and worse for Vince Schultz.

By the time they had left the office yesterday, Lauren didn't know if it was day or night, the weather had turned so bleary. That, combined with the fact she was bruised, battered, and sleep-deprived, had thrown her remaining sense of time even more off kilter.

"Can I come in?" Reese had never breached the sanctity of Lauren's bedroom, ever.

Thankfully, she had on a heavy pair of flannel pajamas. Sitting up, she scooted against the headboard and called, "Come in."

"I just got a call from Church." Reese rushed over to the bed, carrying his iPad. He looked as disheveled as she felt, wearing a ripped undershirt and boxers. "He said there's something coming on we have to watch."

He dropped himself down next to her, positioning the iPad between them so they could both see. Watson squirmed his way up onto the bed and lay across Reese's legs as he hit the television app on his touchscreen.

"What channel?" Lauren pulled the bedspread up around her chest. Her furnace hadn't kicked in and the room felt chilly.

"All of them." Reese's mouth was set in a hard line as he maximized the window. An empty lectern was set up in some unknown office conference room, surrounded by microphones. A ribbon of text scrolled across the bottom of the screen reading: SAM SCHULTZ PRESS CONFERENCE TO START AT 8:30. Obviously, they were late kicking things off. Random noises filled the background: a cough, a whisper, the sound of chairs being moved. The reporters out of the line of sight were jockeying for position in anticipation of the announcement to come.

The great chase and arrest of Vince Schultz had made national news. The twenty-four-hour cable channels had descended on Buffalo, streaming the story live as it unfolded. *That's what every newscaster said,* Lauren thought, staring at the empty lectern, *"Bringing you the story live as it unfolds." Try living it as it unfolds.*

Lauren wondered why Sam Schultz was calling a press conference. He was days, if not hours, from being locked up. What could he possibly throw out to the media that could help his case?

Lincoln Lewis appeared in the far-right corner, leaning over, talking to someone out of the frame. Not exactly handsome, but extremely confident, Lewis stood almost six-five with short brown hair and deep-set brown eyes. He had a way about him that moved juries to disregard facts and evidence, making him the highest-paid defense attorney in Buffalo.

Lauren had come close to propositioning Lewis at a charity benefit over the summer, almost breaking her self-imposed vow of chastity. He'd seemed very receptive as they stood at the bar at the North Buffalo Club, but ever the gentleman, he waited for her to suggest that they go back to her place. Five drinks later she chickened out; the lawyering community in Buffalo was small, and word was sure to get back to her ex-husband. She wouldn't have wanted to hear about Mark banging another female cop. Lewis had slipped her his business card as she excused herself with a regretful kind of smile.

Cops and lawyers, she pondered, *that's all I seem to attract. Maybe I should start dabbling with the guys on the fire department?*

Still, there was something undeniably appealing about Lewis. Even now as he prepped himself, he oozed confidence from every pore, as if giving a news conference was really just a locker room chat between two old hockey buddies. His signature bow tie was red with white pinstripes, very festive seeing how it was now December and the holidays were looming. He never missed a trick. Those subliminal messages he sent out were meant to make you trust and like him. Lauren watched him tap one of the microphones and it gave a squeal of feedback, causing him to jump back slightly, then laugh self-deprecatingly at himself.

"I think we'll get started." Lewis glanced around the room, making sure everyone was ready. *He's thoughtful like that*, Lauren thought bitterly to herself. *Lincoln Lewis can charm the skin off a snake.*

"I want to thank all the members of the media for coming here on such short notice. My client, Samuel Schultz, wants to say a few words. When he's done, he'll take no questions. I'll answer a few the best I can."

From the same side Lewis entered, Sam Schultz and his wife appeared in the frame. Sam kissed her cheek and stepped up to the lectern, leaving her standing off to the right in her deep-blue pantsuit, looking like a grieving widow. Lewis stepped aside for Sam but didn't step down, just repositioned himself behind his client. *To stop him from messing up*, Lauren thought, twisting the edge of her bedspread between her fingers. *To keep him from saying too much.*

Sam looked drawn and tired, huge bags hanging under each bloodshot eye. It looked as though he had aged ten years in the last two days. He hardly resembled the vivacious go-getter ready to step into the district attorney's shoes she'd seen on Saturday night.

Sam Schultz cleared his throat. "Ladies and gentlemen," he began, his voice breaking up, causing him to cough into his hand. He regained his composure and tried again. "Ladies and gentleman, many years ago as a rookie cop I made a horrendous and unforgivable mistake. I panicked and caused a young man to lose his life. Instead of owning up to my actions, I cowardly remained silent and made the decision to leave the police department. Over the years, I have been haunted by my actions, and inactions, that night. There has not been a day that goes by that I haven't thought of Gabriel Mohamed and his family. After this press conference, I have arranged to turn myself in to the district attorney's office and fully expect to be arrested and charged for my crimes."

He paused, and the buzz in the room rose to a crescendo as reporters started calling out questions. He glanced over to his wife, swallowed, and went on. "I'd like to apologize to Gabriel's family, the community whose trust I betrayed, my fellow police officers, and my family. It's too little, too late, I know. But now, today, I fully accept the consequences of my actions, whatever the people of the state of New York deem those to be." A single tear ran down his cheek.

"That son of a bitch," Reese swore, almost jumping off the bed. "He's getting ahead of it. Throwing himself on the sword. That mother—"

"Shhhh," Lauren admonished as Sam stepped down to stand with his wife while Lewis replaced him at the lectern.

Bombarded with questions, Lewis waited like a second-grade teacher would with an unruly class while Sam and his wife disappeared out of view. When the crowd had sufficiently quieted down, Lewis pointed his pen at a female reporter in the front of the room.

"Vincent Schultz has been arrested and charged with the attempted murder of Detective Lauren Riley, not once, but twice. Can you speak on how those charges might be related to Samuel's admission in the Gabriel Mohamed case?"

"No, I cannot. Next question." His pen searched the room until it found a familiar face. "Ken?"

"Samuel Schultz's brother Richard was a Homicide detective when Gabriel Mohamed was killed. Sources within the police department are saying he was involved in a cover-up. Do you expect Richard to be charged?"

Lauren inwardly cringed at the mention of "sources" within the police department. They'd already outed one snitch; hopefully there wasn't another one.

Lewis shook his head. "My client states that his brother Richard had no knowledge of his involvement with Gabriel's death. Richard only learned of it when Vincent was arrested."

The reporter called Ken immediately asked a follow up: "There was no conspiracy with Richard to cover up the death of Gabriel Mohamed?"

"No. Absolutely not. If there was anything Richard had done that had even had the slightest appearance of misconduct, the statute of limitations in New York State ran out years ago on any charges that might have been brought—"

The room ignited with a fresh round of questions being hurled at the lawyer.

"No charges?"

"What about federal law? Could he be charged federally?"

"Isn't he guilty of civil rights violations if he tampered with an investigation?"

Lewis motioned his hands downward in a quieting gesture, trying to regain control. "I cannot speculate what the federal government can or will do. I think that's it for the questions, people" He squared his shoulders. "I'd like to thank you all for attending..."

Lauren stabbed the screen with her finger, cutting off the live feed. "No charges for scumbag Richard," she seethed. "We have to wait for the Feds to run with it, and maybe, just maybe, he'll do a couple years in one of those country clubs they call prisons."

"We should have seen his coming." Reese got up and began to pace the room. "Only murder has no statute of limitations. We should have known. It's our *job* to know this shit." He was cradling his head in his hands, walking back and forth in front of her closet.

"We'll talk to Church," Lauren told him. "There has to be something."

"There's nothing!" Reese's arms shot out wide to illustrate how ridiculous the situation was. "Vince and Sam go to jail, but Ricky covers up a murder and gets away with it."

Lauren's new city-issue cell phone buzzed on her nightstand. She had turned the cracked one over to evidence and gotten a temporary work phone. She looked at the number and recognized it right away. It was Church.

"Did you see the press conference?" he asked. No hello. Right to the point.

"We saw it, all right," Lauren replied. "Tell me Ricky is getting charged with something."

"My next call is to the state attorney general's office."

Lauren's stomach dropped. "That'll be a no, then."

"I'm working on it," Church snapped, then added: "Right now all we have to connect Ricky to the conspiracy is the fact he checked the gun out and it never came back. That's it. Even the Feds are going to want more before they charge him, especially if all three brothers stick to the story that Ricky didn't know anything about it."

"Sam told Vince, but not Ricky? You believe that?" she challenged.

"Ricky was the Homicide detective. We have a picture of the two of them huddled in a police car immediately after the murder."

"It doesn't matter. I have to be able to prove that Ricky knew and conspired with Sam and Vince. Right now, I can't." He took a deep breath on his end of the phone. "I need you two in the Homicide office with every single sheet of paper you have on these cases right now. And get some coffee on the way, because it's going to be a long day and probably an even longer night."

Church hung up on her. She sat staring at the generic phone in her hand.

"Well?" Reese prompted.

"Get dressed," she said and tossed the cell back on the nightstand. "We have to go to work."

46

It still felt odd to Lauren to walk into the Homicide squad, in the middle of the biggest investigation the unit had handled in years, both as an investigator as well as a victim. The smell of old coffee hung around the hallway instead of the freshly brewed scent that had filled the air when she last left. As she made her way to the large main office, Marilyn was at her desk, answering call after call. She looked up, saw Lauren, and stuck her index finger up, signaling to give her a minute.

On the large folding table in the middle of the room that they pulled out for just such occasions, labeled files were neatly arranged in rows. Reggie Major sat at the end of the table with a yellow legal pad, recording every task completed and assigning a new one to anyone who found themselves with a second to spare.

Reggie had close to forty years on the force, with over twenty spent working in Homicide. A scholarly-looking black man with round glasses perched on a long thin nose, he planned on retiring in a year when he turned sixty-two. He had slowed down over the last few years, but he was still in the game.

He looked up from making his latest entry. "You and Reese are wanted in the captain's office, now. The DA and the commissioner are waiting."

"They finish up the warrant for Sam?" Reese asked him.

"That was done this morning." He reached out and touched one of the folders with the tip of his ballpoint pen. "A copy of the warrant, the return, and the list of itemized property seized are right here if you want to look at them."

Declining, Reese waved his hand. "What about Ricky?"

Reggie scanned the list in front of him, flipped a page, then said, "Joy is going to do the warrant at Ricky's house. She's trying to get a good address on him. Apparently, he recently moved. She wants to grab his computer and cell phone."

"Thanks, man," Reese told him. "You're doing a great job."

Reggie pushed his glasses up on his nose. "Ricky worked in this squad with me. We weren't friends—he was too political for my taste—but I had respect for him. I worked that case. The whole squad did. I talked to that kid's mom all those years ago, as much as she could through an interpreter. All she knew was that her only child was dead. She brought Gabriel here to have a safer, better life. Sam Schultz let him die in the street and Ricky covered it up." He shook his head. "This one is personal for me."

"Understood." Lauren wanted to go and give his shoulder a squeeze, but Reggie wasn't the huggy, touchy-feely type. He was doing exactly what he did best, sorting out the facts and keeping everything on track and moving.

"We need to arrest Ricky," Reggie's told them. "No excuses. Now go get busy." He bent back over his files; they were dismissed.

Reese and Riley turned and went back down the hall to the captain's office, passing by their co-workers, busy doing their assigned tasks. Reese popped into the kitchen and grabbed two cups of coffee, handing one off to Lauren. She sipped it. It tasted the way it smelled, old and stale.

Captain Maniechwicz's tiny office was located at the end of the hallway, near the door to swipe in. The door was cracked open a little. Reese nudged it with his hip and they crammed themselves into the back of the room, standing shoulder to shoulder.

Commissioner Bennett and DA Church were positioned in the two chairs in front of Captain Maniechwicz, both wearing severe looks on their faces. When Riley and Reese came in, they swiveled around to face them. Bennett sat very straight, her hands clasped together in front of her impressive dress uniform, with its hash marks and medals. Her black hair was pulled into a neat bun, highlighting her round face. Deep lines etched each corner of her mouth and across her forehead. People said Bennett wore the stress of the job on her face, but this was the first time Lauren had truly believed it.

Captain Maniechwicz, AKA the Invisible Man, sat wedged behind his desk, belly butting up against it, framed by the huge Buffalo Bills flag he had stretched across the window, giving everything a weird red and blue tinge.

The commissioner was the first to speak when Riley and Reese came in. "I'm not happy you two decided to go rogue on this case," she began. "Not happy at all. Granted, the district attorney says the recording and the evidence seized at Vince Schultz's apartment pretty much seals his fate, but civilians could have been seriously injured or killed in that car chase. I can't let that go by without punishment."

They both hung their heads in acknowledgement and out of respect for her position. Riley and Reese had known going in that departmental charges would be waiting for them on the other side, no matter what the outcome of their DNA hunt at the party.

"That being said," she continued, "even though I'll be filing formal departmental charges, I won't be suspending you. I'll leave it to an arbitrator to decide your punishment. You're still witnesses, the most important witnesses, and the district attorney is requiring your cooperation in the investigation."

Church held out two pieces of paper. They each took one. Lauren quickly read over the first few lines. It was a departmental permission to search form, already filled out, for her home and computer, looking for any and all records and documents, written, printed, or digital, pertaining to the Schultz cases.

"Am I the target of an investigation?" she asked, as she had been instructed to do since day one on the job if handed such a piece of paper.

"No, you are not. And neither are you, Detective Reese, but we have to satisfy the court there aren't any documents pertaining to this investigation in your possession that you haven't yet turned over. We're going to have to have a look at your departmental iPads, home computers, and cell phones."

"You already have my cell phone in evidence." She held up the paper. "I would have given permission to search. You don't need the form."

Church raised an eyebrow. "We need to do this by the book, am I right?"

Lauren and Reese nodded in unison. Satisfied they understood, Church continued. "Investigators from my DA's office are working with the state attorney general's office on this, along with the Homicide squad. At some point today, someone will take you home so you can turn those items over. Your friend Charlie Daley is being re-interviewed as we speak."

"You brought Charlie back in?" Reese asked.

"Hail, hail, the gang's all here." Church clapped his hands together. "When we're done here, go find Omar Pitts, my investigator, and he'll tell you what he needs."

"And Ricky Schultz?" Lauren prompted.

"We have enough for a search warrant, barely. Hopefully, his cell phone will yield some kind of communication between the brothers that shows he knew about the murder or that he knew about Vince's stunt to try to get the Murder Book. The judge said no on taking his computer."

"What?" Lauren was stunned. A routine search warrant always included the computer.

"Joy just called. Judge Quinn declared the computer overreached the scope of the warrant. He said if any communications are found on Sam's and Vince's computers, she can reapply."

"I've never heard of such a thing," Lauren sputtered.

"Cell phone, yes; computer, no," Church said. "Joy's restricted to looking for the Murder Book and anything related to your attack. Quinn says right now we have no probable cause to believe he was involved in Gabriel Mohamed's murder, and even if we did, the statute of limitations is up."

"Judge Quinn is still acting like a defense attorney," Reese hissed, reminding everyone which side of the courtroom the judge was on before he was elected to the bench. "Joy should take the warrant application to Judge Reynolds."

"I told her no. Now is not the time to go judge shopping. Besides, another judge isn't going to go against Quinn's decision. We know we can reapply if we need to. We have to come up with something more," the commissioner pointed out.

Reese wasn't convinced. "Yeah, after Ricky gives his computer an acid bath."

"If Ricky was going to destroy computers or phones, he'll have already done it, believe me." Church was stating the painfully obvious. "He's had time to dispose of the evidence. We're just looking for crumbs from him at this point."

"They haven't found the Murder Book yet. What about the tire iron?" Lauren asked.

The dour look on Church's face answered her question before he opened his mouth. "Not a trace of it at Sam's or Vince's. Unless it turns up at Ricky's apartment, and I don't think it will, it's a pretty sure bet it's been disposed of. I can only assume Vince kept Garcia's swipe card in case he thought he might need to get inside the Homicide office again. Garcia's keys weren't found with the swipe, so they were probably tossed."

"Do you think Sam will actually turn himself in?" Reese asked.

"He already did," Church replied. "Along with a news crew from CNN. I have him waiting in the main conference room across the street. Ben Lema is going to take the lead for the interview. I'm on my way over there after we're done. Sideshow circus doesn't even begin to describe it. I've got reporters trying to question our office cleaners."

"Are you going to let Ben make the arrest?" Reese asked.

"If Sam Schultz repeats what he just told the world, yes. My main concern is what Sam told his brothers and when he told them. Especially Ricky."

Reese shook his head. "Sam won't throw Ricky under the bus. He'll stick with the story that Ricky found out everything last Saturday night."

Church's forehead wrinkled. "That's what I'm afraid of. African American leaders in the community are demanding answers and actions. Understandably so. A candlelight vigil and rally are being planned for tomorrow night on the steps of City Hall. We have to show the city that we are committed to bringing all the parties involved to justice."

"The arrest of Vince and Sam will be a good start, but there's outrage that Ricky might not get charged," Bennett added.

"Without Sam outright admitting he conspired with Ricky, we have nothing. And if we can't prove he knew about Gabriel's death, we won't be able to prove he was involved in Vince's attempt to steal the file and his attacks on Reese and Riley." Church frowned. "Sam's a lawyer; he knows what constitutes a murder conspiracy. He can't help Vince, but he'll try to save Ricky's ass if he can."

Bennett stood up. "We're all under the microscope right now. Seems like every news channel on the air is parked outside at this moment," she said, "so act accordingly."

Lauren absorbed that information with dread. Every move they made would be on camera. She'd already seen pictures of herself splashed on the twenty-four-hour news outlets proclaiming her "the beautiful, avenging detective" and broadcasting ridiculous headlines like: NOT EVEN A STAB TO THE LUNG COULD STOP THIS COP FROM SEEKING JUSTICE FOR SLAIN TEEN.

Commissioner Bennet followed up her warning with one more statement. "I'm officially informing you that formal charges are being brought against you. Your union rep should be called. I'll try to have the arbitrator schedule a hearing as soon as possible. And for what it's worth," she added, "I'm sorry I have to do this. But I can't have detectives running around half-cocked along with retired police officers conducting their own investigations."

"Understood," Lauren told her. "And thank you, Commissioner."

"Thank you," Reese echoed, the proper amount of humility in his voice.

Bennett nodded in a way that clearly expressed they were dismissed.

As they were walking out, Lauren took note of how Captain Maniechwicz had said nothing the entire time they were in the office. For once, his silence didn't reassure her.

47

Lauren could see Charlie through the open door to his interview room. Splayed out in his chair, legs apart, arms dangling, he wore a bored look on his face as the investigator from the state attorney general's office questioned him. While it was standard procedure for the AG's office to investigate official police corruption, it was a pain in the ass to have to be interviewed over and over again. After she'd finished her third cup of coffee, Lauren was ready to put on her gym shoes and take a lap around the office before her heart exploded.

The investigator from the attorney general's office had her in the main Homicide office waiting to go over, for the second time that day, the events of Saturday night.

Another video had surfaced of the confrontation in the kitchen. A bus boy had whipped out his cell phone right when Vince and Reese had started tussling. He managed to capture Vince's admission that Lauren's stabbing had been an "accident," but with video as well as audio. Vince's hair drag of Lauren and his subsequent forking were also caught, and according to Marilyn, had already gone viral with over a hundred thousand hits, all before they'd managed to track down the owner of the phone. When Lauren reached back and plunged the fork into Vince's face, the camera jiggled a little as the kid recording yelled, "Oh, damn!" Now she had to break down for the state investigator exactly what was going on, second by second, even though in her mind the video was clear and self-explanatory.

She knew they had Reese in the interview room in the Cold Case office doing the same thing. And he was probably just as happy to be there as she was.

"Here, darling," Marilyn slid a paper plate with three chocolate chip cookies in front of her. "You gotta eat something before you keel over."

"Thanks, Marilyn. You're an angel, you know that?"

Marilyn shrugged her shoulders as she made her way back to her ringing phone. "Someone has to take care of you." She paused as she studied the blinking lines, decided on one, and picked up. "Homicide."

There was a long pause while Marilyn listened to the caller's introduction, then parroted her response into the receiver. "All requests from the press are being referred to our media liaison. Please hold while I transfer you." She gave Lauren a wink and pressed a few buttons only to pick another line and start again.

Lauren smiled to herself as she dunked Marilyn's cookie into her coffee. She really was a lifesaver. Biting down, careful of her tongue, Lauren's eyes picked up on familiar faces as they carried on their work.

Across the room the Homicide squad's big screen TV was muted, playing a live stream from one of the cable news channels. A picture of the three Schultz brothers appeared on the television with the tag-line beneath: CORRUPT COPS TAKE BROTHERLY LOVE TOO FAR?

While she waited for her interrogator to return from the men's room, Lauren made a mental list of the three brothers involved:

279

Sam—ex-cop who committed murder while on the job.

Ricky—retired Homicide detective who covered for his murdering brother while he was working.

Vince—working cop who attempted to continue the cover-up perpetrated by his youngest brother by stealing police property, stabbing a fellow officer, assaulting two fellow officers at a party, then trying to kill them and a retired officer by both ramming them with a stolen taxi and shooting at them.

It was cut and dried when you broke it down, really.

How did I ever manage to get myself involved in all this? She let her head sink into her hand as she leaned up against the wall next to her chair. *Oh yeah, I showed up for work. Big mistake. I should retire and work in the graveyard with Charlie.*

Lauren wondered how Ben Lema's interview with Sam was going. It had been at least four hours and they were still at it, as far as Lauren knew. Lenny the cleaner was going around the office dumping out the trash cans again. Lauren waved to get his attention, then signed one of the words Lenny had taught her: *Hello.* He waved and signed *hello* back before returning to his duties.

It seemed like only five minutes had passed since Reese woke her up, but it was already after six in the evening. It was dark out; the short winter days replacing the lingering autumn ones. It was that season when you went to bed in the dark and got up in the dark, totally throwing off your sense of time. Outside, it was still snowing. Lauren had watched a plow come by a few minutes before, scraping the snow up onto the curb in front of headquarters in huge piles. Lauren speculated what winter would be like in the new headquarters building. Plowed parking spots and sidewalks? Warmth in the winter? Would the new, modern heating system work without all the ghostly metal banging these ancient radiators made to signal the heat was on?

Lauren looked at the time on her phone. Joy had left an hour before to serve the search warrant at Ricky's house. It had taken Joy longer to write up the warrant than anticipated. She'd had a hard time with the address because Ricky had moved twice in the last year, and the utilities for his apartment were in his son's name. Joy finally tracked him down, driving by the suspected apartment and seeing a red car in the driveway with a Buffalo Police sticker on the windshield. She'd run the plate, and it had come back to Richard Schultz, so she snapped some photos of the outside of the house with her cell phone to attach to the application for the warrant.

Armed with the warrant, Joy took two patrol cars with her and told Lauren before she left that she'd text her if they found anything interesting. Coincidently, the picture on the flat-screen TV in front of Lauren flipped to a photo of a young Ricky Schultz in his police uniform. The banner underneath now read: NO CHARGES FOR EX-COP? COMMUNITY OUTRAGE GROWS.

Lovely, Lauren thought as she stared at his piggish face and slicked back hair, *it's a slideshow of scumbags.*

Her investigator from the attorney general's office, Wayne Kencil, came back, buttoning his suit coat all the way up. He was a retired detective from Rochester Police department, very doughy looking, like maybe there'd been a time he'd been into body building but decided he liked chicken wings more. He had close-set, gray eyes that made Lauren want to avoid eye contact with him. *That probably hinders his interview abilities,* she thought. *Having those wolf eyes.*

"I just got a text," Kencil told her, taking his seat across from her. "Sam's been placed under arrest for the murder of Gabriel Mohamed."

I wonder if he took the call while he was sitting on the can? She vowed not to touch his phone for any reason.

"I want to go over this just one more time." He grabbed the iPad he had left face-down on the desk. Turning it around so she could see, the screen showed the new video, stopped right at the moment Lauren had stuck the fork in Vince's face.

She picked up her second cookie, making sure not to offer Kencil the last one. Who knew when she'd get another snack? She wondered if Marilyn had a secret stash of them in her desk. *Probably,* Lauren thought, giving her cookie a healthy dunk in her coffee. *That's how she rolls.*

Lauren brushed crumbs from her mouth with the back of her hand while she chewed. No use hunting for a napkin; any sense of propriety she had possessed had gone out the window on Saturday night. She answered while still chewing. "What do you want to know?"

Before he could answer, Lauren's city-issue phone buzzed in her pocket. Only work people knew the number and not many of them. She slipped it out and looked at her screen. It was a message from Joy.

I GOT NOTHING OVER HERE SO FAR. WE'RE TAKING RICKY'S PHONE, BUT NO MURDER BOOK, NO TIRE IRON, NOTHING WITH THE NAME GABRIEL MOHAMED ON IT.

Lauren texted back right away: HOPEFULLY THERE'S SOMETHING OUR COMPUTER FORENSICS PEOPLE CAN DIG OUT OF HIS PHONE.

Three little dots let her know that Joy was composing a reply. Then: I WOULDN'T COUNT ON IT. HE SEEMED VERY SMUG WHEN WE SHOWED UP. NOW HE'S STANDING HERE STARING AT ME WITH A SHIT-EATING GRIN ON HIS FACE.

Lauren gripped her phone hard while she pictured Ricky with that black stain marring his cheek, smirking at Joy as she searched. KEEP LOOKING.

WILL DO.

Bastard. Lauren wanted to throw her cell phone across the room. *Cocky, smug bastard.* She looked over at Charlie, who was punctuating something he was saying by driving his index finger into the desk. The investigator from the attorney general's office jumped back a little, not sure what to make of a sixty-eight-year-old grave digger with access to a gun, whose work uniform now consisted of a pair of stained denim overalls.

"I just want to go over this video one more time. And the footage from the hotel cameras in the lobby and the main doors. They show a lot, but I need you to put it into context for me."

Lauren put the rest of the cookie down on the desk. She'd lost her appetite. She could only pray the guys down in the lab would find something, anything, on Ricky's cell phone linking him to Gabriel or Joe's death. *What is the context?* she thought bitterly. *That me and Reese will do whatever it takes to make a case? Because right now, as far as Ricky Schultz is concerned, that's the only thing the video proves.*

48

Lauren wrapped her green-and-white checkered scarf around her head and face like a mummy as she and Reese approached the side door of police headquarters the next day. Despite closing off road traffic except for emergency vehicles on Franklin Street all the way from Pearl to Church Street, the media lined the sidewalk from end to end. Across Church Street, media vans took up every available parking spot (and even some that weren't), including blocking the sidewalks.

Lincoln Lewis had brought Ricky Schultz in for questioning. Reese had been finishing packing up his baseball cap collection when they got the texts from Marilyn to get their asses down there.

They'd been at headquarters well into the evening, and sleeping in late that day had been an absolute luxury. Lauren had watched Reese load a box, then his big duffel bag into his car while she sipped her coffee. Watson followed him back and forth to the car, tracking snow across the hardwood floor and spraying her with droplets when he decided to give himself a good shake.

Reese had been living in the house he inherited over by Cazenovia Park before her attack, but it was tiny. Lauren had to fight back the offer of just letting them stay with her because she knew that was the empty nest in her heart talking. Still, it was painful to watch him pack up his and Watson's stuff. Then they got the text messages.

Reese got ready to swipe in the side door, mindful not to kick over any of the plastic soda bottles sticking out of the snow that people used as ash trays on their smoke breaks. One of the report technicians from the Narcotics squad stood shivering just inside the doorway, cigarette posed between her fingers, taking a long drag. She looked up at them, exhaled a cloud of blue smoke and said, "This is nuts. Can't even get down the damn street."

Reese pulled his card through the reader. "Careful. Those cameras can pick up every word you say."

"Yeah? Well, screw them." The chubby middle-aged redhead chuckled loudly. "I got some words for them, all right."

Riley and Reese walked past her into the building, which seemed strangely empty until Lauren remembered all the administrative report technicians had already been moved to the new building, leaving this end of the first floor a ghost town. They took the elevator to the third floor in silence, not trusting that any reporters hadn't somehow found their way into headquarters.

Lauren unwound the scarf, letting it hang around her neck. "They already know what you look like," Reese commented as they stepped off the elevator. "I don't know why you even bothered."

"Maybe I should let them film me. It's better than that stupid departmental picture they keep showing." The department took a photo of every officer and detective in their class A uniform every couple of years. Andy, the police photographer, told her it was so if she ever got in trouble, the brass would be able to put her in a photo array with other cops. Of course, that was also the picture the department released to the press.

They could hear the chaos before they even opened the Homicide wing's door. Every detective working was stuffed in the hallway, talking, drinking coffee, nosing around for the scoop. Every head swiveled to Reese and Riley when they walked in, then the crowd went silent, staring.

For exactly one and a half seconds. Then they went back to rumor mongering, speculating, and gossiping.

"This is great. Downstairs it's a circus, upstairs it's a sideshow." Reese pushed past Vatasha Anthony and Reggie Major, who were standing by the breakroom door, both with coffee mugs in their hands. Vatasha gave Lauren the stink eye as she passed. Almost getting murdered had not warmed their frosty relationship one bit.

"They got him in the big room," Reggie called after them. "Joy's in there with Ricky and his lawyer."

Lauren half turned, "Thanks, Reggie."

The primary interrogation room was straight back through the main office. Another smaller, narrow room was to its immediate left. There you could watch through the two-way mirror and listen through the intercom system that had been installed in the eighties and had never been updated. The state-of-the-art camera inside the room fed into the media center, where you could watch and listen on monitors. The sound was crystal clear and the picture perfect, but it wasn't the same as standing three feet from the suspect, watching every twitch, hearing every stutter—close enough that if the glass should shatter, you could reach out and touch them.

Lauren could see the red light over the interrogation room door was lit, indicating an interview was happening. The door was shut, the frosted glass had a piece of paper taped to it that read QUIET. INTERVIEW IN PROGRESS.

The door to the room next to it was ajar. It had to be kept dark, so you couldn't see through the two-way glass. It was like stepping into the world's smallest movie theater. Standing-room capacity: three. Lauren pushed open the door, slipping inside. Reese followed, shutting it behind him.

Lincoln Lewis was standing in front of the mirror, arms folded across his chest, staring into the glass. He stepped sideways to make room when Riley and Reese came in, but he didn't look away from his client. Lauren found herself sandwiched between Lewis and Reese in the claustrophobic closet. Lewis was wearing one of his simple, expensive suits, complete with his signature red bow tie. Lauren could smell just a hint of cologne on him, mixed with soap, like he had showered right before he had come to headquarters. Lewis had a pair of silver-rimmed glasses resting on his nose that Lauren hadn't seen him wear before, his eyebrows pulled down to the frame as he watched Ricky.

Ricky Schultz was sitting with Joy Walsh, directly in front of them. Wearing the same ill-fitting suit he had on Saturday night, Ricky's cheeks were blotchy, with more angry red patches splashed across them. The mole that Lauren thought he should have checked seemed inked into the side of his face, dark and jagged. It was hard not to stare at it when you looked at him.

Lauren broke the silence by whispering, "Shouldn't you be in there with your client?" You had to keep it down in the narrow space or your voice would bleed over to the interview room.

Lewis shook his head. "He said no. Richard Schultz denies any knowledge of his brother's involvement with the shooting of Gabriel

Mohamed, and he certainly didn't know anything about Vince's attack on you."

Lauren took in Ricky's body language: annoyed, cocky, and angry. He'd been in Joy's seat too many times to say the wrong thing. Of course he'd give a statement denying any knowledge. As long as his brothers kept their traps shut, he'd be just fine.

"You really think that's true?" Lauren asked Lewis.

Now he did look at her. "They found nothing during the search of his apartment. Nothing on his phone and nothing in his personal effects. I have to give it to you, Lauren—you're tenacious as hell. What I can't believe is that you caught the guy who stabbed you, they've arrested the man who killed Gabriel Mohamed, and you're still not satisfied. You have an almost obsessive need to entirely destroy the Schultz family."

"I don't want to destroy anyone. I just want all the guilty people in jail where they belong."

"How noble of you," he mused softly, turning his attention back to Ricky. "But as plausible as it is to believe the three brothers loved each other so much they'd cover up a murder and kill to keep a secret, it's equally plausible that Vince and Sam hid their crimes from their big brother to protect him as well."

Reese made a snorting sound. Lauren gave him an elbow.

The three were standing so close in the darkness that their shoulders touched. Lewis was so tall he had to hunch forward slightly so that his head didn't hit the ancient audio equipment that hung from the ceiling. He wasn't wearing a top coat; he must have draped it over a chair in the office or hung it on the coat tree someone had pulled out of the garbage somewhere and stuck in the corner by the door. Lewis looked like he was watching his nephew's communion video, not the interrogation of a former police officer.

Ricky was looking at Joy with amused contempt. "You think I'd tell Vince to stab a fellow officer? Just to steal a file? On a case I worked my balls off on? Look at my notes in that file. I worked that case hard."

"But your brother Sam was never a suspect," Joy pointed out.

"Why the hell would he be? I'm just as shocked by all this shit as you folks are. My two brothers are going to jail. The people at my mother's assisted living home thought she had a heart attack last night. She's in Mercy Hospital right now hooked up to a heart monitor. She's eighty-eight years old." He thrust his finger toward Joy's face to make his point. "If I'd have known my brothers were up to this, I would have brought them in myself."

She flinched but kept the interrogation going. "What about the pictures of you and Sam in the police car immediately after the shooting?" she pressed. Lauren could see the crime scene photos spread out on the desk next to Ricky.

"It was freezing out. My rookie brother was walking the beat. I let him warm up in my car. He didn't say anything about anything and I sure as hell didn't suspect him."

Convincing. Lauren clenched her jaw as she watched his performance. *But you're a professional liar. Your brothers wouldn't have made a move without asking you first.*

"It's hard not to believe him," Lewis said in the smooth, confident voice that lulled juries to his side.

"He let his brother walk away from murdering a teenager."

"He had no knowledge of that and no history of being heavy-handed when he was on the job. He was a good cop."

"I'll keep that in mind when my doctor checks on how well my sutures are healing next week. Want to see my scars?"

His eyes dancing over Lauren's face, a smile creeping across his mouth as he gave her a quick glance up and down. "That's an interesting

offer. Unfortunately, I'm going to have to take a rain check. Excuse me."
He carefully inched behind her and Reese, making his way to the door.
"It's time I cut this interview off."

"This is wrong, Lincoln," Lauren's voice raised a notch as he got
past Reese and opened the door.

Lewis paused, half in and half out of the room, hand on the knob.
"You got two of the three brothers. You won. Be happy with that." He
slid out, closing the door behind him.

"You okay?" Reese asked. Through the window they could see
Lincoln Lewis enter the interview room and Ricky getting to his feet.

"No." Lauren pushed past Reese out into the main office. Ricky
and Lewis walked out together, Lincoln plucking a camel coat off the
back of a chair as he passed.

Lauren followed them down the stairs, vaguely aware that Reese
was by her side. She was fixated on the back of Ricky's head, with its
greasy comb-over, bobbing down with each step he took. Ricky didn't
look back, didn't acknowledge her in any way, but Lauren knew he
was aware she was behind him. Dandruff was sprinkled across each
shoulder of his suit jacket; his winter coat was draped over his arm.

Greasy, dirty, disgusting excuse for a human being. Lauren tried to mirror Reese's cool, calm exterior, but knew she was only being marginally
successful as they reached the first-floor landing. Outside the Church
Street door, reporters were already pressed to the glass, filming, shout-
ing, and pushing each other for position. Stopping short of the doorway,
Lewis turned back to Reese, "Can we get a little help here?"

"Very little," he answered dryly, then looked down the hallway where
two uniformed officers were milling around by the entrance to the property office. "Hey, guys? Could you make a path for our friends here?"

The two young coppers nodded and proceeded to hold open the
door and simultaneously hold back the press. The shorter officer

yelled at the crowd, "Coming through, people! Don't block the sidewalk! Get out of the way!"

Lewis grabbed Ricky's coat and threw it over his head, covering it as he led him out of the building. The two coppers followed along, cutting a path for them through the cameras and questions. Lauren and Reese brought up the rear, catching the attention of one astute cameraman. "Aren't you the detective who got stabbed?" he asked. Cameras swung around to capture both Lauren and Ricky walking on the sidewalk through the unshoveled snow.

A young Latina reporter stuck a microphone in her face. "How does it feel to watch Richard Schultz walk away?"

Lauren stopped, and Reese did as well, watching Lincoln Lewis rush his client to a waiting black sedan with tinted windows. *How does it feel?* Camera flashes went off all around her. Her eyes narrowed as Ricky was driven off. *He covered up a murder, he tried to have me killed, and he possibly beat Joe Wheeler to death. Two out of three isn't good enough.*

Lauren turned and walked back into headquarters.

This wasn't over by a longshot.

49

Twenty-four hours later, almost to the minute, Wayne Kencil's number flashed across the screen of Lauren's new phone. She almost didn't answer it. Commissioner Bennett had ordered her and Reese to take the next two days off when she went back into headquarters after watching Ricky leave. "I don't want you back in the hospital," she told Lauren in the hallway outside of the Homicide office. "I want both of you out of the public eye. Completely. Go home. Let the rest of the squad take care of this. It's over for you right now. I won't tell you a third time."

Lauren had been pissed, Reese only slightly less, but they'd followed orders and went back to her house. Reese was almost packed to leave but decided to stay one last night. Another day with Watson helped calm her nerves. At least it had, until the AG's investigator called.

"I just got a call from your captain," Kencil sounded breathless. "Seems Ricky Schultz didn't show up for an appointment with Lincoln

Lewis, so Lewis went over to his apartment. You and Reese need to come take a ride with me."

Twenty minutes later Wayne Kencil picked them up in his brand-new maroon Dodge Charger. "The attorney general's office must be doing well if they can afford to give out take-home cars like these," Reese commented from the passenger seat. Lauren sat silently in the back, dread creeping up her spine. She knew Reese was making small talk because he was nervous.

Kencil ignored Reese's comment, glancing up at the evening sky instead. "There's a storm coming. I saw it on the news before I left my house. They say it's a bad one."

It was already dark. Ominous clouds rolled off the lake, accompanied by a wicked wind that stung the cheeks and froze the snot in your nose. Lauren didn't need a weatherman to tell her what was coming. You could feel it in your bones.

Kencil didn't say it and Reese didn't voice it, but Lauren knew they were all thinking the same thing. Ricky had done something very bad, maybe to himself.

They drove the rest of the way to Ricky Schultz's apartment in silence.

A traffic cop had Ricky's street blocked off, keeping the hordes of media vans at bay. The reporters craned their necks to see who was in Wayne's car as they were waved inside the perimeter. News stations monitored police radio broadcasts, heard everything the cops put over the air. Try as the department might to put as little as possible over the air, the media still put two and two together when Evidence, Photography, Homicide, the duty inspector, and a district supervisor were called to that particular address. Lauren put a hand up, blocking her face from the glare of the cameras trained on them.

Another uniformed cop waved them into a space and Lauren wondered if Ricky was feeling any remorse at all. *Probably not,* she thought, opening the back passenger-side door and stepping out into a slush puddle. *For a guy like him, it's always going to be family first.*

But that didn't explain what they were doing at his house now.

Riley and Reese let Kencil lead, following him toward the house. Cops were scattered across the front lawn, talking with their backs to the news cameras, well aware that they had microphones that could capture your conversations from a distance.

They passed the squad cars lining the narrow North Buffalo street, clouds of exhaust pouring out of their tailpipes as the coppers kept their doors locked with the motors running so the cars stayed warm.

Lauren looked up at Ricky's house. It was a typical Riverside double, Lauren knew; she'd answered a hundred calls in houses just like it, with a large front porch and an upper fenced balcony. The upper apartment looked vacant to her; there were newspapers covering the darkened windows. The walkway to the porch hadn't been shoveled, but boots had trampled the snow down into a hard, bumpy packed surface.

A late-model red sedan sat in the driveway, two inches of snow covering the windshield and hood. That told her the car had been sitting there at least a day. Ducking under even more crime scene tape, Lauren grabbed onto the black wrought iron railing as she took the porch steps carefully. She eyeballed the front picture window, covered in heavy drapes. While she and Reese and Charlie were running around, Ricky had been hiding out here, like a rat in his hole.

A young female officer stood at the front door, just inside the frame with a metal clipboard in her hand, dutifully logging in everyone who came on scene. She looked new, and a little frazzled, with her black leather gloves making it hard for her to write. She motioned to two boxes at her feet: latex gloves and shoe covers. "Everyone is down in the basement." She pointed to a door standing open directly ahead of them, in the kitchen. Reese bent down and grabbed boxes, letting everyone pluck what they needed before dropping them back by the officer's foot.

Kencil looked at Lauren and stepped aside. "I think you better go in first on this one."

Lauren noticed a yellow plastic evidence marker bearing a black number 3 sitting just off to the right of the door as she tugged on her shoe covers. Squinting as she stood up, Lauren asked the cop at the door, "What's that?"

"Possibly blood. There are two more drops near the door to the basement, so be careful. And don't grab for the doorknob. More suspected blood."

Swallowing hard, Lauren didn't reply.

It was hot in the apartment; someone had cranked the heat up, amplifying the greasy kitchen smells coming from the unwashed pots and pans sitting on the stove. Lauren could clearly see what looked like two dark, fat drops of blood marked off with their own yellow evidence tents set to the left of the door frame.

Passing by the barely furnished living room, the four of them crossed the stained linoleum of the kitchen floor to the opening to the basement.

Voices drifted up the stairs from below. An ugly green shag carpet covered the steps heading downward into the dimly lit basement. As Lauren descended, she became aware of the faint scent of burnt paper and mold. She used both hands pressed against the walls to steady herself as she stepped down. *A basement office,* she observed absently, *kind of like mine.*

Lauren stopped cold, sharply sucking in a breath.

Every head in the room swiveled to look at her. Frozen in place, she suppressed a gag. Reese and Kencil were trapped on the stairs behind her, unable to get past.

Sitting in a metal folding chair at an old wooden desk, facing a computer, was Ricky Schultz. A kitchen knife was sticking out from his chest, just in front of his left arm, which hung limply down by his side. His head was tilted forward, stringy hair hanging in his face, bald spot uncovered. The nasty dark stain on his cheek was stark against the paleness of his drained face. A red ribbon of blood, now dry, had run down to his hip and along the chair, collecting into a small, black pool on the carpet. An open pack of cigarettes lay next to the blood spot, under Ricky's hand, as if he'd merely fallen asleep and dropped them.

Thankfully, Lauren's left hand was still pressed to the wall, holding her up as her knees threatened to buckle underneath her. She couldn't wrench her eyes from him. His face was the color of cold ashes, gray and dull. Ricky's blue polo shirt had been too small, and his beer belly stuck out from under it in hairy, dimpled folds, covering his lap. On the wall above the computer was the badge-shaped retirement plaque the union gave everyone as a parting gift. It was the only decoration Lauren could see.

"It looks like someone got to Ricky," Joy said, stating the obvious.

"Do we know who was the last person he had contact with?" Wayne Kencil asked from behind Lauren. She still hadn't moved.

"No. He received a phone call to his cell from his mother's aide at seven thirteen this morning. It lasted eighteen minutes. Interestingly enough, he also spoke to our old friend Kevin King at eleven twenty-seven for thirty-two minutes." Joy held up a plastic evidence bag with an old-fashioned gray flip phone in it. "This was on the table in front of him. We took an iPhone off him yesterday for evidence. Lincoln Lewis said he gave this as a loaner until we were done with Ricky's, so they could stay in contact in the meantime. The call log shows all Ricky's calls, the last one around one o'clock this afternoon. That was to Lewis. Ricky was supposed to meet him at Lewis's office downtown at four. He never showed. Lewis called and called, waited until five thirty, then drove out here. He saw the blood on the front doorknob and called 911."

"Where's Lewis now?" Reese asked from somewhere behind Lauren on the stairs.

"In the back of a patrol car. He insisted on coming inside with the first responding officer." Joy wore a disgusted look. "Who was too stupid to tell him to stay the hell out of a crime scene. Lewis saw everything."

"How could this happen? There should have been ten media trucks parked outside this house," Reese said. "We should have his murder live on video and streaming."

"They were parked in front of his ex-wife's house." Joy let the crime scene photographer snake past her in the cramped space. "Apparently they didn't believe her when she told them he didn't live there anymore. They camped out there and only descended on this block when the police radio call came out."

"We were supposed to be going for the trifecta here. We got two brothers arrested and now one dead. Every frigging news station in the country is stationed outside this place right now," Kencil said, anger rising in his voice. "How the hell are we supposed to explain this?"

"As case fucking closed," Reese chimed in, sounding pissed at Kencil's tone. "Someone exacted their own justice on Ricky. They didn't want to wait until you guys in the attorney general's office got your shit together."

Kencil ignored Reese's outburst. "Any sign of forced entry?" he asked Joy.

"No. Other than the knife wound there's no other trauma that we can see." Joy pointed to the weapon. The police photographer bent forward and snapped a shot of it. "But from the angle of the wound, and those drops of blood, I doubt he was stabbed sitting here. I think his body position is staged. I think the killer either talked his way in or pulled a gun at the door, made Ricky come down here, stabbed him, and sat him facing the computer screen."

"That's a hell of a lot of work just to kill a guy." Kencil sounded unconvinced. One of the evidence techs was carefully bagging a cigarette butt from a cheap tin ash tray on the desk. Oddly, the ashtray looked like it was filled with the remnants of burnt paper. A red plastic disposable lighter and an evidence tent marking it item 18 sat next to the almost overflowing tray.

"I doubt the killer carried Ricky down those stairs. The whole scene, the blood drops upstairs, his positioning, screams *staged*," Joy insisted. "The whole thing looks wrong to me."

"A former assistant district attorney would know how to stage a crime scene," Reese pointed out. "Maybe Kevin King knew about Gabriel's murder and Lauren's stabbing the whole time. Maybe he was afraid Ricky would talk."

"I've got a patrol car going to over to King's house to pick him up right now," Joy said. "But he's a lawyer. He won't talk. And I doubt we're going to find any forensic evidence at all if this scene really is staged."

"It is." Lauren's voice sounded foreign and hollow to her. Reese's hand came down on her shoulder, more to hold her up than to comfort her. From the reflection in the computer monitor Lauren could see Ricky's mouth ajar, and his eyes half open, like he was drunk or stoned instead of dead. The killer stabbed him, sat him in that chair, and watched him die.

"How do you know that?" Kencil's voice cut through her thoughts.

She stared straight ahead, reading the message printed across the screen in bold, black type: *You can find out just about anything on anybody using the plain old internet.*

"I just know."

Damn David Spencer to hell. The certainty of his actions washed over her like a wave. His presence in the room was almost palpable; she could practically smell David in the musty basement. Lauren knew right then that David had killed Joe Wheeler. She knew he stabbed Ricky Schultz, then watched him die, choking as he tried to suck in a breath, like she had.

She pictured David sitting Ricky in that metal chair, probably speaking to him in low, soothing tones while he watched the blood drip down the old man's side, onto the shag pile. A criminal justice major would have no trouble figuring out how to muddy up a scene. Her jaw tightened as the truth of the situation hit her. Drop some blood where it doesn't belong, write a cryptic message no one can figure out, confuse the cops. Except for the cop the message was meant for. That cop would know immediately.

The cases involving the Schultz brothers might be over, but David had effectively sucked her back into the sphere of his life. He was teasing her, pulling her back to him.

He killed Joe Wheeler and now Ricky Schultz because they hurt me. He wants to see what I'll do about it. If I have the balls to come after him. He wants me to be a part of this sick game he's created.

"How do you know?" Kencil pressed. Lauren spun around, pushing Reese to turn and go back up the stairs to the kitchen.

"I want to see Lewis," she said, prodding Reese forward in front of her. Kencil called after her, but she ignored him.

Reese looked back at her. "Can you tell me what's going on?"

"Where is Lincoln Lewis?" Lauren demanded of the frazzled young cop still stationed at the door.

"Uhhh—" The poor officer looked from Lauren to Reese and back again.

"That's not an answer. Use your words," Lauren snapped.

"I think he's in Caffrey's Tahoe, right there." She pointed to an SUV idling by the curb in front of the house.

Before Reese could apologize to the female cop for her, Lauren plunged down the steps and over to the Tahoe. She kicked the plastic booties off, sending one into a neighbor's front yard.

Lauren peeled off her latex gloves, dropping them into the snow. Without bothering to look, she stepped off the curb into the street. Reese paused in his pursuit of her just long enough to properly take off the crime scene gear on the front walkway. She didn't wait for Reese to catch up. The patrol cop sitting in the driver's seat didn't see Lauren until she threw open the back-passenger door. "Lincoln—"

"You." The venom in his voice pierced the air. "Officer, I want you to put the cuffs on this woman right now for the murder of Richard Schultz." He tried to pull the door closed, but Lauren threw her hip against it, causing a wave of pain to travel through her entire body.

"You think I did this?" she asked in disbelief.

"Let me guess, your partner back there is your alibi for last night. And the department just had to bring you to the scene, contaminating it. You want to talk about cover-ups?" His usually kind eyes were blazing with an anger she'd never seen in him before. "Let me tell you the one about the totally obsessed cop who wanted the guy she couldn't arrest so badly she killed him, and the Buffalo Police Department covered it up for her. Because she's pretty and blond and breaks big cases. How's that for a cover-up for you?"

Reese hauled her back from the door, allowing Lewis to shut himself in the patrol vehicle. "Don't put on a show," he hissed as he pulled her toward Wayne Kencil's car.

"It was David Spencer." Her breath was coming out in huffs; fogging the air in front of her. "He killed Ricky and Joe Wheeler. That message on the computer was for me."

"You don't know that."

"I do. I said those exact words to him when I went to his house. He sent me flowers in the hospital, Reese. I should have told you—"

"Okay," he said through clenched teeth. "But this isn't our investigation. You have to take yourself out of this. Lincoln Lewis thinks you could be the killer. You really think he's going to keep that to himself? And Kevin King isn't going to talk about what he discussed with Ricky today. King would be more than happy to point the finger at you, if it takes the heat off of him."

If Lauren even remotely thought Kevin King had the balls to kill Ricky Schultz, she might have taken a step back and given him a silent thought of thanks for taking out her garbage and then walked away. There was no redeeming a dirty cop. No sympathy for someone who crossed that thin blue line, no matter the reason. His death could remain unsolved, she wouldn't have lost a wink of sleep over it, and neither would have any of the other coppers on the department.

But David Spencer coming out of the woodwork to kill her suspect? That meant David had crossed over into something far more dangerous than what he already had been. It was what she'd been afraid of since his acquittal last year.

"This case is over. Sam is in jail for murdering Gabriel Mohamed. Vince is in jail for attacking you, and Ricky is dead. The Kinger is out of the DA's office. Case closed for us. Now tell me," Reese said, opening the back door of Kencil's vehicle so she could get in. "No, *promise* me you'll let this go."

Reese hung in the doorway, one arm draped over the door, the other over the frame, boxing her in the back seat. His handsome face was pinched, lip curled into a sneer because the cameras had followed their trek and were now trained on him standing outside the car. But his eyes betrayed the concern and anxiety that was crashing over him. He knew what that message for Lauren meant, maybe better than she did.

Lauren did what she did best when the men in her life wanted something permanent from her, like a promise: she lied.

"Okay, okay. I promise. Case closed." She let her body slump against the seat. "I'll stay home and go to physical therapy and let everyone else worry about this. I'll let Joy and Ben and Garcia do their jobs. Because I have no real choice here, do I?"

His green eyes studied her face. Knowing that was the best he was going to get out of her, he slammed the door and began to walk around to the other side.

She'd try to spare Reese as much as she could. She turned away from him when he got in, looking out of the tinted window at the house. Lauren's forehead fell against the cold glass, her shoulders tense and rigid.

I'm sorry, Reese. But David Spencer isn't going to stop. Not now. Not when he knows he has my attention.

A gust of wind threw a splotch of snow across her window, but she didn't so much as blink. Outside the car, officers still milled about, media people still jockeyed for the best camera angle, neighbors still clustered on porches, huddling together against the bluster. Nothing had changed since she had entered Ricky's Schultz's apartment, yet everything had changed. Her final thought as she surveyed the scene in front of her was as inevitable and as certain as the snowstorm about to come hard at the city off Lake Erie.

Not until one of us is dead.

Acknowledgments

I'd like to thank everyone in my critique group at the Dog Ear's Bookstore in South Buffalo. Your critiques, criticisms, and encouragement have made me a better writer.

A huge thank you to my friends who helped me smooth out my manuscript: Rick Ollerman, Ruth Robbins, Stephanie Patterson, and Michael Breen.

Thank you to my friends and family who have supported me through thick and thin during this journey: Lorri and Lenny Cain, Missy Warnes, Nell Kavanaugh, Maura Krause, Sharon Kysor, Karen Adymy, Tom McDonnell, and Brian Ross.

I am so grateful to live where I do. The Buffalo community has been so incredibly supportive of me and my writing. I truly live in the City of Good Neighbors.

Thank you to my Sisters in Crime: Kathy Kaminski, Barbara Early, and Alice Loweecey for all the advice, support, and laughs.

Thank you, Richard Walter, for all of your help, not just with this book but over the years. You are a brilliant mentor and friend.

To everyone at Midnight Ink, especially Nicole Nugent and Terri Bischoff—many thanks.

Thanks to my agent, Bob Mecoy, and Dana Kaye at Kaye Publicity for everything they do.

To my husband, Dan, for sticking by me and encouraging me. I love you and appreciate you every day.

Natalie and Mary, the sky's the limit for both of you—chase all your dreams!

© Short Street Photographers

About the Author

Lissa Marie Redmond is a recently retired Cold Case Homicide detective with the Buffalo Police Department. She lives and writes in Buffalo, New York, with her husband and two kids. *The Murder Book* is the second novel in her Cold Case Investigation series.